Keeping Her

Savage Brothers MC— 2nd Generation

Jordan Marie

Copyright © 2020 by Jordan Marie

All rights reserved.

No part of this publication may be used or reproduced in any manner whatsoever, including but not limited to being stored in a retrieval system or transmitted in any form or by any means, electronic, mechanical, photocopying, recording or otherwise, without the written permission of the author.

This book is a work of fiction. Names, characters, groups, businesses, and incidents either are the product of the author's imagination or are used fictitiously. Any resemblance to actual places or persons, living or dead, is entirely coincidental.

Cover: Mayhem Covers L.J. Anderson

Editing: Read by Rose and Jenn Allen

WARNING: This book contains sexual situations, violence and other adult themes. Recommended for 18 and above.

❦ Created with Vellum

Dedication

This will be my first book that I released without Susan Frank in my corner. I won't lie. Her loss shook me and left an emptiness that I'm having trouble wrapping my head around.

I hate cancer. I hate that it has the ability to destroy lives and to extinguish lights that we need—especially in today's world.

Spread love. The world has too little of it now, and life is way too fragile.

RIP Susan. Until we meet again and hug it out.

J

Susan Marie Frank-Koczynski
10-7-1970
to
6-6-2020

Blurb

**One kiss from those cherry lips and I knew she was meant to be mine.
I'm claiming her and I won't be letting her go.**

Luke "Grunt" Stafford had one job. He didn't like it, but when your President gives you an order you usually follow it.

He didn't plan on the feisty redhead that showed up and rocked his world.

Jasmine Blake knows how her family and friends see her.
They think she's a wild child rebelling from her parents.

It's not true, but Jasmine has no idea how to explain herself. Being the daughter of Dancer, Savage MC Vice President, is anything but easy. So, after a while, she gave up trying.

Luke caught her eye immediately. She'd sworn off men, but something about him made it impossible for her to stay away.

Luke and Jasmine both have secrets though.
And they just might be enough to get them both killed.

Chapter 1

Grunt

This was a bad idea.

I knew it, but it was like being caught in a fucking tornado on the freeway. You could hide in a fucking ditch, but there wasn't much you could do to stop the shit-storm headed your way.

"Here they come," Jonesy says, and you could hear the anticipation in his voice.

He loves this shit, and it definitely shows. Me? I've got zero taste for it. I support my club, I do what I have to do to keep our territory ours, and the money coming in. This petty fucking shit? Not my cup of tea. Some young punk had to go and piss off Ford, our Prez.

You can't do that shit. Ford was a big guy. He probably tipped the scales at three hundred. Sure, he had some meat on his bones, but he also had muscle. That made him formidable enough, but when you added in his short fuse, you had a recipe for disaster. Ford's temper was scary as fuck. There's not much in this world I'm afraid of. I don't even think you could say I was afraid of Ford, but I fucking knew to be cautious around him. He's an asshole. He's fair for the most part and he takes care of the men in his club, but he is still an asshole. Then again, most of us are—maybe that's why we chose this lifestyle.

"Jesus," I hiss as I get a look at the girl in question.

"Damn," Jonesy whistles. "She's a dead ringer for Lyla isn't she?"

"She sure as hell is pretty damn close," I admit, although I can see a few differences.

Lyla is Ford's daughter. There are few things in this life that Ford will admit to caring about. The club, Demon Chasers MC, and his daughter are the only two. He protects them fiercely. Lyla is his pride and his only child. She's eighteen, but she might as well be six to Ford. In his eyes, she will never grow up—which is bad fucking news. Because Lyla has grown up. She's gorgeous and boys have been sniffing around her for a while. There's only thing that's stopped them from stepping up to try and get her. *Ford.*

Certainly, that's why none of the younger guys in the club have tried. The rest of us view her as either a kid sister or a niece. She's family. That's why so many of us are pissed. Lyla has been crying for a fucking month over some little sniveling asshole. My call would have been to hunt down the little dick-weed and teach him a lesson about hurting women. Ford? Well, our Prez might be a fair man and make good decisions ninety-nine percent of the time. It's that small amount of time when he goes unhinged that gets all of our asses in a sling, and when it comes to his little girl hurting...

He's definitely fucking unhinged.

He's determined to bring the little punk to his knees and that begins—at least in his head—with kidnapping the woman he chose over Lyla. Now, normally, I could get more behind this plan of revenge. But then normally the woman in question wasn't the daughter of Skull, the President of the Devil's Blaze in Kentucky.

Keeping Her

I haven't had a lot of dealings with the Devil's Blaze. We're in Virginia and try to steer clear of the Blaze. We're not allies and once we take little Gabby here, I think the term mortal enemies will more likely apply.

"We're sure about this?" I ask Jonesy, hoping like fuck he'll say no.

"I know you're against this, Grunt," he says, frowning, staring at the girl in question.

"Fuck yeah, I am. This is going to get bloody and you know it will. I'm not just talking a little blood either. We're talking fucking rivers."

"Yeah," Jonesy mutters. "There's no way we're going to talk Ford out of this shit though. You know that."

"Let's watch her for a bit, make contact and tell Ford that we didn't get the opportunity. If we can delay it a bit---" I shrug, not knowing how to finish it.

"For a man that got the road name Grunt because you hate talking, you're talking a lot now," he grumbles.

"When it's important, I can talk and this bullshit? It's bad, Jonesy. I've got this sinking, fucking feeling in my gut that it's worse than we know. I just think we need to be cautious."

"Okay, we'll scope it out and report back, but you need to know, Grunt. We're not going to stop this. There's no way in fucking hell that Ford is going to let this slide."

"Yeah," I admit, knowing he's telling the truth.

"Well, let's go meet this little Gabby chick and see how she likes a real man."

"Man, she's like Lyla's twin. Please tell me you're not going to flirt with her. Lyla's like our kid," I growl.

"She's not Lyla," he shrugs, like that makes it okay.

There's nothing I can say in response to that, so I do what I'm famous for.

I grunt my disapproval, then I follow the asshole over to

where the girl is. As we get closer, I'm still amazed at how much this Gabby looks like Lyla. But, it's the girl that's with her that catches most of my attention. She's got this flaming red hair, pale, almost ivory skin that has a sprinkle of freckles over her body. She's wearing a leather jacket, jeans and a red shirt that shows more cleavage than is decent, but fuck if I'm not enjoying it.

And so is my dick.

Chapter 2
Jasmine

"Gabby, you have to snap yourself out of it," I grumble, taking a drink of my vanilla milkshake. My thighs don't need the shake, but my sanity does.

"I just can't believe Dom ended things like this."

"Maybe after things die down—"

"Don't you dare suggest I wait around for Dom to get his head out of his ass, Jasmine Blake, because if you do—so help me!"

"Cool your tits, chick. I just thought if you love him—"

"I do, but if this is how he wants to treat me, I don't need him," she huffs, taking a large, *loud*, slurp of her coconut milkshake. I wrinkle my nose up at the thought of the taste. I'm a purist when it comes to my ice cream. Give me vanilla, and an occasional chocolate, and I'm good. Every now and then, when I get a wild hair, strawberry is good—but that's it. It's boring, but if my family knew how truly boring I was, they'd all have heart attacks. I give them hell; I know I do. I can't seem to stop myself. It's not that I don't love them, it's not even that they don't love

5

me. They love me, just as much as I do them. The truth is... just complicated."

"Then get back up on the horse again."

"The horse? Ever since you dated that cop-slash-cowboy, I don't understand half of what you say," Gabby complains.

I shake my head.

"I don't think you can call what we did dating and in the end, he fucked me over epically—so..."

"Yeah, did you ever tell your parents the real reason you had all those fines and tickets?"

"It wouldn't have helped matters," I mutter, not looking her in the eye, choosing instead to stare down at my milkshake. "They have come to expect the worst from me. It's easier to just let them believe it."

"Still, he was an asshole. If you told Uncle—"

"Can we let it drop? I get my license back in a couple of months and my community service is almost over. Once all of that is done, Dewayne Lagger will just be a bad decision in a series of bad decisions."

"I still think you're letting him off easy," Gabby mutters and we share a smile.

She's the only person outside my brother Hawk who truly understands me. There are times that I think I would go insane without her. She and Hawk have always been in my corner when no one else was. Admittedly, a lot of those people I've pushed away, but I've tried pushing away Gabby, too.

She just refused to let me.

I'm damaged. I admit it freely. There's something inside of me that just pushes and pushes. I don't know how to stop it.

I never have.

"He'll crash and burn one day," I tell her, and I figure he will. Hopefully when he does, it won't be because my father found out and killed him.

"Hey, there."

I look up to see this hot guy, staring down at Gabby and standing beside our table. He's covered in tatts and wearing a plain white t-shirt, faded blue jeans, and jet-black hair with not exactly a beard, but definitely a day to two of stubble.

I could almost laugh. Gabby has that effect on guys. She always has. She got the best of both worlds. She somehow managed to get her mother's blonde hair with her father's dark coloring. She's got her dad's full lips and though my Aunt Beth is gorgeous, she doesn't have Gabby's curves. Gabby had to get all of those from her dad's family and she works them.

The guy is sexy and definitely rocking a blue-collar vibe. He's hot, I can admit that, but the guy standing behind him is the one that catches my eye. Maybe he does because he's not staring at Gabby like she's a juicy steak he wants to eat. No, he's staring straight at me, his blue eyes boring into me. The other guy might be hot, but this guy? He is off the charts.

He's got soft honey-brown hair that's a little too long, but not so long that you can't tell he gets it cut semi-regularly. Right now, the wind is blowing, and it floats around his face with the breeze. He has an army green Henley on that is long sleeved. His arms and hands are covered in tattoos. The ink disappears under his sleeves. He's definitely hot and he's trouble, especially with the way he keeps his gaze trained on me, smoldering intensity and all, makes me feel alive.

Which is bad.

The last guy to do that, was so bent on destroying my father, he nearly destroyed me. I'm done with guys in general.

"Hello?" Gabby says, and I hide my grin. She's used to guys hitting on her and this one she's apparently decided to play cool and indifferent with. It was probably a good call, because I can even see the surprise that flashes over the guys face.

"I saw you sitting over here, and I have to say you are a nine baby."

"A nine?" she murmurs, as if she's considering the number. "Just a nine? That's disappointing. Maybe you'll find someone better at a different table—or maybe even a different restaurant," she tells him with a saccharine smile. I let out a snort, looking down at the table. When I look up tall, dark and broody is staring at me. I shift uncomfortably in my seat.

"Why baby? I'm the one that you need to make a perfect ten."

"Oh Lord Jesus help us from corny pickup lines," I mutter.

"You don't like my lines?" the man asks.

"They're overdone." The guy that's been staring a hole through me grunts in what, oddly enough, I think might be humor and even though I know I shouldn't, I turn my attention back to him. "What's your name?" I ask him. It doesn't truly surprise me for some reason when he doesn't answer. "What's your friend's damage?" I ask the guy with him.

"Grunt," he answers. "He's the quiet shy type."

"Yeah, right," I mutter.

"You don't believe me?" he asks with a smirk. He has a nice smile, but he's clearly a player. Gabby needs to get back out there, but not with this guy.

"I never trust a man who tries to pick up a woman with cheesy lines," I respond shrugging helplessly.

"I should at least get an A for effort," he reasons.

"Don't know if you know this or not stud, but I'm not sure a man should strive to get an A in effort."

"You'd rather he not even try?" the guy asks. I look at Mr. Broody as I consider his question.

"I'd rather he gets an A in delivery," I finally respond. The man I'm staring at still doesn't talk, but I catch the slight arc of his eyebrow with my answer and the way his lips twitch. Too bad I've sworn off men, because I get the feeling he'd be a fun bull to try and wrangle...

Chapter 3

Grunt

"You better have a damn good reason as to why you didn't bring the girl here, motherfuckers," Ford rages.

"We made contact, Prez, man," Jonesy mutters.

"Then why in the fuck isn't she here?" Ford growls.

"I know you want this shit fixed soon, man, but we have to tread carefully here."

"I want this fucker's head on a pike. The best way to do that is to get this damn girl here—"

"Prez, the DC's have never been about hurting women, despite our reputation. Do you truly think this is the best way to go here?" I try to reason. I know it's not going to help when Ford just stares at me like I've lost my fucking mind.

"If you two lazy fucks can't carry this out, I'll get Hog and we'll do it. Jesus I expect this shit from Jonesy, Grunt, but when did you get so damn soft?"

I snort at his insinuation. I'm not fucking soft. I'm being smart, which is something he's not being and hasn't since Lyla has been grieving this loser ex-boyfriend of hers.

"We'll get her, Prez. Give us a week. We need to do it in a

way that suspicions aren't arose. You don't want the whole fucking Blaze club on our ass, do you?"

"No, I don't. I know you're right. But, hell man, she's grieving over this asshole. How did I miss the fact she had some worthless prick in her life?"

"You still don't have any information on him?"

"No. Lyla refuses. She says he's not worth her time, that he threw her aside for Gabby Cruz and she's done with him."

"This right here is why I've never had kids," Jonesy growls.

"You've never had kids because there hasn't been a woman desperate enough to let you breed her," Ford mutters.

"It's a wonder you had Lyla if you told Sherry that you were going to breed her," I point out.

Ford shrugs, gives a resigned smile. "She was too mercenary to care," he answers and boy do I know what he's talking about.

"Fine, we'll bide our time. I'll let you try to find out who this fuckhead is that hurt my daughter first. You have a couple of weeks. You find him, you bring him to me. You don't, you bring the girl and then he'll come to us."

"Hell, Prez, man I wanted to go on the Chicago run with Tweet and the others. Don't have me running after these damn girls all the time. I'll go crazy," Jonesy complains.

"Bullshit, Jonesy. Since when have you ever hated following girls?" Ford responds, making me laugh under my breath—because he's right. If there's a pretty girl involved, Jonesy is there.

"Man, these chicks are jailbait. Not to mention, one looks just like your daughter. The other one is a redhead and you *know* my history with those bitches. Three words Ford. No. Thank. You."

I smirk as Ford shakes his head. Jonesy's ex was a red head and man did she have a hell of a temper. Of course, Jonesy got his name because he's always jonesin' for the next best thing. Fucker is never satisfied, and his ex's find that out the hard way.

"I'll do it, Pres. I have zero interest in traveling to Chicago."

"You sure? You're my enforcer after all, the boys might need you."

"It's an easy run and through friendly territory. Jonesy here can handle it without me.

"Damn straight I can. I taught you everything you know anyway, asshole."

"Except how to bulk up in the gym," I remind him, and he flips me off. Jonesy has muscles, but as enforcer I make sure that I can take anyone out there in a fair fight and know all the tricks to come out in an unfair one. You might have an off day, and you will eventually go against a man who might be a little faster or a little smarter than you. The trick is to know how to handle yourself so that even when that shit happens you come out the winner. In my world, life depends on that particular talent.

"Fine, it's settled then. Now get out of my sight, the both of you. I got shit to do," he grumbles, going back to the paperwork on his desk and already ignoring us.

"You're not fooling me, you know," Jonesy murmurs quietly after I close the door.

"What do you mean?"

"I saw the way you were eye-fucking that red head. You have your own reason for wanting to tail the girls."

I grunt my answer, because he's right, but I'm not about to admit it. Jonesy's loud, obnoxious laughter follows me down the hall.

Chapter 4

Jasmine

"Is there a reason you're watching me?" I ask Mr. Broody from the other day.

He's been following me off and on since the other day. I've spotted him each time. I'm not sure if he was trying to hide the fact that he was or not. When you grow up in a biker club, you spot a tail pretty easily. My father taught me that special skill. He doesn't trust cops. Then again, he doesn't trust anyone outside of the Savage club. I'm pretty sure he doesn't even trust me, although he does love me. I could complain about that, but I don't understand myself most of the time, not sure I can expect them to at this point.

He looks down at me—because he literally towers over me. He's broad and tall. The kind of man that would make a woman weak in the knees—or wet between the legs. Again, I remind myself that I've sworn off men. Especially when his lips twitch and move just enough to say he's *almost* smiling. I get the feeling that Mr. Broody doesn't really smile at all. This might be as good as it gets.

Too bad it's really damn good.

Keeping Her

When he doesn't answer, I give him the look that I give my brother Hawk. The one where I'm annoyed, but he's not worth the effort or muscle movement to roll my eyes.

"If you're not going to talk, then maybe you should move on down the road because your stalking is annoying," I finally mumble before walking back to the picnic table I was at earlier.

"Where's the girl you're always with?" he asks, following me. I close my eyes for a second, because his question hurts.

It's stupid, of course. I mean, I just got done reminding myself that I had sworn off men. I sure don't want one that has verbal issues and stalking tendencies. Still, I thought he was following me because he liked what he saw and you can say what you want, that's damn good for a girl's ego sometimes. At the very least, I thought he might feel some of the attraction I feel toward him.

Not that I'd ever act on it. Ever.

"That explains it," I mumble, instead of punching him in the balls when he comes to stand over me. I finish settling in on the seat, and don't bother looking up to acknowledge him. There's no point.

"Explains what?" he pursues, proving he might have verbal issues, but he definitely doesn't have hearing ones.

I put down the pencil I just picked up and look at him. I hate that he's so pretty. He looks like he could be a movie star, or on the cover of a GQ magazine. It's annoying. When I'm done swearing off men, I'm going to find an ugly guy. That way I don't have to live with his freaking ego.

"All the guys chase after Gabby. She ignores them all because she only has eyes for one guy. So, if I were you, Mr. Broody, I'd just move along, because it's a lost cause there."

"Why do they chase after her?" he questions, making me rethink the whole he's nonverbal line of thought.

"Gee, I don't know. Why are you?" I lean back to look at him.

He surprises me by sitting down—not on the bench, but on the top of the table, his feet down on the bench part. I take him in, my mind filing away little pieces of his appearance to check out later —if he keeps annoying me that is.

"I never said I was, Red. You did." He doesn't move his gaze away from me and, for some reason, I get the feeling that he's taking notes, too. He's dressed in a black t-shirt today with black pants, motorcycle boots and a wide black leather strap around his wrist. There's an insignia ring on his forefinger and I can't tell what the engraving is, but my interest is piqued. I find myself staring at his hands, probably too long. They're masculine and sexy, callused and tanned. They tell me that he is definitely used to manual labor and I like that. I've always liked that in a man.

Damn it.

I could point out he asked about Gabby, but I don't, instead I lean back, rolling my pencil between my fingers as I study him.

"She's curvy, sweet, funny, and she has the blonde hair and blue eyes that men seem to go gaga over and lose all ability to reason."

"Not me. I'm not into blondes."

"Yeah, baby, tell me another one," I snort.

"I like that," he says, his voice dropping down to a sweet sound that literally forces me to look into his eyes.

"Like what?" I ask, confused, but intrigued all at the same time.

"You calling me baby."

"Are you flirting with me?" I ask him, not quite believing it.

"Is that so surprising?"

"I'm not Gabby," I remind him.

"I've had a couple of blondes in my time. Crazy bitches that get all twisted up in emotion. Not really my type."

"And what is your type…Grunt, right?"

Keeping Her

"You remembered. Should I be flattered?" he asks, those lips of his twitching again.

"You can be whatever you want to be. Last I checked it was a free country, Grunt," I reply with a shrug.

"You can call me, Luke," he says and suddenly I feel like I'm in dangerous territory.

"Is that like some big honor?" I ask him.

"It's my name," he shrugs, studying my face.

"Are you a biker?" I ask, watching him closely.

I see surprise flash in his eyes.

"What makes you ask that?"

"Grew up around them and I'm not stupid," I respond, waiting.

"Now, that's something I never thought you were."

"Mmm-hmm," I murmur. "Are you going to answer?"

"Are you part of the Devil's Blaze like your girl?"

"You've been doing your homework," I respond, surprised, but refusing to let it show.

"Partly, but everyone around these parts know who Skull and the Devil's Blaze are," he says easily. I wonder what he'd say about my dad's club, but I don't go there. I'm not sure what this guy's agenda is, but something is setting off warning bells. Then, a thought pops into my head.

"You looking to sign up with the Blaze?"

"You think they would have me?" he asks, and his lip twitch deepens into a smile. I get a feeling that's a rare occurrence.

"No idea. I don't talk to any of them other than Gabby and her brother. You could always try. You look a little old to be a prospect, though, *Luke*."

"Changed my mind," he mumbles.

"About?"

"I'd rather you call me baby. It makes my dick twitch."

I laugh, surprised and unable to hide it.

15

"Maybe you should see a doctor about that. It could be a serious condition," I suggest, still laughing.

"It could be. You got a PhD in your name anywhere?"

"Afraid not."

"That's okay. I trust you. I'll let you inspect my dick anyway."

I shake my head. I know he's joking but he's back to looking at me, the only thing giving away his laughter is his eyes. Clear, Prussian blue eyes, that I like way more than I should.

"Do you normally get girls using this approach, Luke?"

"Never really tried. Never had a problem finding a girl to fuck though, if that's your question."

I blink at his bluntness, but for some reason I like it. I get the feeling that with Luke a girl would know exactly where she stands.

Again, I remind myself that I've sworn off men.

"What are you drawing?" he asks, switching topics. I look down at my forgotten sketch pad. I suppose he can't tell what it is, but in my mind it's a picture of my little brother, Hawk—although he's not that little anymore.

"Just a picture," I shrug, I gasp as he picks the pad up. I want to yell at him to put it down, but I don't. My pictures are a weakness and I learned a while back that you never show a weakness. It's something that can be exploited.

"Of a man," he says and since I just got the barest outline of his face, it surprises me that he can tell that.

"Yes."

"You got a man?"

"Several of them," I tell him. I'm not really lying. If you count my brother, my father, Uncle Dragon and the other guys in the club, I have a lot of men in my life.

"That's okay. I like a little healthy competition," he says with a grin. "Let's go Red," he adds, sliding from the table, way too gracefully for someone with his size and bulk. Then he tucks my pad under his arm and offers me his hand.

"Go? Where are we going?"

"I'm buying you lunch, and you can tell me all about those other men I have to beat out to get between your legs."

"I can't decide if you're trying to be an asshole or if that's just who you are," I laugh.

"It's who I am, but don't worry, I can already tell that you like it," he says. Then he shakes his hand, his eyebrow cocked in challenge.

I shouldn't do it. I know I shouldn't.

I do it anyway.

I put my hand in his and reluctantly let him pull me from the table, all while reminding myself that I've sworn off men.

Damn it.

Chapter 5

Grunt

"I've had a good day with you, Luke," Jasmine says, and she sounds genuinely surprised. I guess I can understand that. I knew I was drawn to the girl, but even I have to admit that today was better than I imagined it would be.

"Go home with me and I'll make it better."

"God, you're such a flirt," she laughs.

"I'm not flirting, Red. I'm simply stating a fact." I counter. Then, I step into her, closing the distance between us. The sweet smell of her surrounds me. She reminds me of wildflowers on a sunny day. "Come home with me and I'll rock your fucking world," I promise, bending down so that our lips are closer. Like this I can hear her audible intake of breath. With my hand on her neck like it is, I can feel a fine tremor that runs through her. She wants me, and she's not going out of her way to hide it either. Jasmine is different than any woman I've ever met. She's not shy, she's definitely more direct. I like that. I admire the way she doesn't try to hide what she's feeling. I like it even more that she wants me.

I want her too. I wanted her before, but after spending the

day with her, I want her even more. I'm fast approaching the point of no return. I have to have her, taste her and satisfy the curiosity she raises inside of me.

We spent the rest of the day together after talking in the park. I took her out for lunch, and we spent the rest of the day riding my bike and enjoying the scenery. Now we're back where we started, standing a couple yards away from her Corolla. It's a newish model car and a metallic flake blue color. It's cute for a girl, but it doesn't suit Red. She needs something racy.

Red is going to be a major problem. I mean, I'm not a man to have a chick on the back of my bike, but I wanted her there. Hell, I still do.

"I think you need to slow way down." Her voice is quieter, almost as if she's embarrassed to turn me down. I mean, fuck, I would have been fucking ecstatic if she had said yes, but I didn't expect it. Jasmine is a strange mix of woman. She can bust your balls but seem almost fragile the next minute. Maybe it's just a package she's selling and not real, but whatever it is, I'm buying it.

"I'm good at going slow too, Red."

"You realize I'm not the girl for you, Luke," she drawls, her eyes narrowing on me.

"I think I'm a better judge of that than you are."

"You're crazy. I have to go. I'm going to be late and Mom and Dad are already giving me hell as it is."

Jesus. Mom and Dad?

"How old are you?"

"Oh, I know that tone," she laughs. "Is big-bad-wanna-be-biker afraid I'm jailbait?"

"Woman, there's nothing wanna-be about me," I grumble.

"You said you were looking to join up with Skull's crew."

"No, you just assumed that's what I meant," I correct her, and she stares at me and then shakes her head.

"Why do I get the feeling that you are very skilled at getting information and not giving any?"

"Because you're smart," I tell her, smiling. That's something else that's new. I've smiled all evening. Yeah, I'm fucking strung up over this chick. Prez is going to seriously kick my ass for not following the other girl today. I should worry about that, but I'm not going to. I don't actually give a damn right now—probably because I'm thinking with my dick.

A throbbing hard dick that's dying to get inside this sassy little redhead...

"Are you jailbait, Red?"

"What would you do if I said yes?"

"Back off, at least for now. I've done a stint in jail, don't really have an inclination to go back any time soon."

"Yeah, it's not a fun place," she says, her green eyes clouding.

"What does a pretty little thing like you know about jail?" Damn, if I'm not getting the vibe that she does. Seems Red has a lot of layers and damn if I'm not liking every single one of them.

"It's been fun, Grunt, I'm sure I'll see you later," she mutters, turning away from me.

I grab her wrist, pulling her back around. She spins in my direction, her hand coming out to slap against my chest to steady herself.

"What the hell?" she huffs, clearly pissed off.

"You either call me Luke or baby, or some shit like that. The name Grunt never passes your lips again, Red."

She opens her mouth to give me more sass but must think twice about it, because it snaps shut a second later. Then, her eyes narrow, and I swear to God her eyes look like they're throwing fire at me. It's burning me too—right in the fucking balls. When I get a hold of this girl, I may not let her out of my bed for a week.

"How about I don't talk to you ever again? Then, we don't

have to worry about whether I call you Grunt or asshole. How does that work for you, *baby?*"

"I've warned you once, Red. That's the only warning you get. Personally, I want you to push me. I'd take great pleasure in punishing your sweet ass."

"Punishing..." Her eyes dilate as she says that one word, her ivory skin, heating with color. *"My sweet ass?"* she screeches. "Are you delusional? You're not getting anywhere near my ass and if you try, so help me God, I'll cut off your balls and serve them to you!"

"There's my fire," I growl, putting my hand at the back of her neck and taking her mouth, my cock so hard that it's painful.

Jasmine holds her body stiff, not giving in at all. I plunder her mouth with a bruising force, my hold on her neck just as punishing. I don't allow her to get away from me, to run from this. I feel the vibration of her humming and slowly her body softens, and she begins kissing me back. Her tongue fighting for dominance, trying to take over. I don't let her. Jasmine needs to learn that I'm in charge, but I'll give her everything she needs and more.

She will...in time...

Chapter 6

Jasmine

"Will you pay attention to me?" Gabby chastises.

My head jerks away from the window to look at her. I don't even pretend that I was listening. I don't have that in me today.

"Sorry. What were you saying?"

"What is up with you today, Jazzy?" Gabby mutters clearly exasperated.

When Gabby gets upset, her brow crinkles up and her eyes narrow. She really is beautiful, but when she's pissed she reminds me of a teacher I had in grade school. Ms. Hester was so intimidating when she was mad. She walked around with a ruler slapping against her hand and you just knew it was going to come down like the hammer of Thor and get your hand at any moment. Ms. Hester didn't care that the world had shifted away from corporal punishment. She was more of the spare the rod, spoil the child mindset.

"Nothing," I lie. "Just have crap on my mind."

"Shit, is Officer Jerk-Off bothering you again?"

"Nah. It's been silent on that front at least," I mutter, not liking even wasting a moment thinking about Dewayne.

Keeping Her

"That's good. I still think you needed to tell your father what the dickhead did."

"It's not worth it, Gabby," I murmur, picking at the pasta in my plate. We're eating at an Italian place in London. Gabby is getting ready to go back to college. I gave up on college. That's another thing my parents aren't taking that great. Heck, at this rate, I feel like nothing but one giant failure in my parents' eyes. At least they got one perfect child in Hawk. He's getting ready to start medical school in the fall.

"Maybe, maybe not," she says, but I ignore her. She wouldn't understand.

"Well, if it's not Officer Jack Off, it's something. Why are you so quiet? Where's that bitchy Jazzy I know and love?"

I sigh. She's right. I am quiet. It's been three days and I haven't seen Luke again. After he came on so strong, and the great evening we had together, the last thing I expected from him was a disappearing act.

Who does that?

Go home with me baby, I'll rock your world...

And then just silence.

He's another player, just like Dewayne. I have to have something inside of me, some kind of chemical that lures assholes to me like a bee to honey.

"Have you heard from Dom?" I ask Gabby, changing the subject. Once she gets started on Dom she forgets everything else. She'll whine about him for the rest of the day, which sucks, but it's better than me having to tell her about Luke.

"Not a fucking word and I've about had it, Jazz. If he can just throw me to the curb like that, I don't need his ass."

"To be fair, he's in a bad situation, Gab. I mean, his brother is hung up on you."

"I love Thomas, don't get it twisted. But, he's like my brother. Kissing him was like...kissing someone's ears. Kinda

23

gross," she says, scrunching up her face like she just sucked a lemon.

"Hold up," I cry, sliding back from the table to look at my best friend who just apparently grew another head while I wasn't looking. "You kissed Thomas?"

She looks up at me, her mouth open, as if she didn't realize what she just confessed. Her cheeks turn pale pink—and since her complexion makes her look like a bronze goddess, that means if it were me, I'd be red as a beet.

"Well, yeah."

"Oh my God, Gabby! What were you thinking?"

She slaps her fork down against her dish. It makes a large clanging noise that sounds like it might have possibly cracked the plate. I ignore it however, never taking my gaze from her.

"Quit acting like that, Jazz."

"Like what?"

"All holier than thou. Like you haven't done worse!"

"You kissed Thomas!"

"So? I had to see if there was anything there, didn't I? Dom was being an asshole and I just needed to feel… special. Thomas has me on a pedestal. It was…"

"Stupid. Stupid is the word you're searching for Gabby."

"I just needed to feel like someone cared for me, okay? Quit acting like I killed someone, for fuck's sake."

"You didn't kill him, but you might as well have torn his heart out. No wonder Dom walked away. Did you think Thomas wouldn't tell Dom that you kissed? Fuck, you didn't do anything more than that did you?"

"I…"

"Oh my God, Gabby! You Ho!"

"No! I mean we didn't do *that*. It didn't go very far. It was like second base, maybe leaning into the third, but I was drinking, and the phone rang… so it stopped."

"It stopped because the phone rang?"

"Yeah, but it wouldn't have gone very much farther. I was already going to call a halt to it."

"Jesus, Gabby. Why didn't you tell me?"

"Because I *knew* this was how you would react."

"Because you knew it was wrong. I bet Dom lost his shit."

"I wouldn't know. He's not talking to me."

"No wonder. Christ, Gabby. They're brothers."

"I know that!" she cries. "Don't you think I know that better than anyone?" I can see that Gabby is close to crying, so I reach out and pat her hand. I suck at giving comfort. It makes me feel uncomfortable.

"It will be okay."

"I don't see how. Dom won't talk to me, and I'm pretty sure Thomas hates me now."

"Maybe it would be good to distance yourself from them both, Gabby."

"I know. I know what you're saying. I've been trying. I just... I love Dom, Jazz," she says sadly, her voice breaking. "I've always loved him."

"Sometimes love ain't enough, baby girl," I tell her sadly, sounding like some fucking greeting card.

"It hurts."

"I know, Gab, trust me."

"Did you love Dewayne?"

"I thought so at the time, but it's hard to love someone you didn't truly know," I confess.

"Do you think you can ever truly know a man?"

My mind goes to Luke and how he was with me and then going quiet for three days.

"No, I don't," I confess. "And I'm tired of even trying. I'm going to stick with the only boyfriend who never lets me down."

"Who's that?" Gabby laughs.

"My vibrator," I joke, laughing with her. We clink our glasses together in toast and I push all thoughts of Luke from my head. I don't need another man that plays games.

Chapter 7

Grunt

"Why aren't you going near her?" Jonesy asks in that annoying voice he has when he thinks he has something on you.

I snort under my breath, but don't bother answering. My silence just makes the asshole laugh, but I don't have much I can say.

Because I don't know what in the fuck I'm doing.

When I got back to the club the other day, Ford was waiting on me. I should have known he'd be watching the girl too. He wasn't happy that I wasn't there. I tried to play it off that I was watching the girl's friend, but Ford isn't stupid. He knows this girl is under my skin. We weren't fooling one another. He didn't say much, but he did remind me of my oath.

Club first.

Motherfucker, I'm doing my best to put the DC's first, but I miss Jasmine. How you can miss a woman you barely know this hard after three days is fucking unreal, but it's true.

"Go down there and quit being a chump," Jonesy dares me.

"Fuck off," I mutter, the temptation to do that so strong I want to punch him.

"Okay, okay," he says, holding his hands up in surrender. "I'll shut up," he says holding up his hands in surrender.

"Good," I rumble under my breath.

"You think Ford's going to go through with kidnapping this girl?"

"If it's the only way he can get to the guy who hurt Lyla, then yeah, I think he will."

"It's going to cause a club war."

"We've weathered them before." I shrug, feeling older than my years and worn-the-fuck-out.

"True enough. I just can't see why we can't go after the guy directly. Leave this Gabby chick out of it."

"That might be easier if we knew who the guy was."

"Do we know what he looks like?"

"Not a lot, no. Why?"

"Cause there's a guy that just came to their table. It could be him..."

"Good, you let me know. I'm taking a fucking nap," I mutter, leaning back in the truck seat.

We're sitting across from the diner that Jasmine and the other chick are at. Jasmine's body has teased me enough today. She's wearing faded, cut-off jeans and a faded red t-shirt. Her long red hair is just a huge mass of curls that falls around her face and down her back, and I had to stop watching her before I blew my cover. Ford wanted us to follow them without them knowing it, see if we could figure out who the guy is that hurt Lyla. Because of that, we brought the truck to keep hidden from the girls. After three days of being in this cage, I'm ready to scream.

I want my bike and the open road.

I'm lying through my teeth.

I want Jasmine in my bed, my cock buried deep inside of her, and her nails biting into my back. I want her screaming out my name as I fuck her harder and harder, pushing her as far as she thinks she can go and then pushing her beyond that.

That girl is driving me fucking insane.

"Hmm... I don't think that's our boy."

"Why do you say that?" I ask, stifling a yawn.

"Because he just came and picked the redhead up and sat down with her in his lap."

My body goes stiff. I turn to look toward the diner and see this tall asshole with dark hair, with his arms around Jasmine and she's laughing, cuddled up to him, while sitting in his damn lap.

Fuck no. That's not happening.

"Where are you going?" Jonesy laughs, as I bail out of the truck stomping my way across the street.

Ford can just bitch. I'll do this my way, and in the process I'm going to show Jasmine that I'm not about to share her.

Chapter 8

Jasmine

"Hawk! Put me down!"

"There's only two seats at the table," he says, plopping down in the chair and keeping me in his lap.

"Then steal one!"

"I'm the good one in the family. I can't do that. Now settle down, you're causing a scene," he laughs. Gabby laughs along with him and I'm glad to see some of the sadness gone from her face.

"You're a jerk," I mutter, trying to hide my grin. I do love my brother. We're as different as night and day. I'm definitely the black sheep while he's the golden child, but he's always there for me. *Always.*

"What are you girls up to today?" Hawk asks, stealing a bite of my garlic bread.

"I wasn't hungry at all," I huff.

"It's bread, Sis. I'm just helping you to shrink that ass you're always complaining you have."

"I happen to like my ass."

"Today maybe, but you complain all the time."

"He's right about that," Gabby says, smirking at me.

"You're such an asshole, Hawk. Remind me again why I love you," I grumble.

"I'm your favorite person in the world," he shrugs and while what he's saying is mostly true, I elbow him in the gut.

"Ow," he moans, rubbing his stomach—which is mostly rock hard and solid abs. *I'm* the one that should be rubbing my elbow at this point. "Don't make me spank your ass—"

"Let's go, Red," Luke growls, surprising me.

I had no idea he was even around. I turn my gaze toward his voice to find him standing over me and Hawk. He looks good, sadly. He's wearing a worn white t-shirt, the kind most guys where under a regular shirt. He's got on black jeans and his boots again—and this time he's wearing an MC cut, that proclaims him an enforcer of the Demon Chasers. I've never heard of them, but that's not surprising. What pisses me off is that he never mentioned it, let me think he might want to prospect for Gabby's father's club. *The asshole.*

"Red?" Hawk asks, looking up at Luke as my brother studies him.

I can tell Luke has already dismissed Hawk. That's a mistake. Hawk might not look like the guys in the club, but my brother could take any of them—and that's not sisterly pride. Dad's proud of him. I think he secretly wants him to become part of the club, but he's always said our lives were ours to live. My father had his choices taken away from him in his life. He knows how important that is—even when he doesn't agree. He's proud of Hawk. Me? I think he wants to strangle, but he does love me. I've never doubted that.

What I'm unsure of right now is Luke. He's pissed and I mean *really* pissed. His face is locked into place, stiff and unmovable. Anger is radiating from him and firing in his brown eyes. My first reaction shouldn't be that he's extremely hot when he's mad. I also shouldn't feel myself get wet when I stare at him like that. I've always known I'm different from other girls. It turns out that I might be twisted.

"Are you stalking me again, *Grunt*?"

"Grunt?" Hawk's body grows stiff beneath me, but I ignore my brother. If Luke can be pissed, so can I. He's basically ignored me for three days and now he shows up, acting like an overbearing asshole—ordering me around and not even saying hi first.

Definitely an asshole.

"I told you what would happen if you called me that. Now, get your ass out of this fuck-head's lap and get over here."

"I'm quite comfortable where I am, thank you very much," I sass back, with a saccharine smile plastered on my face.

"If you don't get over here, you'll be uncomfortable for a week because I'll leave blisters on your ass."

"I'd like to see you try. You lay a hand on me and I'll gut you like a pig, Grunt. *Annnnd...I'll do it smiling.*" I add the last part, by drawing out the word and showing that the idea brings me nothing but pure glee.

Hawk laughs, probably because he knows I can do it. You don't grow up around the men I did, who live the lives they live and not know how to defend yourself. Especially since so many of their women were in danger in the past. They take self-defense classes seriously and bring them to a *whole* new level.

"We'll play our little love games later. Now get your ass over here," Luke huffs, but I get the feeling he's wanting to laugh at my comeback. I saw a spark in his eyes and that spark fuels my anger.

"*What?*" I screech, sliding off of Hawk's lap, slapping my hands on my hips and stepping up to Luke. "Who in the fuck do you think you are?" I snarl, my anger beginning to rise to what my family likes to call the danger zone.

Keeping Her

"The man that's going to tame you if it kills the both of us," he growls back.

"Tame me?" I screech.

"Who is the guy?" I hear Hawk ask Gabby.

"No clue, he showed up a few days ago and got Jazzy all hot and bothered and then ghosted her," she says.

I jerk my head to look at her, my eyes going wide. "I did not get hot and bothered over him!"

"Oh, please. You so were! You've been pouting for three days. You've barely paid attention to anything I've said since you met him," Gabby whines.

I can't believe she just outed me. *Who does that?* I'm pretty sure there's a girl code about that shit.

"I've been ignoring you because there's only so much I can handle about you *mooning* over Dom. You need to kick his ass to the curb and move on," I snarl, and okay, that was harsh, but I'm pissed, and she started this shit.

I turn back around to see Luke nodding at his buddy Jonesy, and I narrow my eyes at them.

"What?" My question is more of a demand, because I want to know what's going on. It feels like they're communicating with each other about something and since he already lied to me about being part of a club, I'm not big on trusting either of them right now.

"We're leaving. Say goodbye to your girl," Luke orders.

"I'm not going anywhere with you, you idiot," I argue.

"I don't think I'm her girl anymore," Gabby says, and I close my eyes, because I know I'm going to have to grovel to get her over being pissed. Gabby can be a bit of a drama queen, even though that's what most think I am.

"And I don't think she wants to go with you," Hawk announces, standing up.

Oh shit.

Jordan Marie

I know that tone and I need to do something quick. The problem is, Hawk's not wrong. The last thing I want to do is go anywhere with Luke.

Damn it! How do I get in these situations!?!?!

Chapter 9

Grunt

"Kid, this ain't none of your damn business. You need to step back," I mutter. I just want to collect my woman and get the fuck out of here. Now that we have the kid's name who has hurt Lyla, we can get shit handled without involving Jasmine's friend, which is good, since she looks like she already wants to kill me. I don't need to piss her off any more than I already have.

"If it involves Jazz, it involves me," he says, folding his arms at his chest.

"Is this one of them, Red?"

"One of them what? Will you start making sense?" she mutters, and I swear to God, if I didn't want to strangle her right now, I'd kiss her instead.

"One of your many boyfriends."

Gabby gasps, and the boy laughs, surprising me. Maybe he thinks it laughable that I called him a kid, but hell, that's what he is. A damn kid. I doubt he's even old enough to buy his own fucking beer.

"Oh God," she mumbles, covering her face.

"Many boyfriends, Jazz? How many do you have?"

"Shut up, Hawk."

"You need to leave, Gru—"

"Baby, I've been pretty damn understanding to this point, but if you call me Grunt one more time, I'm throwing you over my shoulder and carrying you out of here and when I get you back to my place, I'm going to remind you exactly who I am," I warn her.

"I think I liked you better when you didn't talk," she mutters and Jonesy, being the dick that he is, laughs.

"Let's go."

"If you think I'm going anywhere with you after three days of silence you're insane. I don't know what kind of games you like playing with a girl, but I don't like them."

I rub the back of my neck and let out a frustrated sigh. Why can't I be attracted to a boring, calm, whiney bitch like the blonde? She wouldn't give me lip and she'd be a decent lay. I could even forget her through the fucking day and most of the night. I'd probably even manage to like her—at least when my cock was in her mouth and she couldn't bellyache me to death.

"I've been busy, Red. I'm not like the boys you fool with that aren't out of school. I have commitments and a job," I breathe, trying to find patience, but the longer she's standing closer to *Hawk* than to me, the harder it is.

"Oh," she mumbles, as if that just occurred to her. "You know what? That's another thing. You didn't tell me you were part of an MC. You let me think you were looking to sign up with Gabby's father's club."

"Daddy wouldn't have him," Gabby says, and I roll my eyes. Yeah, I couldn't fuck her even if I taped her mouth shut.

"I didn't say I was looking to sign up. You just assumed and I didn't correct you."

"I..." her mouth snaps shut, and she narrows her eyes at me. I know I've made my point and so does she, but she's clearly not happy about it. "Whatever, you *still* could have called me."

"I didn't have your number, woman. Now, will you get over here?"

"I don't think she should. We don't know a damn thing about you, and I don't really like your attitude," Hawk says, grabbing Jasmine's arm to hold her back—not that she was coming to me, like a smart woman, but still, I don't like that he thinks he has any control over this situation.

"Ask me if I give a fuck what you think, pretty boy."

"Pretty boy," Hawk laughs, taking a step toward me. He's got balls, I'll give him that. It will be fun to squash them under my boot and watch him cry like a baby, when I take Jasmine out of here.

"That's what I said. You sure ain't a man. You're walking around in a suit that probably cost more than most people make in a month and meanwhile Jasmine here is wearing shit clothes. You don't deserve her."

"Oh my God! My clothes are not shit!" Jasmine huffs.

"Babe," I laugh, shaking my head.

"What? I look perfectly fine!"

"He's right, Jazz. Those cutoffs are older than I am and I'm not too sure that shirt isn't too," Gabby says, resulting in Jasmine rolling her eyes.

"Give me a break. Not everyone can be you. I mean who wears a freaking white pants suit to east spaghetti? If I did that it would be all over me," Jasmine huffs.

"Baby," I laugh, loving the show she's got going on right now.

"If you don't like the way I dress, *Grunt*, you're welcome to leave. That way you don't have to see me again," she says so sweetly it could give me a toothache. Then, she turns around to grab her purse with an annoyed breath.

"I warned you, Red," I growl from behind her, wrapping my arms around her. She lets out a startled squawking nose, just as I pick her up.

"What are you doing?" she demands, and I have to concentrate, because all I can think of is how good it feels to have her back in my arms.

"You and I are going to have this shit out, Red."

"Jazz do you need me?" Hawk asks, but I don't turn around to look at the fucker.

"Uh..."

"Call him over here and you'll get pretty boy hurt, Red. I can think of nothing better than to smash his face in and break his hands because they were on your body," I murmur for her ears only, leaning down to deliver my warning against her ear.

"I..."

"Not kidding, Red. Try me." I pull back and stop walking so she can look at me. She studies me and I let her, wondering if she's going to push me. I wasn't lying. I want to smash that damn boy's face in more than I've wanted anything in my life—except for maybe Jazz herself.

"I'm okay, Hawk," she says, looking over my shoulder. She stretches up to do that, causing her to shift in my hands and my hand squeezes her ass cheek. Firm, soft, lush ass that fills my hand and makes my dick cry.

I'm in deep shit with this woman.

"Good choice, Red."

"That remains to be seen," she sighs, settling down so that her head rests against my chest. That simple movement eases something inside of me and I instantly relax. "You really are a jerk," she mutters.

"I know." I smirk, but I don't look down to see her reaction.

"Good." She lets out a soft sigh and for some reason that quiet sound is beautiful to me.

Fuck...

Chapter 10

Jasmine

"This is your place?" I ask, looking around the living room. It's surprisingly roomy but absolutely no design aesthetic. There's barely furniture at all. A large couch on one wall and a television on the opposite one. The kitchen is separated by a small breakfast bar and there's a mini fridge, a sink and cabinets. *That's it.* I don't see a sign of a stove. There is a microwave.

I suppose Luke is the ultimate bachelor—at least that's what I'm seeing here.

"Not fancy enough for you, Red?" he asks, studying me. I release a breath, letting him know how annoying he's being.

Not that he cares.

"If you're going to be an asshole, I'm leaving," I mutter. "I don't care what your place looks like. I just meant...."

"What?"

"It doesn't look like you spend a lot of time here," I respond finally, with a shrug.

"I don't. I'm at the club most of the time. Some of the guys bought campers and live at the club or in the compound itself. I do that until I start needing to be by myself. Then, I end up here."

I nod, because there's not a lot more to say to that.

We left Kentucky and passed the Virginia state line, driving through downtown Norton—which reminded me of most downtowns back home in my part of Kentucky...*small*. I should have probably been nervous going with Luke. At the very least, I should have worried about crossing state lines with him, but for some reason I'm not. Well, I'm not worried about *Luke*. My father and Uncle Dragon? That might be a different story. I need to text my brother and make sure he keeps his big mouth shut. I don't want Dad coming down on me, at least until I find out what Luke's game is. He's part of an MC club and he's suddenly showing up wherever I am. Maybe I'm wrong to think that's bad news—but, I don't think so.

"Why am I here?" I finally ask, turning around to face him, and pulling my attention away from his place.

"You belong here."

He says the words matter-of-factly, as if it's written in stone somewhere. His arms are crossed at his chest, daring me to argue.

"Really?" I look around, not sure how to respond to that.

"If you don't like something here, change it," he shrugs.

Those words definitely set off warning bells. *Lots of them.*

"Why would I change it? I'm not staying."

"You are," he argues, not changing his stance even a little.

"Now, you're insane. I have a life in Kentucky, Luke."

"We're not that far from Kentucky. You can visit."

"I can... *Are you insane?*"

"If I am, you've made me that way," he says with a shrug.

"Uh...wrong. We barely know each other. You just showed up all stalkerish. Which is another thing we need to discuss. You hid the fact you were in a club, and you show up unexpectedly not once, but twice. Just what are you up to, Luke?"

"I don't know what you mean," he replies, but he shifts on his feet and something about that doesn't seem right either.

There's a lot to take in with Luke and none of it is truly adding up. Which means...

He's lying.

I don't know how I know. I just do. So, I call him on it.

"Bullshit. You're lying. You were following me. Am I getting in the middle of some club war? Is that why you kidnapped me?"

He blinks, face exposing his shock and then he shakes his head.

"You're not part of a club war, Red. How could you be? You're not even part of a club, you're just friends with someone that is, and damn it, you aren't kidnapped."

"Fine, then, I'm going home—"

"But you're not leaving either," he says, interrupting me, and I look at him like he's crazy.

"You can't keep me here against my will, Luke."

"It won't be against your will. We both know that, Jasmine. You want me."

"Is this your idea of dating a girl? Take her out, ignore her, and then show up three days later like a reject from the Tarzan movie and all, *Me, Grunt. You, Jasmine. You mine,* shit?" I yell.

I'm really starting to hate the way he makes me feel like I'm always screeching. I am *not* that person. I'm usually cold and detached. It's a finely honed trait that took me years to master. My mother hates it and my father is right there with her. Yet, Luke manages to make me sound hysterical at the drop of a hat.

"That's it," he growls, walking over to me so purposely, my heart begins beating double time. I back up, out of self-preservation.

I stop when my legs hit the back of the couch.

"What...what are you doing?" I sputter.

"Making sure you remember my fucking name," he barks,

and before I can respond, he moves his hand behind my neck, holding my head prisoner, so that it's impossible to move. Then, his lips crush mine, his tongue thrusting into my mouth and taking over every instinct I have of survival, leaving me wanting nothing more...*than more of him.*

Chapter 11

Grunt

There's only so much a man can stand. Watching Jasmine standing there, giving me hell, not scared, not cowering, but blasting my ass, is a turn on that I can't even begin to explain. I'm the muscle behind the Demon Chasers. I can be fucking intimidating and I'm used to people falling in line with what I want.

Not my Red.

She wants to bust my balls constantly and maybe that shouldn't make my dick hard, but it does. She's smart too. There's no fucking denying that. She's too close to the truth when it comes to how we met. I want to be able to tell her the truth, but I can't. I'm not dumb.

Just horny.

So, I give into the only option I have.

Fuck her stupid.

I wrap her hair around my hand, the feel of it reminds me of silk. I tug it roughly, making her gasp and then I kiss her with desire and more than a little anger. Most women would hate it, but my Red, she's not most women. She's right here with me, her tongue fighting for domination that I will never let it have. We kiss like we're going to war, and fuck, maybe we are. Our lips clash so hard, our kiss so intense, I swear I can taste the coppery flavor of blood mixed in. Which is possible, since teeth are definitely involved. My Red is a wildcat.

We break apart and she just stares at me, her breathing as ragged as mine, her eyes shooting fire.

"Take those fucking shorts off, Red," I bark, my voice dark and demanding control.

"Take your pants off," she counters.

"That's not the way we play this, baby. You can give me hell anytime you want, but in this, I'm in control."

"Only if I give it to you," she says, stubborn to the end.

"You either give it to me, or I'll take you home. There's no in between with me Jasmine."

"I don't—"

"And, in case you were wondering, I'm not taking your ass home. Now, take off those fucking shorts before I cut them off of you."

"You wouldn't dare," she gasps.

"Try me."

"This is not the way to a girl's heart," she mumbles, her hand going to the button on her shorts.

"It's not your heart I'm trying to get to," I respond. Her hand stalls on her zipper. Her eyes narrow and I wait for her to tell me to go fuck myself. I fully expect it. Instead, she continues taking her clothes off.

"That's a good thing, because there's no way in hell you could touch that anyway," she mumbles, as she quickly shimmies out of her shorts.

I wonder if she realizes that she just threw down a gauntlet.

"I'll get you to give me your heart, Red. Don't think I won't."

"You're dreaming, Grunt."

Keeping Her

How a damn woman can be so defiant, standing there in nothing but white lace panties and a faded red t-shirt, I don't know. Yet, here she is, pushing me again and from the smirk on her face, she knows it. That's the only reason she insists on calling me by my road name. That's okay. Two can play that game. She wants to piss me off by not using my name, I'll give her something to *grunt* about.

"Always pushing me. You don't know when you're in danger, baby," I rumble under my breath as I step into her. Her eyes dilate and I think maybe she finally senses the danger. With Jasmine though, you can never be sure.

I move my hand from her hair, down to her ass cheek, grabbing the fleshy globe and squeezing it tightly. I hear her breath stutter as she exhales. My fingers push underneath the lace fabric, and I'm instantly rewarded with a warm gasp from her swollen lips. I press against her ass, letting them caress the tender valley, teasing her and maybe warning her. I see the uncertainty in her eyes, but I also see the hunger. She wants me maybe as much as I want her, but I find that doubtful. This woman sets my blood on fire.

I lean in, kissing her neck and nibbling my way to her ear, biting down on the lobe, causing her entire body to tremble against me. I grin as she hisses.

"Turn around and lean on the side of the couch." I'm speaking quietly, but you can't deny the command in my voice. Jasmine needs to know who is in charge here.

She rubs her lips together, moistening them. Her gaze is locked onto mine, as if she's trying to figure out who I am. I'd wish her luck, but I'm not even sure of who I am around her—and that's just the damn truth.

"You're very bossy," she complains as she turns around.

"You have no idea, baby. At least not yet."

She turns around, facing the side of the couch. I step even

closer, my body pushing into her, letting her feel my hard cock that is pressing against my jeans, dying to come out—dying to get inside of her.

I push my leg in between hers, smiling as her body quivers and she steps her legs apart, making room for my invasion. She grinds down on my leg, surprising me. I smile, letting my hand move along her side, petting her.

"Does my woman want to ride my leg and make herself come?"

"Your woman?" she huffs, continuing to grind her pussy against me. "You're full of yourself, Luke."

"That's okay, baby. Soon you'll be full of me too," I tell her softly, placing a kiss on the side of her neck. "You're going to want to take your shirt off, Red. So, do yourself a favor and take it off now."

"Why should I?" she asks, defiantly. "Especially since you've yet to take one single piece of clothing off."

"I don't need to take anything off for what I'm going to give you this time. Now stop fucking questioning me, woman," I growl, thinking it's going to be an adventure to get this woman to settle down.

"Right now, I'm trying to decide why I want you," she mutters, jerking her shirt over her head, revealing a plain white bra that somehow manages to be sexy—probably because it's Jasmine wearing it.

"The bra too, baby. I'm going to fuck you hard and quick. You're going to want to play with your nipples."

"Shouldn't you be doing some of the work here?" she mutters, unlatching the bra.

"And I would have, but you had to push me. Now, this ride will just be a short, hard one. Also, you need to behave, or I won't even let you come."

Her fingers stop at the latch of her bra, as what I said to her settles.

Her eyebrow lifts, as if she can't believe what I just said. I take my index finger to the clasp that she's holding but hasn't undone yet. I flick it quickly so that it releases.

We stare at one another and I wait. Then, she lets it drop to the floor.

"You better be worth this crap," she mutters.

I have to fucking hold back a laugh. Jesus, this woman...

I grasp the panties on her hip and rip the flimsy fabric, leaving the scraps to float down her leg, to pool at her feet.

Her gasp is audible as a shiver moves through her body.

I undo my belt, then release the button and zipper on my pants. The sound of the zipper sliding down seems loud and she looks over her shoulder to watch.

"Turn back around, Red," I order.

"I want to see."

"This isn't about giving you what you want. It's about *taking* what I want."

"You're being an ass. I think you just don't want me to see you because you won't measure up to your promise," she argues.

I lean over her, knowing she can feel my hard length rubbing against her ass. I pin her against the side of the couch, as I slide two fingers between her legs, seeking out her pussy.

A growl releases under my breath before I can hold it back. She's soaking wet for me. I push them inside of her and instantly her heated flesh sucks at my digits, trying to hold onto them. She starts rocking her hips, trying to fuck herself using my hands. I might let her some other day, but not today. I take my hand away, rewarded with her whimper of frustration. I push against her again. I press the back of her hand against my palm, placing them against the back of the couch.

"You better hold on, Red. I'm not doing this gentle."

"I didn't ask for gentle—"

Her words break off in a cry as I wrap my hand around my dick, position at her wet cunt and slam inside of her.

"You're going to learn, Red, that I call the shots when it comes to us fucking," I growl, slamming into her over and over. I'd worry but she's thrusting out to meet me, wanting what she's getting and silently begging for more.

"Shut up, Luke, before you piss me off," she hisses. I grab her hair in my hand and slide out of her pussy, until just the tip is inside. Then, I slam home again, hard and fast, not stopping until I'm balls deep.

"Oh fuck," she puffs, her breath coming in ragged bursts.

"What do you think now, baby?" I ask, tugging on her hair that I have in my tight hold, bottoming out, I stop, not moving. "Do I *measure* up?" I growl into her ear.

"Luke," she moans, as I rotate my hips, scraping her walls with my dick. She's fucking tight, literally choking my dick.

"What's wrong, Red?" I tease, reaching around her to tease her pussy, my fingers grazing her slick cunt. Her entire body quakes beneath me.

"Stop torturing me, Luke, please," she begs. "I need more."

"That's my good girl. I'll give you more. Now, bring your hand down to your pussy, where mine is," I instruct. She quickly does as I ask. Her fingers grazing against mine. I move giving her room to work her pussy. Then, I move her hair, exposing her shoulder. I begin fucking her harder, my eyes closing at the pleasure I'm experiencing.

"Luke," she cries as her orgasm starts.

There's nothing fucking sweeter in the world than hearing Jasmine call out my name as she comes. It's so fucking good my heart stutters in my chest. I pound her harder, feeling that familiar heat moving through me, starting at the base of my spine.

"I'm never letting you go, Red," I growl as I unload inside of her, painting her womb with my cum, emptying myself into her with each fucking stroke.

"Luke," she cries again, as we finish together. Her body slumps against the couch and I lean over her. I come so hard that my damn balls hurt.

As I slip from her body, I hold my hand between her legs, feeling my cum leak from her body and refusing to let it.

"Christ, Red," I rumble against her ear, placing a kiss on her shoulder. I don't know what I want to say, but I think she understands, because her hand comes up, her fingers tangling in my hair and she hums her approval.

I close my eyes at the sweetness of her touch. I told her I was never letting her go. I don't know if she took me serious or not, but she should have.

There's no way I'm letting her slip away from me.

I'm keeping her.

Chapter 12

Jasmine

"Hawk, just promise me you won't say anything to Mom and Dad right now," I plead, closing my eyes. My brother is being a jerk and there's nothing I can do to call him on it, since I need him to cover for me.

"You're in Virginia with a man you barely know, Jazz. Fuck, you *know* Dad would lose his shit, Jazz."

"I wouldn't say that I *barely* know him," I mumble, my body growing warm from the memories of the day before.

It's the next night and I'm still in Luke's house. He was gone this morning, but before he left he made me breakfast in bed and got me off with his mouth. We haven't had sex after that first, intense time. Instead, he held me all night and I slept. I slept like a baby. I felt safe and content.

I can't remember feeling content, at least not in a long time and never this satisfied. I'm not talking physically either—although I can say Luke does that and more. This is a soul-deep satisfaction, a happiness that doesn't fade with the sunrise, it just gets better. I didn't know that was possible.

Keeping Her

"Sis, be serious here," Hawk growls, clearly not happy with me.

"I am being serious. I really like Luke. I need time to figure out exactly what he's doing and how he feels about me," I return, hating the fact that I sound like I'm whining to my brother. I don't whine. I really need for him to sit on this, though. If he doesn't, it could all end way too soon.

And it wouldn't end well for Luke—of that much I'm sure.

"You don't think Mom and Dad are going to blow a gasket when you don't come home? They're only going to buy that you're staying at Gabby's for so long, Jazz."

"I know. I'll think of something. I just need you to sit on this. At least for a little while, please?"

"If Dad or Mom ask me point blank, I'm not going to lie, Jazz, not even for you."

"Then it's a good thing you're going back to school and won't be around," I mutter.

"Won't help. Unlike you, I talk to our parents every night."

"Yeah, I know. You're the golden child. I'm the black sheep," I mutter, trying to ignore the bitterness that tries to rise up.

"Stop being like that, you know Mom and Dad love you. They'd do anything for you."

"Except believe me."

"Jazz—"

"I don't want to talk about it, Hawk. Will you please just stop giving me this grief and sit on this for a little while?"

"You have to check in with me every day," he mutters.

"Hawk—"

"Every single day, Jazz."

"Fine," I huff.

"Good. You know I love you, Jazz, right?"

"You realize that you're my *little* brother, not my big one, right? It's not your job to rescue me," I mumble, instead of answering his question.

"Someone has to rescue you, you never look out for yourself," he returns.

"I'm hanging up now. Luke will be back soon."

"Take care of yourself."

"Always," I tell him and then, with a sigh, I close my eyes and pinch the bridge of my nose. "And Hawk?"

"Yeah, Sis?"

"I love you bigger than outer space."

"Love you, Jazzy," he says as he hangs up. I can hear the smile in his voice and because I can, I smile too. As brothers go, I'm pretty sure I won the lottery.

Chapter 13

Grunt

"What in the fuck were you thinking?"

Ford's bellowing reverberates off the cement walls of his office. Really, the walls are made up of cinderblocks. The whole compound is. Ford figured it'd be harder to burn that way. We slapped plywood and stained it, with sheet insulation under that in most of the place, but stone walls are the norm for Ford's office and the kitchen. The bar is like that too, though we did smooth plaster over that and it looks cool. For the most part it's a no-frills place. We come here to meet, drink, get high and fuck. Most of the time we do all four.

"Ford—"

"I told you to bring me that Gabby chick and you refused—"

"Now, hold up, man, I didn't refuse," I argue, even knowing that arguing with Ford is bad for your health.

He slams his hand down on the table. "Now is not your time to talk asshole. You want to explain to me why you have that redhead in your house while you still have all of your teeth and can talk plain?"

I rub the back of my neck and finally just shrug and say fuck it.

"She belongs to me."

"Belongs…"

"I wanted her, so I took her and I'm keeping her."

"Jesus, couldn't you have decided this about someone that wouldn't give me grief when it's discovered?"

"It's not going to cause you grief. Red is only a friend to that Gabby chick. She's not part of the Devil's Blaze. She'll be inconsequential and probably not even on their radar."

"You can't be that naïve," he accuses me.

It's not that I'm being naïve, but I doubt they'll even notice if Jasmine isn't around, especially if I make sure she reports back to her friend that she's healthy and happy.

"Red will make sure Gabby knows she's fine. I'm not some stupid, wet-behind-the ears-holding-my-dick-in-my-hand prospect, Ford. I know what's at stake here and I will always put the club first," I growl back, irritated that he's questioning me. There's a little voice inside of me saying that maybe I wouldn't. Maybe, just maybe, Jasmine would come first now, but I squash it down.

Ford stares at me and then finally his tense body relaxes ever so slightly. He stretches out, leaning back against his chair. He lights a cigarette and after taking a deep draw from it, he lifts his hand up to muss up his long hair. I watch him and wait. I can tell what he's thinking, but for now at least, we've said our peace.

"This might work to our advantage. You can use her to get Gabby to come to us," Ford says with a grin, but I immediately shake my head no.

"I don't want to use Jasmine in this shit storm, Ford. She's my property. We can deal with the fucker who hurt Lyla another way."

Keeping Her

"Your property. *Fuck*. Are you claiming her as your old lady?" Ford asks, and there's shock reflected on his face.

Hell, he's no more surprised than me. How many times have the two of us had the conversation where we swore we'd never get tangled up over a woman? We'd both seen too many good men end up with their asses in a sling—or worse. Shit, I never knew a woman like Jasmine existed, but I sure as fuck refuse to walk away. If having her gets me killed? We all fucking die sometime, at least my ride will be sweet.

"Yeah. Which makes her part of this club and under our protection," I grouse, making a split-second decision. It feels right though, and as it settles inside of me, as I understand the step I just took, I like it even more.

"That's fine. Claim your woman, but that doesn't preclude her from being valuable to us. You've made it clear how you feel about this shit, Grunt, but I'm going to find out who this asshole is and if I have to use your woman to do it? So be it."

"You're going to cause World War III, over some young punk that doesn't deserve to breathe Lyla's air, Ford." He just stares at me, and then I see the pain behind the anger.

"She's pregnant, Grunt. My little girl is knocked up and some fucker not only broke her heart, he turned his back on her after leaving his bastard inside of her. I want him torn apart limb by limb. I want to cause the asshole so much pain he begs for mercy and even then, I won't give it to him."

"Christ," I exhale, thinking things just got a lot more complicated. Before, this was just about bringing the kid before Lyla and letting her spit on him, maybe beating the shit out of the kid. Now? Fuck, there's going to be blood. There's no way to get around it. "I'm not going to use Red," I mutter. "At least not directly, but if she invites the girl down and she's on our turf," I mumble, trailing off with a shrug. I realize I'm splitting hairs and I also know that Jasmine is going to hate me if her girl gets hurt during all of this. The club comes first and even if I don't like dealing with all of this shit, Lyla is one of our own. I may not like how Ford is going about all of this, but I understand, especially now.

"Lyla's too damn young to be having a baby," Ford rumbles, scrunching his hair and suddenly looking older than he should.

"You were only twenty when you had Lyla," I remind him.

"Lyla is barely eighteen. She had plans, Grunt. Hell, my baby was innocent before this asshole came along."

I don't argue. He's right. Lyla was. Then again, with most of the club watching her, she didn't have a choice but to be innocent. This asshole would have never got to her if she hadn't been spending the summer at her mom's.

"So, what's the plan?" I ask, not really wanting to know.

"You make sure Gabby and your old lady keep in touch. For now, we'll sit back and watch." I let out a breath, because we both know what that means. I also know that Jasmine isn't going to like it. "I know what you're thinking, but we only have one other play."

"Forget all of this shit?" I suggest.

"Get Jasmine talking about her friend's man. You get his name or any other shit about him and I'll leave the girls out of it."

Fuck...

He smiles because he knows that's what I'm doing. I get up and leave, because I know that Jasmine may never forgive me when she finds out I'm using her to get information.

Motherfucker.

Chapter 14

Ford

"What were you and Grunt talking about, Daddy?" Lyla asks, coming into my office a mere minute after Grunt disappeared.

"Club business, Princess."

"Don't hand me that bullshit. You were talking about me. *I heard you.*"

"Eavesdropping on your old man?" I grumble, looking at my daughter.

I've not done much in this world to be proud of. I have two things that fall into those categories. One is the club and the other is my daughter. My father always said that I didn't have enough good in me to amount to a hill of beans.

I guess if there was any good in me, it was all Lyla. She wasn't planned, and instead the result of a wild party with Sherry Bryant. Sherry is an artist, extremely high class and nothing I'd tie myself to long term. I'm definitely not the man she wanted for more than a wild couple of nights, either. Sherry wasn't happy when she found out she was pregnant, and if she'd had the money alone to get an abortion, I might have never known. I begged her to have Lyla. She only agreed after I told her I would set her up for life, if she would give me my child. I don't regret it. Lyla has a relationship with Sherry, although it's not constant. Lyla has no idea that I had to pay her mother to keep her and I'd never tell her. I learned a long time ago that if you stir in shit, it smells worse and worse.

"Don't hand me that, Dad. If I didn't, I would never know what you're planning—"

"Butterfly—"

"Don't you, Butterfly me. I know you're doing everything you can to find out who the father of my child is, but it's useless. I won't tell you."

"Damn it, Lyla," I growl.

"It's none of your business!" she huffs with her hands on her hips. With her long blonde hair and sparkling blue eyes, she reminds me of her mother so much right now that I could almost smile. Sherry is a good-looking woman, too bad she's like me and that's about all that's good about her. "*I* was the one that got played. *I* was the one that made the mistake and *I* will be the one to deal with it," she announces. She might look like her mother, but fuck if she doesn't sound like me. I take pride in that.

"Come here, Butterfly," I tell her, holding out my arms. Lyla looks at me, and then all at once that mask she tries to wear, cloaking her emotions, slips. On her face, I can read sadness, despair, and more than a little fear. Just like that, she's my little girl again. As she walks to me and slides into my lap, I hug her tightly, squeezing her to me. My eyes close at the sweetness, the love I feel at having my daughter come to me.

"It's going to be okay, Lyla," I murmur, cradling her once I've pulled her into my lap. She settles in and I kiss the top of her head.

"I know," she whispers. "You won't let it go any other way,"

Keeping Her

she says, sadly, but showing that she has all the confidence in the world in me.

"Damn straight," I respond gruffly.

"I don't want you to go crazy, Daddy," she says, squeezing me tighter.

"Butterfly, he hurt you. He lied to you and then when you needed him most, he left you alone. He needs to learn not to fuck with a woman's heart. More than that, he needs to learn not to fuck with *my daughter's* heart."

"How do you know he lied to me?" she sniffles and my heart squeezes in my chest, because I know she's crying and that's the last thing I want. When I find this bastard, he'll be lucky if I don't tear his head off and feed it to my damn dogs. I'm going to do that to his dick anyway.

"Because I know you. You never would have been with him if he hadn't."

I don't know shit about raising kids. Everything I learned was just from being there for Lyla. Because of that, the two of us talk about everything openly. There aren't secrets. I was there when she started her period and I was the one to make sure she had tampons or whatever she needed. Sure, I sent a prospect to go get that shit, but still it was me that gave them to her, me that made sure she had ice cream. She's never hidden anything from me....

Except this bastard.

"He didn't exactly lie to me, Dad," she mumbles. "I was just stupid and naïve."

"Give me his name."

"No, this is the way it has to be. I don't want you or the club getting involved. You won't believe me, but he's a decent guy, and if I told him about the baby, he'd come back."

"Then, why in the fuck won't you tell him?" I ask, pulling away to look at her. I hold her face in each of my hands, not letting her turn away from me. "I thought you told him about the baby and then he ran."

"No, I was going to tell him about the baby, but before I got the chance, he decided to tell me how he was in love with Gabby and was using me to get over her. He said he realized that was a shit thing to do and that it was over. He wanted to end things before anyone got hurt."

"Lyla," I sigh, not sure what I want to do now, but I'd like to take my frustration out on this asshole.

"He was actually very nice about it and maybe if I hadn't asked him..."

"Asked him what, Butterfly?"

"I asked him how he could sleep with me and make love to me all this time if he was truly in love with another woman..." she murmurs, her voice cracking and so quiet that I have to strain to hear it.

"Butterfly..." I murmur, my heart torn. As her father, it's up to me to protect her and keep her from hurt. That's always been my job...

"I look like her, Daddy. All this time, I was in love with him and he was with me because..." she breaks off, taking a shuddering breath, her body trembling against me as she lets herself cry. *"I looked like her."*

I hold Lyla closer, letting her cry it out. I'm going to kill this asshole.

Kill.

Him.

Chapter 15

Grunt

"When you said we were going on a ride, I don't know what I expected..."

"Yeah?" I laugh, knowing what is coming next.

"Miniature golf, Luke? *Really!?!*"

"You don't like golf, Red?" I laugh as she puts her ball down and tries to judge the best way to get the ball into the clown's mouth for the final round.

"I didn't say that and since I'm beating your ass, I think you can tell I like it," she mumbles. "It just doesn't seem like your idea of unwinding."

"Okay, I'll bite, baby. What do you think I do to unwind?"

"I don't know," she says with a shrug, turning to look at me. She's smiling, there's a twinkle in her eyes and I see the happiness there and my chest grows tight. Jasmine has no idea how beautiful she really is. "I imagined something a little more...*manly*."

"Are you having doubts about my manhood, Red?" I question with a knowing smirk. I woke her up this morning with my head buried between her legs. I'm pretty damn sure she can't have complaints in that department—purely judging by the way she screamed out my name as she came, but with Jasmine, anything is possible.

"Mmm... no...," she says, and for some reason, I get the idea that she's toying with me.

"Would it make you feel better, if after we left here, we went to the garage at the club and I rebuilt an engine or something for you?" I mutter.

She scrunches up her nose and shakes her head no and for some reason that makes me laugh.

"That's so boring and messy really. Although, if you were naked and covered in oil, that might be a *little* sexy."

"Fuck," I hiss, wondering how this woman can make my balls ache in the middle of a place that's swarming with screaming kids. She knows her power over me, too, because when her gaze drifts up from my hard cock, which thankfully is mostly disguised by my pants, she's smiling at me.

"Got a problem there, Grunt?" she teases.

"What did I tell you about using that name, Red?"

"Maybe I want punished," she murmurs, giving up all pretense of golfing and walking toward me.

"Christ woman, didn't you get enough this morning."

"Not even close," she says, shaking her head no.

"You're playing with fire, Red. Be careful you don't get burned."

"What happens if I get burned?" she murmurs, studying my face.

"Red," I groan, knowing this woman has me by the balls, but not really giving a fuck. I haven't been inside of her body since that first night. Somehow, I can still taste her on my lips. I need her and I've been denying myself, trying only to give her pleasure —maybe because I know that I'm going to use her to find out who this asshole is that hurt Lyla. It's not right and I know she'll get hurt, but I don't have a lot of choices right now.

Keeping Her

"Grunt," she sing-songs.

"Luke," I correct her.

"Whoopsie, I guess I messed up, didn't I?"

"Jasmine," I mumble when her hand comes down between us. She flattens her hand against my cock, pressing in against the rigid outline.

"Are you going to punish me now?"

"Is that what you want, Red? Do you want me take you right here where anyone can see me fuck you?"

She looks up at me then, and I swear to God her fucking eyes are glowing. Her teeth come down on her bottom lip and damn, I can see the hunger on her face, and I know it's the same reflected on mine.

"Well, maybe not *right* here..." she murmurs, looking around.

I pull her up in my arms, holding her under her legs and across her back. Golf all but forgotten, the clubs falling to the concrete with a clang. I can barely hear them, the sound of Jasmine's soft laugh is echoing in my ears as she kisses on my neck, not giving a damn who is watching us.

I take her behind the building where you rent the golf balls and clubs, thanking God it's there. Luckily when we get there, it's empty. I let her slide to the ground, wedging her up against the building and my body. My head goes down as I undo my belt, unable to wait a minute longer.

"Take those shorts off, Red," I order, my voice rumbling out like a hungry lion on the prowl.

"Way ahead of you, baby," she replies and my gaze jerks away to look at her. Her shorts are undone—she's kicked them off, along with her panties. From where I'm standing, I can see the wetness against the lips of her pussy. Her breathing is ragged, and her nipples are so hard they're pushing against her shirt. All this and I haven't fucking touched her. What is it between us that ignites like this? I can't wrap my head around it.

She's a fire in my blood and her heat burns me, makes me whole.

"Tell me you're ready for me, Red," I practically beg, grabbing my cock and rubbing the head against her wet entrance.

"Carrying me over here was foreplay, Luke. Quit talking and fuck me," she coos into my ear, bringing one of her legs up to rest on my hip. She bites into the lobe of my ear as I push inside of her. She cries out in pleasure as I bury myself to the hilt. "So good," she moans, as I put my hands on her thighs and heft her up. She locks her legs around me and somehow my cock shifts deeper.

"So fucking good," I breathe out my agreement, as I take a minute to just savor how she feels, not moving a muscle. Her body trembles, the walls of her pussy flutter against my cock, and her fingernails bite into my back.

"I need you to move, Luke," she whimpers, already trying to rock against me and move on my cock.

"You're like a kitten with claws, so sweet to pet..." I grunt into her ear, as I start fucking her.

"God," she moans, her entire body trembling. "It feels so good. *You* feel so good," she whimpers, as we move together. It's then that it hits me. I've never believed in it before, but if love is real, then I could love Jasmine.

I start moving faster, her pussy clenching on my shaft as I fuck her harder.

"Don't stop," she moans. "Don't ever stop."

"I'm not going anywhere, Red. Not going anywhere," I promise her, as I grind against her. I kiss along her neck, letting my teeth tease her skin, while I never stop thrusting in and out of her, pushing us both to the edge.

"Luke," she cries, as her orgasm starts to build. I bite down on her neck, her body jerks in reaction as I suck on the tender skin, marking her. She comes in that moment, her pussy gripping my hard shaft so tight it's like she's choking it. I continue fucking her, my own orgasm beginning, and I let her pull me over the edge with her.

My eyes close and I moan as I pour into her, painting her womb with my seed. I don't know how I'm going to manage it, but when all this is over, it has to end with Jasmine by my side.

There can be no other alternative.

Chapter 16

Jasmine

"You know, Luke, I think there might be something wrong with us," I mumble with a sigh, as I finish buttoning my shorts. I adjust my clothes so that I don't look like I've just been fucked within an inch of my life, up against a building, in broad daylight. I mostly fail, but I'm okay with that.

The thought makes me smile.

"Why's that, baby?" Luke asks.

I turn to look at him, my heart stumbling in my chest. His head is down, his eyes focused on securing his belt. He doesn't even realize he used the endearment but something about it, after what we just did, warms me, fills me with...*happiness*.

"Do you realize that we seem to enjoy getting off in public?"

"You complaining, Red?" he asks, his eyebrow cocked up in what can only be described as arrogance.

That look shouldn't turn me on—especially since I can still feel his cum leaking from between my legs—but, it does. I'm a wreck.

"Just an observation," I respond with a shrug. He closes the small distance between us. His arms go on either side of me, his palms resting flat against the side of the building, trapping me.

The masculine scent of him, the worn leather of his cut, his aftershave and the smell of sex, combine and float on the breeze around us, making me drunk. I lick my lips, wondering if he'll want to go for round two.

"I'll fix that tonight," he says, gruffly.

I smile, I can't help it.

"You like that," he says, and I could deny it, but why?

"Oh yeah," I confirm.

"I knew the moment I saw you that you were going to be trouble, Red."

"Considering *I'm* the one that has been kidnapped, I think you got that all wrong, Luke."

"I told you, you're not a prisoner," he mutters and clearly it upsets him that I keep referring to it like that.

"So, I'm free to go?"

His brow wrinkles and his eyes grow darker, filled with intent.

"Do you want to leave me, Red?"

I sigh, my hand comes up to run my finger across the name on his cut. I don't know who the Demon Chasers are. I'm not sure it would matter if I did. Are they friend or foe to the Savage Brothers? *Do I really want to know?*

I wish I paid attention when Dad talked about the different club names, but I just never did. He wanted to keep that stuff far away from my Mom. It wasn't because she minded, but more so because he didn't want her involved. He always said he had caused her enough pain in her life. I never understood that completely until Dewayne felt the need to tell me. That's just another reason to hate the bastard.

"Red?" Luke prompts me, before I can get too lost in my thoughts.

"No, but I do have things I need to do, Luke. I have a job interview coming up—"

"You don't need a job."

I roll my eyes. "I *want* to work."

"Then, there are jobs here in Virginia too."

"You've got an answer for every problem, don't you, Luke?"

"I can try," he says, leaning down to softly kiss my lips. I let him, because I need that connection with him.

"I'm supposed to have lunch with Gabby this week. She's going through a hard time. She's probably the only friend I have in the world. I don't want to stand her up."

I watch something pass over his face. I don't know what it is and couldn't name it if I tried. Something about it is unsettling though.

"Invite her up here."

"No way would she be able to get away. Her dad would have a cow."

"So? I get the feeling neither one of you do what your fathers order, Jasmine."

"Maybe not," I reluctantly agree. Still…"

"Invite her up. If she wants to come, we can go get her and take her back home when it's all done."

"When it's all done?"

"Your lunch I mean," he says, turning away.

"Hey," I respond, grabbing hold of his cut and pulling.

He turns back to look at me and where once I saw warmth and hunger in his eyes, now they seem closed off.

"Don't do that," I tell him.

"Do what?"

I want to beg him not to pull away from me or shut himself off. I could be overreacting, because I can feel those old wounds left over from Dewayne. They're raw right now and I feel exposed. I know that's because I care about Luke. I vowed that would never happen again, and yet here I am. Still, I'm not going to beg. Luke will either care for me, or he won't.

God I hope he will.

"Don't shut down. I'll ask Gabby if she wants to come visit."

"Sounds good," he says and maybe he's trying to smile, but his face is tight with irritation. I don't want to rock the boat anymore today. So, I decide to change the subject.

"I'm hungry," I tell him. "Someone made me work up an appetite," I add, wrapping my arms as far as I can get around him and hugging him tight.

"Is that so?"

"Definitely," I hum.

"Then, let's go find my girl a hamburger."

"And a milkshake," I add.

His eyes finally warm back up and in turn, warm me.

"And a milkshake," he says, running his hand through my hair. "Hey, Red?"

"Yeah, baby?"

He stares at my lips and then slowly brings his eyes up to mine.

"I like when you call me baby," he says and although I know that's not what he started to say, I like the smile on his face. So, I go up on my tiptoes and kiss him.

"I aim to please." I murmur against his lips.

"Oh, don't worry, Red. You do that and more," he says. For some reason, that feels like the biggest praise I've ever received in my life. He drapes an arm around my shoulder. I put one around his back, and we walk over to the main part of the park together.

I can't remember ever experiencing anything better.

I'm not sure I ever will.

Chapter 17

Grunt

"Okay, Gabby. Yeah, I'll talk to you soon."

I look at Jasmine as she hangs up the phone. Her face is a mixture of concern and disappointment.

"Not coming?" I ask and maybe I shouldn't be, but damn I'm relieved.

"Not right now. She's having men trouble again."

"Again?"

"Yeah, a long story but Gabby is pretty much always having men problems."

"I see," I mumble, liking this Gabby chick less and less.

"What's that tone about?"

"What?"

"Oh, come on, Luke. Whenever you hear something you don't like or are resisting saying something negative, you get that bored sounding tone."

"Learn that much about me already, Red?"

She frowns, looking down at me.

We're lying in bed. After a full day of miniature golf, sex, food, and more sex, we came home and crashed. After a nap, she called her girl and I just watched her. I could watch her for hours and never grow bored.

"When someone is important, you learn everything you can about them, Luke."

Fuck.

My girl knows how to punch you right in the gut.

I hook my hand against the side of her neck and pull her head down to me, kissing her. When we break apart, I rest my forehead against hers. Jasmine has a way of uncovering emotions that I'm definitely not used to feeling.

"That's a nice kiss," she murmurs.

"It was," I agree, reluctantly letting her pull back so I can look at her.

"So, tell me," she murmurs, pulling her knees against her chest.

"Do you really want to get into this right now, Red?" I mumble, flopping back on the pillow and throwing an arm behind my head to angle so I can see her better.

"I think I do," she laughs.

"Just that maybe she has men trouble is because the word *men* is plural," I respond.

"Ohhh...so she wouldn't have trouble if there was only one man in her life?" she says with a grin, which lets me know she has a snappy comeback.

"Probably not as much. Although I suspect she's fucking around with boys. I don't know a man alive that will share a woman they care about."

She moves around, dropping down on all fours and crawling over me, straddling my lap, making me hate the sheet between us even more. My cock stirs to life. You would think the damn thing would be worn out, but I don't think that's ever going to be possible around Jasmine.

"What about your nonstandard relationships, Luke? Those

have an extra man or woman involved, sometimes more than one."

"A couple of my brothers have gone that route. One worked out to where everyone seems happy, the other blew up so horribly that the shit storm that ensued still has people in its grip," I respond, distracted as my hands slide along her soft hips, enjoying the feel of her skin against my fingers.

"You don't sound like a fan," she says thoughtfully, her voice tender as her fingers trace imaginary lines through the hair on my chest.

"I don't play well with others, Red," I grumble, the pads of my fingers trailing against the softness of her stomach. One day soon, I'm going to take my time kissing every freckle on her body. Fuck, they turn me on.

Everything about Jasmine turns me on.

"I happen to think you play very well with me, Luke," she teases, her hips rocking against my hard cock which has found a home between her legs, her pussy grinding against the hard ridge. It's good, but nowhere near as good as being inside of her. Still, it wouldn't take much to come like this...*not much at all.*

"Take this sheet out from between us and I'll show you how well I can play with you, woman."

"In time. I'm kind of enjoying myself here," she says, starting to ride against me, her breasts swaying with her movements, her hair pushed away from her face. Jesus, she's magnificent.

"I'm never sharing you, Jasmine. You want to know what it feels like to have two dicks in you at one time? I'll get inventive, but I'm never sharing you," I warn her, my voice verging on the edge of being ferocious, as a wave of possessiveness comes over me so strong that I can't control it.

She stops, looking down at me, her eyes dark, erotic pools that make me feel alive.

"What if I already know what that feels like?" she asks. I

Keeping Her

ignore the jealousy that spikes up inside of me, tapping it down with the knowledge that no matter what happened before me, she's mine now and no one but me is ever touching her again.

"I'm going to ask you never to tell me about it so I don't kill them and wind up in jail, unable to fuck you and keep you satisfied," I growl.

Her body stiffens against me and I silently curse myself, wishing I'd kept my mouth silent.

"Jasmine—"

"It wouldn't matter to me, Luke."

"What wouldn't baby?" I ask her, sensing something big brewing behind those beautiful eyes of hers.

"If you were or had been in jail. I wouldn't give a fuck. I wouldn't think less of you. Good people go to jail," she adds, her voice dropping down. "Good people do bad things for the right reasons, too. It doesn't make them bad."

I lean up, taking her mouth. I kiss her, while rolling over so she's on the bottom and I'm above her once we finally break apart. Her eyes are stormy.

"You don't think I know that, Jasmine?"

"Some people don't," she murmurs.

"Then, those people are idiots. What's going on in that head of yours, Red?"

"I just, I..." she breaks off, as if she's struggling for words. "I just needed you to know that."

"I know it. As far as I'm concerned, baby, the past is the past, in case you were wondering. All that matters to me is that I'm your future. If some man was an idiot and let you get away and didn't appreciate you, then that's on him. Don't get me twisted up with them."

"I could never do that, Luke. You're a good man. I may not know much, but I know that. You would never use me," she says, and she has no way of knowing the way those simple words cut straight into my heart.

"Jasmine—"

"I feel safe with you," she adds, her face clouded with emotion that I can't begin to name.

"Red, baby—"

"I think I could fall in love with you one day, Luke," she whispers as if she's confiding in me. My heart literally fucking squeezes in my chest. "It scares me."

"Don't be afraid, Red. I'm not going anywhere. You're safe with me," I promise her.

"I think I'm starting to believe you…"

"Good, because I'm not letting you go," I vow.

I pull the sheet away from her body, my fingers moving between her legs, caressing her pussy as my lips begin sucking on her nipple. Her moan of pleasure is my reward, and the sound is so sweet it wraps around me.

"Luke…"

Her broken cry feeds my soul, and I as work her, stretching her channel to accept me, I vow that whatever I have to do to protect Jasmine, I will. I don't know how I'm going to do it, but fucking hell….

I will find a way.

Chapter 18

Jasmine

"I'm surprised your watchdog let you stay here alone," Gabby laughs, as I watch Luke walk away.

I let out a sigh. It's crazy. He just left and I already miss him.

"He didn't want to," I murmur, smiling as I remember our conversation earlier.

"Oh, girl. I know that look," Gabby says, and I look over to find her studying my face.

Shit.

"What look?" I murmur, trying not to sound panicked.

"You're in love."

"Don't be silly. I barely know him," I respond, looking down at the menu and praying I'm not blushing.

"Girl, please. You've been basically living with him for a week now."

"You mean he's been holding me hostage for a week," I lie.

"That kiss goodbye he gave you doesn't look like you were being held a prisoner," Gabby says, deceptively mild.

"What kiss goodbye?"

My head jerks up and when I see my mom standing there, I close my eyes, wincing.

This is great.

I stand up, even though I really just want to run away.

"Hi, Mom," I mutter, hugging her. She puts her arms around me, holding me tight. I close my eyes again, but this time out of gratitude. I take in the scent of Mom's shampoo, the light perfume of her body spray, and the sweetness that somehow emanates off of her.

My mom is one of those truly good people. She rarely says a bad thing about anyone, she's sweet and kind and even donates her time at the local nursing home. She's one hundred and fifty percent love and light.

Between me and my brother, Hawk is definitely more like Mom. Me? I have that taint of darkness that my dad always says he carries. He said Mom's goodness, her light, always drew him to her. I wish I could have been more like her. I know if I had, my father would have been prouder of me. There's nothing I can do though. I am who I am—even if it makes my parents want to pull out their hair.

"Don't you Mom me, just where have you been hiding this past week, Jazz?"

I know it's strange, but while I've been at Luke's, not one person has called me Jazz and I liked it. It's weird. That's been my nickname since before I could talk. It's still true though. Every time Dad or Mom call me Jazz, I feel like I'm failing to live up to someone they miss daily. I know they don't mean to put pressure on me, but it does just the same.

"Hey, Aunt Carrie," Gabby chimes in, trying to rescue me. I appreciate it, even if I know it's not going to work. Mom loves Gabby. She wishes I could be more like her, of course Mom has no idea the havoc Gabby usually leaves in her wake, but I don't guess that matters. Mom's not really her aunt either, but both clubs are super close, as well as the wives of the members. So, the family is just kind of big and extended, which is awesome and irritating, depending on the day.

"Hi, Gabby. Is your mom joining us, today?"

"Nah, she couldn't. Dad wanted her to go with him to Georgia. Uncle Torch and Aunt Katie were going. So, they got on their bikes and headed out. She said to tell you she loved you though."

"That sounds good. I need to try and talk Jacob into a road trip soon. He's been working too hard."

I wait for Mom to get settled. The waiter comes and takes her order and while they're talking I look around me. We're eating outside on the patio in downtown London. Kentucky really is beautiful this time of year and I love this town. Gabby doesn't live here, but she's not too far away. We meet here most of the time. It's not that I wouldn't come to her, Mom and Dad know I would be safe traveling in Uncle Skull's territory. It's that Gabby likes being here, because she's more apt to run into Dom. I don't know what's going to happen with those two, but whatever does...*it will be messy*.

"And what were you talking about when I showed up," Mom questions, staring at me. I'm glad I have my sunglasses on. If I didn't, I would be terrified she'd see the panic in my eyes.

"Nothing really."

"Jasmine," Mom warns, in that voice which all mothers seem to have down pat.

I sigh.

"It's just a guy, Mom."

Clearly that was the wrong thing to say, since I immediately see censure on her face.

"I worry about you, Jazz. You're going to have to figure out what you want out of life soon."

"You act like I'm a hundred years old, Mom," I mutter with a sigh.

"No, but you're too old to have no direction in life," she argues.

"I have direction, you just don't like it," I respond, wishing I had never talked Luke into letting me come back.

"A direction other than quitting school and working at a dead-end job."

"Mom—"

"And definitely not one that ends up getting you arrested for parking tickets and assaulting an officer."

"And I'm out of here," I growl, standing up.

"Jazz—"

"I'll call you later, Gabby," I mutter, grabbing my purse.

"Jazz don't leave like this. I'm sorry, I just worry about you. You need to start making adult decisions. Your father and I won't be around forever."

I stop walking. I shouldn't, but I do.

"What's that supposed to mean?"

"We're not going to be able to bail you out forever, Jazz," Mom says, and I snap. I shouldn't. I should hold it in, but sometimes you just can't. I have in the past, but being with Luke has allowed me to feel a certain amount of freedom. He accepts me for who I am. Hell, he more than accepts me, he *likes* me.

"I didn't ask you to bail me out the first time, Mom."

"We couldn't let you stay in jail—"

"You didn't have a problem letting me stay that first night," I remind her, and even though I didn't ask them to bail me out, it hurt that no one bothered to.

Not even Hawk.

"Your father felt you needed to learn a lesson," she says, and I ignore the pain that hits me.

"Well, you two can breathe easy. I did learn my lesson. I

learned that I should have taken the baseball bat to Officer Dewayne's balls and not just his damn squad car."

"Jasmine," Mom says, but I don't want to listen. I just keep walking. Luke will have a cow, but I'll call him and have him come pick me up later. Right now, I need to cool down.

Chapter 19

Grunt

THERE ARE A LOT OF THINGS THAT I DON'T UNDERSTAND about Jasmine and plenty of things that I'm just learning. Yet, as I walk up past the dam to find her sitting on the concrete spillway, the sadness on her face nearly guts me. I vow to find out every little thing I can about her to protect her from this kind of pain. As I get closer, the tears on her face are evident. She's not sobbing like most women I've met do when they are upset. No, not my Red. She's just staring out, like she's looking at something that I can't even begin to see, while silent tears are running unchecked down her face.

"How did you find me?" she asks, surprising me, because I didn't think she had noticed me yet, and I did my best to keep my approach silent.

"You left your phone at the restaurant," I tell her, holding it up in my hand. She turns to stare at me, and I have the strangest urge to kiss her tears from her face and make her promise me to never cry again. Instead, I take a few more steps, bridging the distance between us, but not touching her—at least not yet.

Keeping Her

"Gabby told me what happened and that you would probably be here."

"She knows me," Jasmine murmurs. "She might be the only one who ever has."

"I'd like to think I belong in that number, Red."

She gives me a sad smile, but she doesn't say anything and that bugs the fuck out of me. I let it go, though.

I walk closer, sitting behind her on the concrete. I take a deep breath. The scent of rain in the air and the sweetness of Jasmine intermingle. My eyes close with pleasure, as I pull Jasmine's body back into me, kissing the side of her neck gently.

We don't talk for a few minutes. I let her have her silence and I try to figure out the best way to approach the subject so that I can help her.

"Want to tell me what happened, Red?"

Her body relaxes against me and I should feel relief at that, instead it makes me feel like the fight has left her, like she's given up on something and I don't like that at all. My Red is a fighter until the very end. It's one of the things I love about her.

"The same thing that always happens when I'm around my parents. They point out everything I've ever done wrong and instead of telling them that they're wrong, I take it and remain silent."

"If that's how it goes, then why in the fuck did you give me head just so I'd bring you to Kentucky to have lunch with her?"

A startled laugh bursts from Jasmine's lips and she pushes her head back against my chest, tilting up to look at me.

"Is that what you really think?"

"Are you going to deny it?" I challenge her.

"I sucked your cock because I enjoy it," she counters. "You would have taken me to Kentucky to see my mom regardless."

I kiss her, just a small kiss, barely tasting her lips, but allowing my tongue the pleasure of teasing her just a little. Our foreheads rest against each other. I keep my arms wrapped around her, giving her a gentle squeeze. It's an admission that she's right. I'd give Jasmine anything she asked if it were in my power.

"You're trying to make me fall in love with you, Luke," she murmurs.

I'd be a damn liar if I denied the shot of pleasure her words shoot through me.

"Is it working?" I ask her.

"Yeah," she says and fuck, that feels good.

She turns back around, and we sit like that, staring out over the water. It's getting late. I don't have a watch and don't want to yank out my phone to check, but I'd guess it's around six. I hate that Jasmine spent so much time alone today. I'm not leaving her alone anymore. I didn't want to today. I did because I didn't want her parents to see me and start asking questions. She may not be part of the Devil's Blaze, but they still might know enough to be dangerous to the overall plan.

But, fuck if I know what the plan is anymore.

Jasmine has changed everything.

"It's beautiful out here," I murmur, holding her tighter, kissing the top of her head and just trying to be here for her, enjoying having her in my arms and hating that she's sad—all at the same time.

"I don't see beauty," she whispers, her voice so steeped in sadness that I don't know how to fix it.

"What do you see?" I ask her.

"I see a place where demons live," she finally answers after several minutes of silence.

"What demons do you have, Jasmine?"

"Plenty," she replies, giving a self-depreciating laugh that holds no humor. "But mine don't live here. These belong to someone I love."

I ignore the jealousy that I feel. This seems more important. Instead, I move my head so that my lips are at her ear.

"The fact that you're the one here and they're not leads me to believe they're yours, Red."

"Maybe a little of both," she admits.

"Are you going to tell me about your demons, Jasmine?"

"Not today. Maybe someday."

"Why not now?" I ask, wishing I could see her face, but content enough with just keeping her close.

"Because I want you to like me first," she says, shocking the hell out of me.

I could tell her that's already happened, but in this mood, with whatever is haunting her, I don't think she'd believe me. So, I remain quiet.

For now.

Chapter 20

Jasmine

"Shouldn't we be heading back?" I ask, and for some reason, I'm anxious to get back to Virginia.

"I'm enjoying spending time with my woman, is that so bad?" Luke asks, turning his gaze to look at me.

"You could spend time with me back home," I mumble, then I kick my own ass, because I referred to Luke's place as home.

What is going on with me?

I have to just be over-emotional right now. Fighting with my parents does that to me, and Lord knows that every single time we get together anymore, it's a fight.

"You're so damn beautiful, Jasmine. You make me ache every time I look at you," Luke says, his voice dropping down to this rumbly tone that sends shivers over my skin and fills me with hunger. I crave Luke. I've never felt anything like it before.

"Luke, in case it has escaped your notice, I'm a sure thing, you don't have to butter me up," I mutter, looking out at the stars.

We're still at the dam. We left to go pick up some takeout, but Luke insisted on coming back here to eat. Now, we're lying back on the concrete watching the stars. I could tell him that I don't like this place, but I know Luke. He would expect me to tell him why.

I'm not ready for that.

I'm not sure I'll ever be.

"Who did it, Red?" Luke grumbles and I can tell he's pissed. There's one thing about it, when Luke is pissed, it makes sense to pay attention.

"Who did what?" I ask, squinting, as my forehead creases in confusion. I can't help but wonder what has set him off. Up until now, Luke has been relaxed and even loving toward me today.

"Made you feel like you weren't worthy, or belittled you," he mutters, sitting up. I sit up too, but before I can manage to put distance between us—which is my first instinct—Luke reaches over and somehow half lifts my body, so I'm secured in his lap, facing him.

"Luke," I can't help but gasp, my knees pressed into his sides, my hands braced on his forearms.

His eyes are intense, heated and definitely pissed. His hands are holding onto my hips firmly, and I can feel the heat from them —it seems to burn me.

"Who did it? Tell me and I'll take care of them."

"Take care?" I squeak, sensing a thread of violence running through him that I've never detected before. I've seen him angry, but this is different.

He's pissed.

"Who hurt you?"

"I don't know what you're talking about," I lie.

"Don't try to bullshit me, Red. Was it your family?"

"Luke, let's just—"

"Tell me who. You wear that tough exterior of yours well, but you're not fooling me. Not after today, so talk to me."

"What if I don't want to talk about it?" I grumble, getting pissed off, because he's not letting it drop.

"Tough shit, we're going to."

"Why? Because you say so? I hate to break it to you, Luke, but just because you want me to talk about something, it doesn't mean I will."

"You will, because that's what people in relationships do," he argues.

"How many relationships have you been in?" I ask him, my eyes narrowing.

"Jasmine—"

"How many?" I insist, my voice filled with a mixture of anger, curiosity and fear.

Shit, what if he has a wife?

"Damn it, woman!"

"Oh my God!" I screech, pushing away from him and trying to get up. His hold intensifies to bruising force and he refuses to let me leave.

"Red—"

"Are you married?" I cry. "You are, aren't you? I should have known. No one looks the way you do, fucks the way you do, and manages to—"

"You like the way I fuck, Red?" he asks, a smile pulling at his lips.

I slap my hands flat on his chest, the sound loud, my palms burning from the impact.

"Don't pull that shit on me! You're married."

"Oh, for fuck's sake. I'm not married," he growls.

"You have a woman you fuck regularly, then," I mutter. "Whatever—"

"Yeah, I do have a woman I fuck regularly," he admits, and my body goes solid. There's a pain that bubbles up inside of me that fills my entire body with a sick feeling. It spreads over me like a virus, threatening to drag me under. My stomach churns.

Keeping Her

"I knew it," I groan, my voice little more than a hoarse whisper, because I'm pretty sure I'm going to be sick.

"There's this crazy-ass redhead who blew into my life and I can't seem to get enough of her. I fuck her every chance I get and when I'm not fucking her, I *think* about fucking her. She's like a fire in my blood and she's burning me from the inside out. I'm obsessed with her," he growls as I go still, listening to him.

"That doesn't sound like you like it...or me...I mean, if I'm the redhead you're talking about and I assume I am, although you know what they say—"

"It's you and right now, I honestly don't know if I like it or not, Jasmine. You're driving me crazy. I'm trying to make shit better for you and you go off like a crazy woman."

"Luke—"

"You're making *me* crazy."

"You make me crazy, too," I mumble.

"At least there's that, I guess," he grouses.

"So, you're saying you don't have someone important in your life?"

"Jasmine—"

"I mean, besides whatever you and I have going on," I add, blushing and not really knowing why.

Luke lets out a grunt under his breath, his hand going to the back of his neck and he rubs it, his face appearing frustrated. This tingle of fear begins at the base of my spine.

"Luke? *Are* you in another relationship?" I ask.

His hold loosens on me, his eyes downcast as he wrestles with whatever demon he has nipping at his heels. I immediately leave him, standing up, needing the space between us. I rub my suddenly sweaty palms on my pants and wait for him to answer. I feel as if my entire future hinges on his answer.

"Shit," I hiss, when he looks up at me.

I may not know a lot, but I know when a man is wearing guilt like a badge on his face.

Shit, shit, shit!

"It's not what you think, Jasmine."

"It never is," I whisper, feeling like the world is falling down around me.

How could I allow this? How could I allow Luke to become so important to me, and know so little about him? What in the world was I thinking? Didn't my time with Dewayne teach me anything? That sick feeling in the pit of my stomach explodes.

I turn away from Luke, unable to look at him.

"Damn it, Jasmine stop!" he growls, and until just this moment, I didn't realize I had started running. He grabs my hand pulling me back around. I ignore the pain I feel, I let my anger feed me.

"Will you talk to me?" Luke growls, but I shake my head no.

"I've heard enough," I yell.

"Bull—," I take off running again. I've had enough. I just can't handle anymore. Luke's arms come around me from behind in a giant bear hug.

"You have to listen to me, Red," Luke mutters, his breath hot against the back of my neck as he tries to lift me and pull me back.

I don't let him finish. I don't have to listen to a damn thing he has to say.

Luke is a big man, but I grew up among some of the biggest, meanest men God ever made. They also take women being able to protect themselves seriously—after what happened with their wives, they had to. So, I call upon all those long lessons that Dad and my uncles gave me. Skills that my brother helped me hone constantly.

I bend low, pushing my weight and forcing him to let me plant my legs on the ground. I let out a wounded-sounding breath

Keeping Her

to throw him off. I turn into him, bringing my elbow up as I go. My elbow connects with the upper part of Luke's throat, making him stumble and loosen his hold.

I pivot quickly, straightening out my left hand, and holding it stiff. Uncle Dragon always told me that being left-handed was an advantage because most men looked for their attacker to be dominant with their right hand.

I'm praying he's right.

I strike out, catching Luke's nose. Bullseye. I wince as blood spurts out, but I can't let myself feel guilty. He deserves this. I've had enough of men playing me for a fool. I promised myself it would never happen again.

"Fuck, woman," he growls, his head going down as he holds his nose.

I get enough distance to give me sufficient room to get power and then I bring my leg up and connect with his groin. He doesn't go down, but he stumbles and that's enough. I take off running and I don't look back. I don't stop until I find Gabby's car that she lent me earlier. I can hear Luke yelling, but I ignore him, starting up her car, shoving it into reverse, squealing tires and peeling out with the smell of rubber behind me, leaving Luke behind.

Chapter 21

Grunt

"Holy shit, what happened to you?" Jonesy says when I walk in. Ford lets out a wolf whistle, and I ignore them both. I grab a cold beer from behind the bar and snag a bottle of Ibuprofen that Tank keeps behind the counter to treat his hangover—which he has often, because Tank likes to drink almost as much as he likes to fuck.

"Fuck off."

"Seriously man, what happened? Who do we need to kill?" Ford growls. "I told you motherfuckers to stop going out unless you had someone with you. We have a target on our backs," he adds. "Every son of a bitch around wants a piece of the empire we've built."

I close my eyes.

"It was Jasmine."

They go silent and just like I knew all along—they're not going to let that shit go.

"*Your redhead did that shit?*"

"Holy fuck, Momma always told me to stay away from redheads, but holy hell."

Keeping Her

"What did you do to piss her off?" Ford asks, staring at me. He's studying me and I guess I should worry about what he sees, but right now I'm too messed up in the head to think about it. I grunt, not wanting to get into this shit, especially right now. "Did you tell her why you were following her?"

I tighten my hand into a fist, a new surge of anger thrusting through me with such a white-hot fury that my hand literally trembles. I slam it against the bar, causing the contents on it to rattle.

"I didn't tell her shit about Lyla," I snarl, pissed off. This is just a reminder of the secrets I'm keeping from Jasmine, and it's clear, especially after tonight, that my Red isn't the type of woman who likes secrets.

"Then what?" Ford presses and if I didn't love my brother, I'd hate the fucker right now.

"I made the mistake of trying to tell her about Daisy."

"Oh fuck, Grunt. I thought you were smarter than that," Jonesy replies. I take a swig of my beer and hold my head down. Just that small movement hurts like fuck, but I ignore the pain.

"I did too."

"Damn boy, what got a hold of you?" Sledge asks. Sledge is one of the original members. He and Ford started the club together. He sits in on votes and always attends church, but he retired from a position in the club years ago. Ford didn't like it, but Sledge was dealing with personal shit, so no one questioned him. Craven took over as VP, but he and Ford are like oil and water sometimes. They both want the same things for the club, they just don't agree on how to get it.

"His girlfriend," Jonesy laughs.

"Holy shit. The girl has skills," Sledge says and he's not wrong. Someone trained Jasmine and trained her well. That makes me jealous, I'm not even going to bother denying it. "When do we get to meet her? I want to see this chick."

"Never, judging by Grunt's face," Ford laughs.

"How'd you piss her off?" Sledge pushes. I grunt, refusing to answer again. I should have known Jonesy would answer for me.

"He tried to tell her about Daisy," Jonesy answers.

Sledge frowns, and then he takes a drink of his whiskey, releasing a breath after he swallows it down.

"Women get peculiar sometimes," he says, sagely.

"You mean hateful," Ford laughs.

"That, too. Good you found out what she's like now, boy. You don't need that kind of shit in your life. There's too many women out there that's willing to give you what you want and only use their mouth to suck your dick and not give you shit," Sledge responds.

I scoot my seat back, the sound of it scraping against the concrete abnormally loud. I walk off, without saying a word.

I don't want another woman.

I want Jasmine and I'm going to fucking have her. If she thinks this ended shit, she's fooling herself. She's not getting away from me.

Not now... *Not ever.*

Chapter 22

Jasmine

"You broke his nose," Hawk laughs, sounding abnormally happy about that.

"And probably his dick," Gabby adds, and I pinch the bridge of my nose, wondering why I said anything.

"That's my sis," Hawk replies, definitely proud.

"Can we please change the subject?" I pout, ignoring them both, and taking an over-filled spoonful of vanilla ice cream.

I'm curled up on Hawk's sofa. Hawk is sitting beside me, spread out with his feet on the coffee table—boots and all. Gabby is on the floor across from us, sitting with her legs under her. I drove straight here from the dam and I cried myself to sleep.

My big plan consisted of hiding out here for a few days and trying to figure out what I was going to do with my life. It sounded good, except I forgot Gabby practically lives here and she showed up this morning. I kind of figured she would, but then this evening my frustration got worse. My dipshit brother—whom I normally adore, but not right now—decided to come here and add to my misery.

"Hey, you okay?" Hawk asks, and this time you can't mistake

the concern in his voice. My hand trembles. Mostly I want to cry and tell him that I'm not okay. I want to tell him that I feel like my world is ending. I want to confess that somehow, despite my past, I let my guard down and I'm hopelessly in love with Luke and he lied and I'm pretty sure, destroyed me.

"Sure. I'm always okay," I fib.

"Bullshit," Hawk murmurs and he doesn't know the half of it, but I don't reply.

"I love you guys, but do you think...just maybe, you could listen to me and drop the subject?"

"You liked him," Gabby murmurs, her face sad. Maybe it's because she knows what a broken heart feels like. Maybe she's putting herself in my shoes and imagining Luke is Dom. Whatever it is, the sadness on her face is enough to cut open the wounds that I'm doing my best to bury in ice cream.

"I need to go to the bathroom," I mutter, slapping my bowl down on the table by the couch.

I try not to run, but I don't think I achieved my goal. I slam the door with an echoing thud, and then slowly slide to the floor

I allow some of my tears to fall. I hate them almost as much as how much I *want* to hate Luke, but I still let them fall.

How could I have been so stupid?

You would think that after dealing with Dewayne I would have learned my lesson.

Maybe I'm just as stupid as everyone is always accusing me of being.

I don't know how long I sit there, but eventually I get up. I splash water on my face and dry my eyes. Then, I vow that I will hold my shit together until everyone leaves. I'll crumble tonight when I'm alone.

I walk back into the living room, trying to pretend I'm not dying inside.

Keeping Her

"Gabby, do you still want to rent my apartment out?" I ask her, hoping I don't sound as fake-cheerful as it sounds to my ears.

"Huh?"

"You mentioned it before. I'm thinking of moving," I tell her as I turn the corner to face them again.

"Where are you moving to?" Gabby asks, just as the doorbell rings. I ignore Hawk's heated stare, even though I can feel it. I stare at the door instead, wondering just how much worse today can get. With any luck it's my parents on the other side, desperate to tell me what a failure I am.

Might as well get it the fuck over with.

"Not sure," I respond, opening the door. "I'm thinking I might move to Vegas, try my luck there," I add looking over my shoulder.

"You're not moving to Vegas."

My body freezes as I hear Luke's voice. Slowly I turn around to see him standing in front of me. His eyes are bloodshot and there's a deep bruise under his eyes, his nose is puffy, but still intact...

Darn it.

Chapter 23

Grunt

How you can be pissed off at a woman and fucking glad to see her, all at the same time, is beyond me. She looks good, even with her eyes swollen. She's been crying. I hate that, but fuck, I'm taking that as an encouraging sign that she cares.

She didn't break my nose. Maybe that's a sign that she likes me after all. Because suddenly, I'm firmly convinced that she could have if she wanted to.

"What are you doing here?" she says, her voice thick with anger, that is in direct contrast to the paleness of her skin.

"I came to take you home," I basically growl.

"That's cute, but I am *home*."

"The fuck you are and while we're on the subject, you're not moving to Vegas."

"Oh wow, I'm glad you cleared that up for me. You just forgot one thing, *Grunt*."

"Don't make me spank your ass, Red. Your little boy toy behind you probably wouldn't like it."

"Boy Toy?" the man behind Jasmine asks, laughing. I'm ready to face-plant my fist into that fucking smile he's wearing.

"It seems to fit."

"Quit threatening Hawk. *He* belongs here—*unlike* you," Jasmine exhales, sounding fed up. I ignore her, my anger pointed at the man behind her. He seems like an easier situation to fix.

I can just kill him.

Right now, I'm thinking that will make me feel better.

"Hawk," I scoff. "What kind of fucking name is that?"

"It's better than...what was that you called him, Jazz? Grunt?"

Jasmine hangs her head down.

"Grunt you need to leave, and Hawk back off."

"Spoilsport," the man pouts, but goes back toward the living room.

"At least you have him trained," I joke.

"Oh, that's rich coming from you. Tell me, how does it feel to get your ass handed to you by a girl?" Hawk taunts.

That's when Gabby wraps her arms around Hawk and pulls him back into the room.

Fuck, could this asshole be the man that hurt Lyla?

Suddenly handing the prick over to Ford doesn't seem like that bad of an idea.

"You need to leave," Jasmine repeats, sounding tired, and bringing my attention back to her.

"That's not going to happen, Red. We need to talk, and this time you're going to let me explain before trying to break my nose, and permanently de-ball me," I grumble. I hear that motherfucker laughing in the background, and the idea of turning him over to Ford is getting more and more appealing by the second.

"If you don't leave, I *will* permanently de-ball you. Believe it or not, I was mostly taking it easy on you the last time," she brags, and I'm pretty sure she's telling me the truth.

"You don't want to do that, baby," I tell her, wedging my body between the door and the frame so she can't close it on me.

"Trust me, *Grunt*, I really do."

"No, you don't. You're going to want me to have my balls in good shape and we both know that. Now, quit acting like a bitch and let's talk this out."

I see the shock move over her face about the same time anger sparks in her eyes. My dick twitches in reaction. Jesus, there's nothing sexier than watching Jasmine's face come alive with anger—except maybe when it's passion.

"Are you fucking kidding me? Why don't you go home to your wife and pull your shit on her, because I'm not—"

"Red, I told you I'm not married," I growl her anger beginning to fuel mine. This damn woman is more stubborn than any I've ever met in my life.

"Your whore then," she spews out with hatred.

"She's not a whore, damn it, Red. Her name is Daisy!"

"I don't give a fuck what her name is. You should have told me about her! I never would have..."

"What, woman? You never would have spread those legs for me if you'd known about her?"

Her entire body flinches like I just slapped her and the look of hurt in her eyes is unlike anything I've ever seen. It's haunting.

"Yes!" she snaps, and although the anger has come back, the hurt is still in her eyes. I rake my hand through my hair, feeling frustrated.

"Fuck, Red, this isn't what I wanted...this is not what I wanted to say. I came here to explain," I mutter, wondering how things got so out of control, especially so quickly.

"There's nothing to explain. I thought you were different. It turns out, you're just like all the rest," she says.

I take this moment to make myself a vow that if I ever find out who the fucking shit for brains was that hurt her, I'm going to double his pain for every tear he made her cry. I should be pissed at Jasmine for jumping to conclusions about me, but I didn't explain it very well in the beginning and I know without a doubt she is carrying some major scars from her past.

"Fuck, Red, you're a hard woman."

"Obviously not hard enough. Will you stop standing in my doorway please? If not, I'm calling my dad and I really don't want to do that."

"Your dad? Your dad a cop, Red? That seems like something you should mention since you're accusing me of keeping secrets."

"I'm not accusing you of keeping secrets, you *are* keeping secrets," she mutters. "Hawk, call Dad and ask him to get over here. Tell him I'm having biker trouble."

"Cops can't do shit to me, babe. They can try, but you better believe, I'll be back for you."

"Dad's not a cop, Grunt. He's much worse. And I could hate you even more for what you're forcing me to do," she murmurs.

"What am I forcing you to do, Jasmine?" I ask her, my voice deceptively soft.

"Call my father and admit to him that I screwed up yet again," she murmurs. Her words aren't what cut me though. It's the tears I see shining in her eyes that my girl refuses to shed.

"You didn't screw up, baby. You can trust me," I tell her, my gut clenching, because that's not being completely honest with her. Am I fixing one mess, just to have a bigger one down the road? I can't help it though. I'm not giving her up.

I can't.

"Hawk!" Jasmine yells. "Are you calling?"

"Calling, Sis."

"Sister? That's your brother?" I ask, feeling better at least about that. Jasmine doesn't answer. Instead she turns her back to me, walking away.

"Hey, Mom, is Dad around?" Jasmine's brother says into the phone, but at this point Jasmine could call in the entire police force in the state of Kentucky. I don't give a damn.

"Don't move, Red," I growl.

She turns around and looks at me.

"Can't you just leave me in peace, Luke?" she whispers, the words broken.

"I've come to take you home, Red. I want to introduce you to Daisy."

"I don't have any inclination to meet your other woman, or hell, I guess I'm the other woman. Whatever, I'm out of this ride."

"Daisy is my daughter, Red."

"Uh…Dad…I'ma' gonna have to call you back," I hear her brother say in the silence. I ignore him. Instead, I'm staring at Jasmine who looks at me like I've lost my mind and hell…

Maybe I have.

Chapter 24

Jasmine

"If you're lying just to get me to Virginia, Luke, I'm going to kick your ass," I mumble staring out the passenger window of his truck.

"I'm just glad you're using my name again," he replies, but I don't turn to look at him.

My head is a mess and I don't know what I'm doing here. All I know is that after he dropped his bombshell about his daughter, he refused to leave unless I went with him. I knew that even though Hawk hung up with my parents they would come over. I didn't have much choice. I either went with him or stuck around for the war that was surely to be raged when Dad saw Luke in my living room.

I chose the easier option.

It's not that my father would be against me dating a biker. I think he might even like Luke, if he gave him a chance. But, he wouldn't give him a chance and that doesn't have anything to do with Luke. It's much more to do with my past choices. I know eventually, I'm either going to have to ignore it and let time heal the open wounds between my parents and I, or confess to them.

Since that last option holds about as much fun as a colonoscopy without medication, I'm ignoring it for now.

"How have I practically lived with you and not known that you had a daughter?" I mumble more to myself than to him.

"There's no practically about it, Red. You have been living with me and you're going to continue to do it," he rumbles.

"We'll see," I tell him, still trying to wrap my mind around everything. "Why did you keep her a secret, Luke? Were you ashamed of me? Or..."

"Or?"

"Am I just another in a long line of fuck-bunnies for you and you figure there's no reason for me to meet your daughter?"

"Damn it, Red."

"I'm not judging, not really. I just need to know the truth. Whatever else, I think I deserve that."

"We've only been together for a couple of weeks really, Jasmine. I figured I had more time," he responds, clearly uncomfortable.

When he puts it like that, it's hard for me to believe. This man that has sunk inside of my heart, broken through every defense I thought I had—defenses that disappeared with one look at him—has only been in my life for a short time.

How did I get this messed up, so quickly?

"So, you were trying me out."

"Fuck no," he growls, slapping his hand against the steering wheel. I look over at him, the vehemence in his denial shocking me. He spares me a glance, our gazes connecting for a few seconds before he turns his attention back to the road. "Nothing about what we share has been or ever will be about me trying you out, Red. It's just...women get funny about this sort of thing. I wanted to give you time to get to know me."

"Time?" I question. "But I didn't know you. The man I thought you were wouldn't..."

Keeping Her

"Wouldn't what? Hide things from you until he knew that you were addicted to the things he gave you enough to stay? I fucking am that man, Red. I'm willing to get you addicted to my cock, my mouth, my fingers, the shit I can buy you, hell, I don't care. Whatever I need to do to make sure you stay in my bed, I'm doing and that includes keeping the secret that I'm a—"

"Wow, you have a great opinion of me, don't you Luke? You think I'm a bitch that will like how you work your cock so much that I'll put up with your little girl."

"Jesus, why are you so intent on busting my balls, woman? Anything I say, you're bound and determined to twist up and make it ugly."

"I'm not *making* it ugly, Luke. It just plain is. It might surprise you, but I don't have to like how my man fucks me to like his child. I even think it's possible to be in love with a man even if you're not impressed with his bedroom skills."

"Bullshit."

"It's true. Sex doesn't have to be the major draw in a relationship, you know. Some couples can't have sex, do you think it makes them love each other less?" I mutter, turning back to look out the window.

"I think sex is required for a healthy relationship, you're damn straight. If something happened and one of us wasn't able, we'd find other ways to keep that part of our relationship vital, but I wouldn't give it up, hell no."

"You don't know what you're talking about," I mutter, rolling my eyes. "Sometimes it's just something you have to accept. What if you were in accident or wounded in battle or something and unable to...you know," I mutter, suddenly wishing I hadn't even started this conversation. "Do you think that injury should be the end of your relationship?"

"Fuck no," he growls.

"Then you agree—"

"I agree that if I couldn't fuck you with my cock, I still have fingers, and if I didn't have those then I could still eat out your sweet cunt," he argues.

I ignore the flush of heat his words give me, and the wetness I can feel as my mind takes his words and creates a vivid picture of him doing each of those.

I squirm a little in my seat, and I don't need to be looking at him to know he sees me and understands what his words do to me.

Bastard.

"It wouldn't be the same. I mean, there wouldn't be any pleasure in it for you—"

"Red, if you think having you come all over my face, or hearing you call out my name as you climax wouldn't bring me pleasure, you're wrong."

"Sure," I mutter, wondering if Luke knows the right thing to say to win every argument, while also thinking about how annoying that is. "I'm not even positive that I like you, you know," I announce, wanting to wipe the smile that keeps pulling on his lips. I've tried not to look at him, but I can't seem to help from stealing glances here and there.

"You can think that, baby, but I'll remind you that you do later."

"Oh, will you stop. Everything is not about sex!" I huff, getting pissed off. "I don't think I want to be with a man that could go without talking to his daughter for at least a week."

"I spoke to Daisy every day, spent time with her, too."

"How is that possible? You were with me the whole time?" I question.

"Not the whole time, Red. I went to the club, most of the time before you were even out of the bed."

I stop for a minute, thinking about what he said. Then, it hits me.

Keeping Her

"Your daughter lives at the club?"

"Yeah. Why wouldn't she?"

"She lives at the club," I stress again, wanting to make sure I understand exactly what he's saying.

"Yes, Daisy lives at the club."

"Your daughter lives at the club, but you have an apartment that you took me to?"

"You're not part of the club, Red. At least not yet."

He's thinking he's upset me by not bringing me to his club, and that's not it. I don't know what Luke and I are together yet, but I know that only two kinds of women are usually at the clubhouse. Club twinkies or old ladies. Kids are at my dad's club, but usually only on days marked for family—admittedly, with my uncles, most every day is family day, but there are still rowdy parties that the kids are specifically banned from—and glad for. I once caught Freak and Nikki getting a little too wild with some other guys from another chapter. I hadn't seen a real-life orgy before. And, I guess that's probably not what this was called, since Nikki was the only girl involved. But one girl and six guys together, seems like it *should* be an orgy, and it was certainly interesting to watch...*at least until my Uncle Dragon caught me.*

Poor Freak was in the doghouse for months, not to mention he and Dad were both super pissed at me. I tried to explain that I couldn't help it. It was just one of those things you couldn't look away from, but I think that made it worse instead of better. I was only fourteen and that, too, made it worse. I have a sneaking suspicion however, that if I had been my brother, they wouldn't have minded quite as much. Uncle Dragon and Dad are great men, but they're more than a little sexist when it comes to the women in their lives.

That thought almost makes me smile.

I miss them. I miss the way life was before I discovered how cruel people were, how cold and calculating others could be.

Before the blinders were ripped off and I saw my super-hero Dad as nothing more than just a normal, mortal man.

"So, Daisy's mother lives at the club?" I ask. I mean, I don't care. My dad is the vice president of the Savage MC. I know how this shit works and what the men do with the twinkies. I'm not stupid. It's not my favorite part of the club, but some of the girls are really nice and Vida started out as a twinkie, until one of the men claimed her as an old lady. Still, I don't know any of the club girls raising a daughter inside the club. I'm sure it's probably done, but I've just never seen it.

"Daisy's Mom left and followed a couple members to a different chapter," Luke replies, surprising me even more.

"Hold up, she left her daughter behind to follow other club members."

"Well, yeah."

"She left her daughter behind," I mumble, wondering what kind of bitch could do that. I try to pride myself on not being judgmental, but this isn't a damn dog, or another man. This is her daughter we're talking about. Then, a thought occurs to me. Luke and I haven't talked ages.

"Wait...How old are you?" I ask him, as he pulls up to a stop light that's red. He turns to look at me, and it's dark really, but from the glow of the lights I can tell that he's got confusion written all over his face.

"Thirty-five and so help me, if you decide that's too old for you now, Red—"

"Don't be stupid," I mutter. He's older, but he's not that much older than me, and I like that he's in his thirties really. Guys in their twenties have definitely been immature...*and evil.* "I'm just wondering how old your daughter is?"

"Why does that matter?"

My eyes widen in shock. "It matters!"

"She's five."

"She's five..."

"Yeah."

"That poor baby," I murmur, my stomach instantly tying in knots.

"Sorry?"

"You should be," I mutter under my breath.

"Red, stop talking in riddles. What are you talking about now?"

"A five-year-old shouldn't be alone in the club, who takes care of her when you're not there, Luke?" I ask him, unable to keep accusation out of my voice.

"The same people that take care of her when I'm there," he grumbles.

"What does that mean?"

"The girls watch after her," he shrugs.

"The...you let the club girls watch her?"

"Why not? I figure they know more than I do," he mutters, and I don't think I'm imagining how uncomfortable this topic is making him.

"Why not..."

"Red—"

"Luke, I made a mistake," I murmur. "I need you to turn around and take me back home."

"The hell I will."

"You're not listening to me. I can't do this."

"I'm hearing you just fine. You just aren't making any sense. You're already *doing* this. You're not running away from me now."

"You're misunderstanding me. I don't want to be with you anymore. It's clear we're too different."

"What the fuck are you talking about now?" he questions angrily, then he shocks me even more by yanking the truck hard to the right and going off the road without slowing down. He slams his brakes so hard that my body propels forward, even with the seatbelt. I brace myself against the dashboard as we careen into the overgrown grass away from the main road.

"What is your damage? Are you trying to get us killed?" I cry, my heart beating so hard that I wouldn't be surprised if it didn't beat out of my chest.

"I'm trying to figure out why you keep trying to invent reasons to be pissed at me," he roars, and I snap. I don't need this shit. I thought Luke was special and it turns out he's just a moron.

I quickly undo my seatbelt, almost simultaneously opening the door and then jumping out of his truck. I'll walk to the nearest store and then have my father come and get me. I'll take hearing what horrible choices I make over this shit any day of the week and twice on Sunday.

Except, I barely make it two feet in front of the truck when Luke's hand wraps around my waist and he drags me back against his hard body, pulling me to the side of the truck. He pins me between him and the truck. I swallow down my nerves as I get a look at the anger shining in his eyes.

Shit.

Chapter 25

Grunt

I pin Jasmine up against my truck. I've had enough of this bullshit. I was hoping to wait until we got home to have this out, but if she wants to be a bitch, then I can show her how big of a bastard I can be.

I grab her wrists, holding them behind her, refusing to let her move an inch.

"Let me go!" she hisses.

"Not on your fucking life. We're going to have this out once and for all. And I'm warning you Jasmine, you're going to quit running away from me."

"The hell I am! We're done!"

"Baby, we aren't done, we're nowhere close to that."

"That's where you're wrong. I'm never going to be with a man who doesn't even want to take care of his own daughter!"

I stare at her stunned.

"What the fuck are you talking about, woman? I love Daisy."

"Yeah, right," she responds, disdain on her face, her voice full of derision.

"You haven't even met her, but you think you're qualified to make judgments on what kind of father I am?"

"She sleeps at a club with twinkies taking care of her, instead of her father who is off fucking a woman who is good enough to be in his bed but not meet his daughter. That's all the information I need, *Grunt*."

"Jesus Christ. You give me a damn headache, Red. First you're pissed because of Daisy and now you're pissed because you don't think I take care of her."

"I don't think, I know. How did your parents take care of you? If you tell me they left you alone with twinkies to raise you, I'm calling you a fucking liar."

"What the hell is a twinkie?"

She blinks, her face is glowing in anger. If I wasn't so pissed at her I'd enjoy it.

"A club whore!"

"I thought you said you weren't part of the Devil's Blaze," I respond, starting to catch on that little Jasmine here knows exactly how a club works. I should have seen it from the beginning. Damn, maybe I am as stupid as she accuses me of being.

"I'm not," she says, her eyes narrowing. "That doesn't mean I'm stupid to the way clubs run. Gabby and I have been friends for a lot of years," she responds, and I guess she's right about that. Still, something tells me that my Red is keeping some major secrets.

"My club has good women in it."

"I'm sure it does," she snaps.

"And Sledge's old lady looks out for Daisy when I'm not there. Hell, they know more about raising a girl than I do. I don't see the problem," I grumble.

She goes still again, not talking, and I figure that I somehow fucked up yet again. So, I wait, because I'm sure Jasmine will tell me soon enough.

Keeping Her

"Who raised you? Club girls?" she asks.

"What?"

"It's a simple question, Luke. Who raised you?"

"Why does that even matter?"

"Because it does. Who raised you?" she asks again, her face thoughtful.

"I swear woman, you're giving me a headache. I like it better when your mouth is so full of my cock you can't give me shit," I growl.

"You did not just say that to me."

"I did and what's more I meant it!" I bark.

"Well, if that's all you are looking for, Grunt, they make these dolls you can stick your dick into that *can't* talk."

"And those are looking better and better," I lie.

I shouldn't be turned on right now, but damn it all to hell, I am. The madder Jasmine gets, the more fire her eyes and mouth shoot at me and I'm probably a twisted son of a bitch, but it makes me hard has fucking nails.

"A word of advice, Luke," she bites out through clenched teeth. "Keep your dick away from my mouth right now because if it gets anywhere close, I'll bite it off."

"Point made," I mumble with a wince. "Did you know you alternate between calling me Grunt and Luke when you're pissed?" She lets out a breath of air that sounds like a pissed off bear. "Or maybe you are doing it enough so that I call you on that shit and spank your ass."

"In your dreams," she mutters, trying to jerk free of my hold.

"Is that what you're doing, baby? Do you want me to spank you?" I murmur, leaning in to breathe deep against her neck, taking her scent into my lungs like some fucking addict—because I am. I'm addicted to Jasmine.

"Let go of me and I'll show you," she taunts, pulling against my hold.

"I don't think I have to let you go to see. I have a way of checking without one word being passed between us," I tell her softly.

I feel her body tremble against me, watch as her eyes dilate. My gaze drops down to take in the way her chest moves as her breathing becomes ragged.

"Luke, stop," she responds, but her voice is threaded with desire and the tone of it feels like a caress.

She rubs her lips together and I can feel the war inside of her. I know she's trying to fight this pull between us. Hell, that's probably the smart thing to do. I should do that too. I should have from day one, but I can't.

"You don't mean that, Red," I argue, my hand going to the button on her jeans.

Her eyes close, and another shudder moves through her.

"This doesn't solve anything, Luke," she argues, but all I can think is that she didn't say no.

"Maybe it will solve everything," I respond, as I release the zipper on her pants.

"I don't see how."

Her voice is soft now, barely a whisper, and her skin is heated against my fingertips.

"This is how you and I relate the best, baby."

Her body bows, her back presses against the fender of my truck, and I release her hands as her upper body reclines back on the hood, her hair surrounding her beautiful face like a damn halo.

I push her pants down, and she moves her legs as far apart as she can. It's not much, but it gives me room to slide my hand under her panties and cup her sex. I lift her higher on my body, wanting her comfort above anything else and I groan as the wetness I find there greets me when I caress the lips of her pussy.

Keeping Her

"I think that's physical, not truly relating, Luke," she whines, her hips thrusting out, seeking my attention.

I push my fingers inside of her and she rewards me with her cry of pleasure. I tease her, curling them inside, petting her tender walls, pushing her to get even more lost in the passion we share. She's mostly hidden and this time of night the road is barely traveled, but every now and then a car passes, the lights abnormally bright. If it wasn't for that, I'd have her take her shirt off, play with her tits and watch them bounce as I fuck her hard. I don't want some asshole seeing them though. They're mine, for my eyes only. Jasmine may not accept that claim just yet, but it's true. What is between us is too fucking powerful to deny.

I tear her panties loose, then quickly undo my pants. I keep them on, doing just enough to get my dick out. I want them off, but that's not going to happen, at least not right now and I've got to have her. There's no waiting, we're both too far gone. I take my cock in my hand, it's so hard it's throbbing and my pre-cum has coated the head. I rub it against her pussy, not entering, but gathering her sweet juices on my cock, loving the way it feels to tease her.

I could make her come like this. Fuck, I could come just as easily.

"Quit torturing me, Luke," she pants, her hands slapping against the fender of my truck.

"But it's so fucking fun," I moan, pressing my head against her clit. She's so wet it slips easily back and forth and I grunt as I feel my balls tighten.

Everything about her is so damn perfect.

"Damn you—"

Her words break off in a cry as I plunge inside her tight little cunt, stretching her as I claim her, not stopping until I'm balls deep. My hands go to her ass, to lift her even more. I groan because that simple action joins us more. I feel like I'm pushing against her womb.

"Oh God, yes," she moans, her fingernails biting into my back with a force that I can feel—even through my leather cut. "Fuck me," she begs, her hot breath against the side of my neck, as our bodies begin to move. She tightens her legs around me, allowing me to take all of her weight, knowing she's safe.

She'll always be safe with me. I make that vow silently, but it's one I intend on keeping.

"That's it, baby, squeeze my cock," I order, my voice dark and clipped because I'm doing my best not to come like a damn chump. I need to make sure my woman gets off first. Her pussy grips me like an iron fist, a hot, slick impossibly wet fist.

It's heaven.

She meets every thrust I give, grinding her sweet little cunt to get what she needs. I find myself watching her, unable to look away. Slowly her pleasure-glazed eyes open, and she looks down at me. My heart clenches in my chest and I know that I will die before I ever give this woman up.

"You feel so good, Luke."

"You can't leave me, Jasmine."

Her thighs tighten against me, her eyes cloudy. She stops her movements, but I take over, using my hold on her hips to push her against me, as I continue ramming my cock in and out of her, my climax already causing my damn balls to ache.

"Luke," she hums my name like a damn wish. As if it's the only thing that can save her—or maybe that's what it feels like because that's how she feels to me.

She's my deliverance, redemption... fuck, anything and everything begins and ends with this woman.

"You can't leave me, Red," I growl.

"Damn you," she says. "Damn you." Her body trembles and I

feel the muscles of her pussy contracting around me. "Damn you," she says again as her orgasm takes over.

"Kiss me, baby. Kiss your man while I paint your fucking womb with my cum." I keep pounding into her. "I'm going to come so much it will be leaking out of you for fucking days," I grunt, right before her mouth slams down on mine and her tongue pushes into my mouth, attacking my own.

We fuck, our kiss just as wild, like the animals that our passion has reduced us to. And I come. I come harder than I ever have in my life. For a minute it even feels like I want to fucking pass out, so great is the pleasure—my hunger for this woman overpowering anything and everything.

We continue kissing even after I've filled her completely, our combined juices running along my shaft and down her thighs. I'm still moving in and out of her at a much slower, leisurely pace, coming down slowly and riding out the storm we created.

When we break apart to take air into our lungs, I still kiss at her lips slowly, nipping them, unable to fully let them go.

"Luke—"

"Don't Red. Not right now. This moment with you is too perfect. Let's go, we'll clean up and in the morning I'll take you to meet Daisy," I tell her.

She stares at me, her eyes cloudy. The sound of cars going by echoes around us, but we both ignore them. I feel like everything hinges on her next words and I only breathe easier when she finally says them.

"Okay, Luke. Take me home."

I kiss her again, trying to show her how much her words mean, without speaking, because I don't think I could tell her.

I'm going to make Jasmine want to stay with me. I didn't lie to her. I'll use the way we fuck, the way I make her feel, anything and everything I can do to make her as addicted to me as I am to her.

Chapter 26

Grunt

"I think there's something wrong with us," Jasmine murmurs against my chest sometime later.

We came home, showered together and fell in bed. I made love to her again, going slowly and memorizing every glorious inch of her. She's been quiet, I know she is still sorting things out and working through it all in her mind. I'm letting her have her space with that, but I'm not giving up having her in my arms.

"Why's that, Red?" I ask, my head on the pillow, head tilted so I can see her. My fingers reach out and delve gently into her curls—for no other reason than I just need to touch her.

"I think we've had more sex in public than we've had in your bed," she laughs, turning so her chin presses into my stomach and she's looking at me.

"Our bed. I think I like the sound of it being our bed much better."

"Yeah, right," she responds, all but rolling her eyes.

I move my hand to cup the side of her face, refusing to let her look away.

"I'm serious, baby."

"Luke, this has happened really quick and until tonight, I didn't even know you had a daughter."

"You can't deny this feels right, Jasmine. Whatever else is going on, there's a pull between us that we can't get away from."

"It might be better if we could," she murmurs.

"No way. I like having you with me, Red."

"Your nose would argue," she responds, reaching up to touch it gently. "I'm kind of sorry about that, by the way."

"Kind of sorry?"

"Well, you did kind of deserve it. You should have told me about Daisy, instead of making me think you had another woman."

"Fuck, woman. Do you think with the way you wear me out that I could have energy for someone else?"

"You're so romantic," she mutters, shaking her head.

"I'm just me, Red, but you have to know that I want you, hell I'm obsessed with you."

"Yeah."

"Is there something wrong with that?" I ask her, when she looks at me, almost...*sad*.

"What could be wrong. Every girl wants to be wanted by a hot guy."

"Red—"

"You don't have to introduce me to your daughter you know."

"Woman—"

"I know, I know. I got pissy and upset, but only because I thought you had been lying to me and I let that anger fuel me when it came to Daisy."

"Red—"

"But you're right. It's none of my business where or how you raise your daughter. It's not like we're much more than fuck-buddies. So, I mean, that's probably not the kind of girl you should be letting her meet and I'm sorry if I made you feel like you had to."

She stares up at me expectantly after saying all of that and barely taking a breath. I just look back at her, saying nothing while my brain processes everything she just said.

"Well?" she prompts after a little more of my silence.

"Oh, sorry, I didn't realize you were going to let me talk."

"Don't be a smartass, Luke."

She gets up, clearly annoyed with me, and I let her for two reasons.

One, she ruined a good sex buzz and I'm pretty fucking annoyed with her right now and two...Well, two is that she's naked and watching her move naked is a damn good show. I frown as she throws my shirt on over her body, but at least it's *my* shirt, so I don't demand she yank it back off.

"I was just being honest. Seems to me you have all this figured out and there wasn't much more to add."

"Okay, then," she says, bending down to the small dorm room fridge I have and grabbing a cold water out of it.

"*But*," I finally say, stressing the word. "If you are going to let me talk, let me go on record as saying we're not just fuck-buddies. If all I wanted was to fuck a woman, I wouldn't leave the club."

"That would probably be better than this dump," she mutters under her breath.

"I told you if you didn't like something here to just change it, Red."

"Why? I'm not staying."

"You are."

"Excuse me?" she asks, her brow creasing.

"Red, we've had a good run here. I fucked you hard and came so much my eyes rolled back in my head. I ate that sweet pussy out in the shower, and I can still taste you on my tongue. I fucked you again and then you sucked my cock and swallowed down my cum. How about you put a cap on your sass until tomorrow."

"Put a cap on my sass?"

"Yeah, babe. I want to sleep with you in my arms tonight and then, when the mood strikes me, fuck you again. What I don't want to do is fight with you over something we both want in the first damn place."

"And what do we *both* want, Luke?"

"You here with me and not in some Podunk town in Kentucky around people that don't appreciate you."

"They appreciate me," she grumbles.

"They love you. I haven't seen a hint of appreciation."

"You haven't even met them," she says with a sigh, her body relaxing slightly.

"I know they made you cry. That's all I need to know right now."

"I'm over-emotional."

She looks at me as if she's daring me to argue.

"You are, but from what I saw, you had reason."

"You don't know the whole story, Luke. You might not like me or take my side if you did."

"Oh, I like you baby. That's not changing. And, I'll always take your side, even if I think you're acting ape-shit crazy. I would just spank your ass in private for it."

"You have an answer for everything," she says with a laugh.

"I try."

"And you're not fooling me, either." She smirks at me. "You're just trying to find reasons to spank me because you like it."

"And you'd let me, because you like it too," I respond, grinning at the way her cheeks deepen in color.

"You're entirely too cocky. And just think, when we first met I thought you didn't know how to speak."

"Come back to bed, baby. I miss you."

"Oh please, I just got out and I'm hungry, which means you're taking me out."

"Taking you out? What the fuck for?"

"I'm hungry and you don't have a stove—or food for that matter."

"I bought some of those microwavable mac and cheese things you like," I mutter, not wanting to leave.

"I don't want food you have to nuke, I'm *hungry* Luke."

"Okay that settles it. Tomorrow you order a stove or whatever else you need to make this place comfortable."

"Uh... that could be *very* expensive."

"You think I can't afford it?" I ask, annoyed.

"I have no idea one way or the other," she says with a shrug. "I'm just thinking this place is kind of shit, so it's probably not worth it, especially since you live at the club the majority of the time."

"That was before you. I like having you alone. I like the way you walk around naked, fuck me loud, and most of all I like the way it feels to open the door up after club bullshit and find you waiting for me."

"Oh Lord, you're as bad as my father and uncle," she says, shaking her head.

"What do you mean by that?" I ask, finally sitting up in bed, because it's clear that Jasmine isn't coming back until I take her to get something to eat.

"Sexist pigs."

"Are we getting ready to argue again?" I laugh.

"No, I doubt it would do any good, anyway. Are you going to get dressed and take me to find food?" she says, shaking her head, a smile playing on her lips.

"All jokes about your hometown aside, mine's not a lot better. There aren't many places open this time of night, woman."

"I saw a Taco Bell..."

"You better make it worth my while when we get back," I warn her.

"I'll see what I can do," she says with a grin, knowing she's won.

What she doesn't know, and I'm not about to tell her, is that I'd give her anything she asks for as long as she smiles at me exactly like she's smiling at me right now, while wearing nothing but my t-shirt...

Chapter 27

Jasmine

I'VE NEVER DONE IT, SO I COULDN'T SAY FOR CERTAIN, BUT I imagine walking into the main room of the Demon Chaser's compound was a lot like walking in front of a firing squad. As clubs go, this would be like the Economy Inn of clubs.

Concrete and cinderblock walls are the décor of choice. It's dark as fuck. The lights are cheap florescent shop bulbs. I can't be sure, but from the looks of the place, I think it used to be some kind of old garage. It's not very big, which I imagine is why so many campers and RV's are out front.

Maybe I've been spoiled by my dad's club and Uncle Skull's, but the DC's definitely need to concentrate on upgrading their digs. Or not, I guess… it's all relative. If they're happy, it doesn't matter. Still, it's dirty as hell in here. I fight to keep my nose from curling at the smell. It reminds me of a boy's locker room after a big game.

I might be a little judgmental because of all the eyes staring at me like they want me to die. You would think that would be stretching it, but it's clearly not. There are seven women in here. Each and every one of them are looking at me like they'd enjoy cutting my head off and feeding it to the tigers. Of course, I don't know if the DC's have tigers, but if they do, I just might be in trouble.

One thing is very clear to me.

Luke might be a favorite among the club whores.

That doesn't exactly fill a girl with happy, warm thoughts of puppies.

I call upon years of experience of being a bitch—and the daughter of the Savage MC VP, and I give them a fuck you smile, while slipping my hand in Luke's back pocket, pressing against his ass with my fingers. It's a universal sign of ownership and damn if I don't enjoy the hate that comes hurling my way when I do it.

Luke looks down at me, his brow furrowed, his eyes asking an unspoken question. Men can be so damn clueless. I try to look up at him in innocence. I'm not sure I completely pull it off, especially when the creases in his forehead deepen.

"You okay, Red?" he murmurs for only me to hear.

"Peachy," I respond, cheerfully. His lips twitch as if he's fighting a smile. His eyes sparkle and it makes my stomach feel as if it has butterflies in it.

"Why is it you make me want to spank your ass just by smiling at me, Red?"

"Because you're obsessed with sex and don't really need a reason to spank me?" I ask, blinking like I'm the innocent one in this party.

He lets out a large bark of laughter and before I can even react to it, he captures my mouth and kisses me soundly. I should pull away and try to prepare myself for meeting everyone here at the club. Instead, I lose myself in his kiss, groaning as his tongue thrusts in, searching mine and immediately showing his dominance—and I surrender, loving this side of him in ways I can't begin to explain.

"Damn, Grunt, let the girl up for air."

I reluctantly pull back as the woman's voice interrupts our kiss.

Luke lets out a breath of frustration and it makes me smile, laying my forehead against his chest, because it does sound like a grunt and I'm beginning to understand his road name all too well.

"Gina," Luke mumbles as his fingers scrunch in my curls. Then, he kisses the top of my head. I pull back to look at him, wondering what in the world I'm going to do with him. Finally, I reluctantly go to Luke's side where he puts his arm around me and holds me there—like I'd try to escape. I'm not going to do that; if last night taught me anything, it's that walking away from Luke might be impossible.

"Is this the girl that Sledge says has your dick in knots?"

I blink, more than a little shocked as I look over the woman. She's got bleach blonde hair that's a little too fried from the coloring. There's nothing soft about it. She's older, I couldn't really venture a safe guess because she's spent a lot of time in the tanning bed. Her skin almost glows orange and it has a leathery sheen to it. She's wearing a cut that proclaims her property of Sledge.

This is the woman that takes care of Luke's daughter?

Okay, maybe I'm being a judgmental bitch, but in my defense, if there was anything at all friendly about this woman maybe my reaction would be different. There's not, though. Hell, she seems more predatory than the club twinkies over at the corner of the bar whispering furiously to each other even now.

I have no doubt that they're whispering about me either. I also wouldn't be surprised to find out that they're led by the fake blonde in front of me.

"I've done quite a few things with Luke's dick, but tying it in knots isn't one of them. It works too damn good to try and damage," I respond, my tone even.

Keeping Her

"Shit, Red," Luke mutters. He doesn't laugh, but I can feel a silent chuckle move through his body.

"I'm Gina. My old man, Sledge, is one of the founding members here," she replies, and there it is.

She's drawing lines in the sand. I couldn't care less. I'm not looking to sign up as a permanent fixture with the DC's. It does make me wonder why she seems to be more than a little intimidated by me. I mean, she doesn't know me. I've never spoken to her. Plus, Luke and I haven't been together long enough for her to wonder what I am to him.

I don't get it.

"I'm—"

"This is my old lady, Red," Luke replies completely interrupting me. My body physically jolts, my back locking into place.

His old lady?

"You gave her your cut?" Gina asks, her eyes going wide. Mine don't, I'm not about to betray my shock in front of this chick because she's looking for signs of weakness. I *know* she is, even if I don't understand the why.

"I did. Giving it to her tonight at the party."

Oh fuck. There's a party tonight?

"That's a surprise," Gina says, and her gaze rakes over me as if she finds me lacking.

I mean damn, I don't look my best, but I look good.

I have my hair pulled back in what looks like a simple pony tail, but in reality, took time to tease and fluff, to make the curls appear as if they're always manageable. I'm wearing a red turtleneck sweater, which might be a tad warm, but looks damn good on me and shows off my girls to their best advantage. I'm also wearing a black vest, which doesn't scream biker. It screams fashion runway in Milan, and I had to save up for freaking months and months to buy it. I have on my best pair of faded jeans, they hug my ass and are worn in just the right places. I look hot, damn it, and probably better than trash-can Barbie has in her entire life.

I don't know why she's determined that her and I are meant to be enemies without even really talking, but whatever. I can roll with it.

"That's my Luke," I say—a little too sweetly. "He's full of surprises," I add and then I slap my hand against his chest. To the outside world it looks like a touch of familiarity, a close couple. Yet, I slap him a little too hard, because you don't pull this shit on a woman. I don't know if I'm more upset about the fact that he'd planned on giving me his cut tonight, or that there's a party.

"Well, I guess congrats are in order, honey. You've managed to do what every woman here has tried to do for years," Gina says, turning her attention back to me.

"What's that?"

"Tie Grunt to their bed and keep his interest. The girls and I were starting to wonder if it was even possible."

Luke lets out that snort of air again. To be fair, if he has to deal with women like this on a daily basis, I can see why he does little more than snort. Sometimes there are just no words.

Unless, of course, you are me.

"Oh that's easy," I tell her. "I never tried to tie him to my bed."

"You don't? Like to leave it all open? A girl after my own heart," she says and Luke's hand tightens on my shoulder, but I knew without feeling that or even looking that he wasn't happy with me. I can just sense the change in him. It's weird, like we're connected and I should worry about that instead of putting Gina here in her place, but I've never been smart when dealing with people.

"Oh hell, once it's mine, it's mine, I'll cut a bitch if she tries to touch it," I tell her, my voice friendly enough, but my face leaving no doubt that I'm telling the truth.

Keeping Her

"Then—"

"I just knew better than to try and tie Luke to any bed. He ties me to his," I tell her. I look up at Luke like a besotted school girl—which sadly isn't that hard to do. He's looking down at me, his lips relaxed in a smile and his face happy. Damn it, even his eyes are sparkling with it. "Sometimes he keeps me tied to it for hours and hours."

"I—"

"The men here in Virginia definitely have stamina," I tell Gina, cutting her off. "Either that or I just hit the hot biker jackpot." I shrug.

"Jesus, Red," Luke says. "Let me go introduce you to Ford and the others before I take you in the back and show you that you hit the jackpot."

"Are both offers on the table?" I reply with a grin, all too happy to be taken away from Gina.

"What am I going to do with you?" he asks, when we're finally clear from her.

"I have a few ideas," I say mildly.

"I bet you do."

"Don't think you're going to get away with not explaining about the cut and why you're bringing me to the party, Luke darling."

"I didn't figure I was, Red. It's okay though."

"It is?" I ask, looking up at him.

"Yeah, babe, because I really dig the way I get to fuck you after I let you bust my balls."

I roll my eyes. "You're an asshole."

He laughs but doesn't say anything and all I can do is sigh, because it's this very moment that I realize I'm completely in love with Luke.

Shit.

Chapter 28

Grunt

I'M NOT A MAN THAT'S GIVEN TO NERVES. I'VE CHARGED INTO a warehouse full of drugs with guns pointed at me and my brothers and not blinked an eye. I've spent time in jail with some badass motherfuckers and not worried a fucking bit.

But bringing Jasmine to my club has me sweating. She handled Gina like a champ and managed to turn me on at the same time. I should have known Jasmine was capable of that.

"You've been kind of scarce the last two days, Grunt. Was wondering if you were going to show tonight."

I look over at Sledge. His words are relaxed, his face not so much. The SOB is miserable as fuck. He knows it, hell we all know it. We've all wondered why he tied himself to Gina. She's a good tumble in bed, but that's about it when it comes to her appeal. She's taken the position of old lady to heart though and the other girls respect her, especially since she used to be one of them. Since Ford is single, she's pretty much head honcho with the women and it's a role she enjoys. She might not be my favorite person, but I have to admit she's good to Daisy, sweet to her and I know Daisy needs that. I know shit about being a

Keeping Her

parent. I never had a mom, and I didn't want that life for Daisy...

"Had shit to do."

"There was a time when men put the club before their own personal shit," Sledge says. I know the bastard is baiting me.

"You got a problem with what I do for the club?" I ask, my voice a low, deadly rumble.

"Seems to me you—"

"I wasn't asking you, Sledge. I was asking Ford. I mean you did step down as second just so you could deal with your personal shit, right?"

Jasmine tightens her hand on my arm but remains silent.

"Grunt," Ford says, sounding tired. He doesn't say anything more than that, but that's okay. Sledge and I are busy staring at one another. It's a pissing contest and I refuse to lose.

"Jasmine, nice to finally meet you, Grunt's told me quite a bit about you," Ford says, and fuck, that makes me break eye contact and look at Ford to see what he's up to.

"I doubt that," Jasmine replies, already making me wonder what she's going to say next.

"You doubt me?"

"Maybe you're trying to be nice," she hedges.

"I'm not nice, unless a woman asks me to be."

My hand tightens into a fist. What the fuck is Ford doing? He's clearly flirting with Jasmine. I can't figure out my club tonight, but I'm wishing like fuck I hadn't brought Jasmine here.

"That will never be me. I prefer to have a man I don't have to ask anything of," she announces with a carless shrug. "I just meant that Luke and I haven't known each other long, I doubt he has much to tell you—if anything—about me."

"So, you're used to having a man trained to give you everything you want without having to tell him?" Sledge asks.

"Motherfucker—"

"If you think that, then you don't know Luke at all. He's more the type to tell you what you're going to get and then give it to you."

Ford laughs. I hold my head down and pinch the bridge of my nose, thinking I should have brought Daisy to the house instead of going about it this way.

"Is that how you like it?" Ford asks. Fuck me...*Am I going to have to shut my own President down?* He's clearly hitting on Jasmine and I don't like it.

I don't like it one fucking bit.

"Never have been. But I like it the way Luke gives it to me, any way he does," she says, and I'll remember those words. I'll remember them because of the pleasure they give me. I'll remember them because of the way she effectively put Ford in his place. A lot of women in my world would step over a man to get to the President. Jasmine is clearly unfazed. She's here with me and fuck, she's making that known. She turns into me, and I look into her eyes, thinking I like anything she gives me too—any way she wants to give it.

"I want to meet Daisy. If you can tell me where—"

"I can take you, Red—"

"The name is Jasmine," she tells Gina, who showed up right behind us, but has kept quiet. She's standing behind Sledge, but carefully not touching him. I never noticed that kind of thing before I met Jasmine, but I am now, and something seems strange about it. "Only Luke can call me Red."

Gina cocks an eyebrow up. She's not used to having women talk back to her. I probably should warn her to tone it down. It's not that I don't think Jasmine could handle herself, it's just that Gina won't exactly fight fair and she can be a cold-hearted bitch.

Jasmine starts to walk away, but I grab her hand, not letting her leave.

"I'll take her," I interrupt.

Keeping Her

"But I can—"

"I'll take her, Gina. I didn't get to see her yesterday." I turn around, leading Jasmine down the corridor where Daisy's room is.

"Well, don't get her too excited. It's time for her to be in bed."

"It's barely six in the evening," Jasmine says, turning to look at Gina.

"Yeah, but there's a party tonight."

Jasmine's body jerks in my hold. Clearly she doesn't like it. It's not sitting well with me either. I never thought about the fact that Daisy wasn't around when the parties were going strong. I just assumed she was playing and being seen too. Now, it's beginning to dawn on me how lax I've been. Hell, Jasmine was right to be pissed at me. I'm starting to get pissed at myself.

"Of course there is," she mutters.

"Red," I respond quietly, not sure of how to defend myself and kind of resenting that I have to. I'm not used to answering to anyone.

"No," she murmurs, as we reach Daisy's door.

"No?" I question.

"Don't bring me to meet your daughter and expect me to not react to the things I see. I don't know your daughter, Luke. We can end this here and I'll walk away and never know her. I'm okay with that, because I haven't met her. I'm not attached. But, if I walk through this door and meet your daughter, I'm probably going to get attached. That means I will have opinions. What you choose to do with them, is up to you, but I warn you that I will give you a piece of my mind. So, you decide now, how this plays out."

"Red? Baby, when haven't you given me a piece of your mind?"

"Then, you shouldn't be surprised, should you?" she huffs.

I bring my hand up and press my palm against the side of her cheek, looking down at her and wondering if it would even be possible to go back to a life before Jasmine was part of it. Somehow, I don't think it is.

"That's where you're wrong, Red. You're constantly surprising me."

"Don't try to be nice to me right now, Luke. I'm pissed and I need to direct that on you."

"Why?" I laugh.

"Because if I don't, I'll probably kill your buddy's old lady and I'm sensing that would be bad."

"It probably would be," I say with a chuckle and bend down to kiss her. "You ready?"

"As I ever will be, I guess," she says, sounding like she's getting ready for a firing squad.

"She'll love you, Red."

"Yeah, but how am I going to feel about you when all this is said and done?" she asks, and I can't stop from worrying about that myself.

Chapter 29

Jasmine

"Daddy!"

I heard the little girl's cry and there was so much joy in it that my heart squeezed in my chest. Then, I heard footsteps, obviously bare, padding over in the dark room toward the door. I frown, looking around the room, but before I can piece it together, I watch as Luke lifts this beautiful little bundle in his arms. She's curvy, with strawberry blonde hair, and if she tightens her little hands any harder on her daddy's neck, she might choke him.

"Hey, sunshine."

"I missed you," she responds, her voice muffled because her face is pressed tight into Luke's neck. I feel around on the wall for a light switch and eventually find it. I give it a flick, but nothing happens. I do it again and get the same result. I'm concentrating on what I'm doing and therefore, my attention is focused completely on it and not Luke and his daughter.

"It's blown," the little girl says and my head jerks back around and thanks to light from the hallway, I see the prettiest brown eyes staring at me.

"What is?" I ask, kind of mesmerized by the little girl. She really is beautiful and looks so much like her dad that it's almost uncanny.

"The light blowed. Auntie Gina is gonna get me a new bulb."

"Oh, she may have forgotten because of the party," I tell her, putting a smile on my face. I'm suddenly nervous being the primary focus of her attention.

What happens if she doesn't like me?

Should it matter? Will it matter to Luke? Does he truly see me as something more than just a passing fling? Does he want me as part of his life?

Am I even ready for any of this?

Too late I realize that I should have asked all these questions earlier. I didn't and now I'm stuck.

"It blowed last week when Daddy took me to McDonalds. Are we going to McDonalds, Daddy?"

"Haven't you had supper, Sunshine," Luke asks, his voice gruff.

"Aunt Gina brought me cereal," she says, and I grin—mostly because I like cereal for dinner sometimes, too.

"Daddy has to meet with Uncle Ford," Luke says, regretfully. "How about—"

"I could take her to get something to eat…" I suggest, feeling weird about asking, but not really wanting to stay here either. Luke just stares at me and I'm beginning to feel even more uncomfortable. "It doesn't have to be away from here, I meant to the kitchen or somewhere," I mumble.

"Who are you?" Daisy asks, tilting her head to the side to look at me.

"I'm a friend of your Daddy's," I answer, suddenly thinking I'd rather face down all of Luke's club than this one small five-year-old. "My name is Jasmine."

"Like the princess on 'Laddin."

"I guess so," I respond with a smile.

"You don't look like her," she argues, her hand tentatively reaching out to touch my hair.

"I don't guess I do," I laugh.

"You look like Ariel," she says, her fingers continuing to play in my hair.

"So do you," I murmur, touching her hair gently which is lighter than my copper curls, but still similar. It would appear that Luke has a type.

"I want to be Merida," she announces letting go of my hair. Luke lets her down on the floor and I crouch down so that we're more eye level. I have no idea what I'm doing, but I've always liked kids—my brother is still a kid, a *big* one.

"She's my favorite," I say with a sagely nod, appearing completely serious.

"Mine too! I have the movie! Daddy bought it for me. Do you want to watch it with me?"

"Jasmine has to—"

"I'd love to," I tell her, interrupting Luke. I'm rewarded with his muted grunt, so I know I didn't make him happy.

I lift my gaze to look up at him while he's standing behind Daisy. "I can watch with her while you meet with Ford and the others," I shrug. His eyes narrow, he's clearly not happy. Sadly, for him, I'm all out of fucks to give. "You could take us to the kitchen first though."

"The kitchen?" Luke asks, the annoyance heard plainly in his voice.

"Daisy's hungry and everyone knows you can't watch a movie without snacks, Luke."

"Snacks!" Daisy agrees, excitedly. "Can we have snacks, Daddy?" she asks, turning to look at him.

"How can I refuse my two best girls?" he finally says, picking Daisy back up in his arms.

"Yay!" she squeals.

"Yay," I murmur.

Luke shakes his head. "You win this one, Red," he mutters against my ear as I stand up.

"I didn't realize we were battling, Luke," I keep a smile on my face as I follow them out of the dark room.

"Then you better get with the program, baby. You better get with the program."

If ovaries can tremble in need and explode at the same time, for some reason, mine just did...

Chapter 30

Grunt

"Where's your woman?" Ford asks right away and I sit down, exhaling a breath and wondering if killing my Prez would get me put in charge of these fuckers, because that's the last thing I want.

"What's your interest in her?"

"Excuse me?"

"Don't hand me bullshit. You were straight up eye-fucking my girl and flirting with her. You might be my president and I'd die for you and this club, but Jasmine is off limits," I growl, laying my cards on the table.

"She's a hell of a woman, your Red."

"That's right, *my* Red," I rumble.

"I don't think I've seen you this possessive over a woman. Hell, Daisy's mom would fuck others in front of you and you didn't give a damn."

"Daisy's mom wasn't important. Red is."

"She gave you a kid," Jonesy says, reminding me of something that I already know.

"And I paid her to keep the kid and not get rid of it. I love

Daisy," I respond, scratching my fingers in the stubble on my face. I do love her, but I'm starting to see that I've been a shit father. I don't have experience at it, and I sure as hell haven't seen it done. I get the feeling I'm coming up short in Jasmine's eyes though, and I don't like it. I don't like the way my daughter has been living either. Until Jasmine came along, I didn't notice it. What worries me the most is that I might never have seen it.

"You look like a man in deep thought, Grunt, my man," Ford says, and I nod.

"Women will do that shit to you. They're not worth it," Sledge all but growls.

"Better not let Gina catch you saying that," Jonesy laughs. This bitter look comes over Sledge's face, but he doesn't say shit.

There's definitely something not right with those two. Apparently, I've not only been blind about my daughter—but blind about what's going on in the club.

"Since you have the balls to call me out, I suppose that means we're going to see more of this chick around here," Ford digs, and I get the feeling he's nudging to find out exactly where I stand.

"If you quit trying to fuck her, maybe," I mutter.

"If you don't trust her..."

"It's not her I'm having trouble trusting."

"See, the bitch is already causing trouble. Coming between members of the club. Cut her loose now," Sledge growls, slamming his hand down on the table.

"Call her a bitch again and it's the two of us who are going to have problems, Sledge," I warn him.

He narrows his eyes at me, his brow creasing in anger, and I don't take my eyes off of him.

"Calm it down boys. I'm just giving Grunt here, shit. I got to admit that I like the redhead though. She has spunk. It's good a man finds a woman who stands up to him. Keeps you sharp."

Sledge gets up from the table with a snort of disgust. "I got shit to do," he mutters walking off.

"What's his problem?" Jonesy asks. Ford watches his old friend walk away and gives out a weary sigh.

"Not my story to tell," he says, but then he turns his attention back to me. "It's clear you think you and this girl have it good," he says, and I purse my lips, but nod my head slightly, agreeing. What Red and I have is good.

Damn good.

And I'm not giving it up.

"She going to give you shit when you find the kid we're after?"

"She's separate from all of that bullshit, Ford. She's mine," I tell him, getting tired of going over this.

"You fucking know that won't fly with her when she finds out you were using her to get close to her girl."

"If it comes out, Red and I will deal with it," I respond, my voice tight while I deal with this knot of dread in my gut. I'm not a praying man, but I'm praying like fuck that she never finds out.

"It will come out," Ford replies, like he can tell exactly what I'm thinking. "These things always do."

That's exactly what I'm fucking afraid of.

Chapter 31

Jasmine

I smile because Daisy is a beautiful little girl, who is curled up to me and already snoring. My heart is filled with emotion that I'm not sure I want to name. I need to step back and see what I'm doing here. I went in headfirst with Luke and it seems to be going at the speed of light. I'm beginning to wonder if meeting Daisy tonight was smart. I like her, a lot—maybe more than I should. She's sweet and accepted me without question. I wasn't expecting that and now that it has happened, I'm not sure how I feel about it.

"You're nice, Jasmine."

"So are you baby," I answer as she snuggles into me.

"Oh no!" she cries all at once, jerking up in the bed.

"What's wrong?"

"I left Bear-Bear in the kitchen," she says.

"Oh, we can get him tomorrow," I murmur, reassuringly. "He'll be okay until morning."

"But, I can't sleep without Bear-Bear," she says, shaking her head stubbornly. I resist the urge to laugh, because she's so headstrong. Luke has no idea what he's in for. He could probably ask my father for advice. I sigh when I think about Luke meeting my parents. I'm getting too carried away. I think I need to take a step back. I mean, I just found out he had a kid. That was a big secret he was keeping. If he can keep that a secret, what else don't I know? That thought is scary to say the least.

"I don't think Daddy wants us to go out when there's a party going on," I stall, thinking back to some of the things I'd seen over the years. I don't think Daisy's delicate eyes should see that at all. I can't see Luke not worrying about this before. I think that's just another reason I should slow things down.

"But Bear-Bear," she whines, sounding so pitiful that it hurts my heart.

"What if you stay here while I go get Bear-Bear?" I suggest.

"Will Jasmine get in trouble?" she asks, suddenly speaking in third person and making me giggle.

"Nah. We'll keep it a secret, okay?"

"Okay!"

She's so excited at the idea of getting Bear-Bear back that she's practically bouncing on the bed.

"You stay here, deal?" I ask. I don't like leaving her alone, which is silly since she lives here. I at least made sure she had a light now.

I know that part of the reason I'm thinking of pulling back is seeing how Luke's daughter is living. All signs point to the fact that she loves her daddy a lot and he's good with her. Yet, the fact he was unaware of the light in her room, or the fact she was forced to go to bed early when there were club parties... And hell, I can't imagine this club is that much different from the one I grew up with—which means there's always a party—is anything but good.

I have a lot to work through.

"Deal," she agrees and then gives me this huge hug, and before I realize it, I return it, closing my eyes.

Whatever I'm going to do about Luke, I need to do it soon before I get too attached to Daisy.

It doesn't take long to get to the kitchen and grab the bear. I get a few weird looks from people I don't know. I don't do much more than spare them a passing glance, making sure my bitch face is there for all to see. A few of the guys leer at me. I ignore them too. Luckily they don't press the matter and mistake me for club twinkies.

I'm not in the mood for that bullshit tonight.

I start to go back to Daisy's room, but I'd like to see Luke again. Maybe I'm just checking up on him. There's a party going on, and he's a single biker. I'm a big enough bitch to admit that I'd like to see what he's doing.

I walk to the entrance to the room we were in when I first got here. I scan the area quickly, only to realize that Luke is sitting at the table practically right in front of me. He's talking to the men I had met earlier.

Luke is not happy—as in he's pissed and that is radiating from him.

I'm about to walk over and announce my presence. But I hear something that I can't ignore. He's telling his president that I'm his.

A smile plays on my lips, because I can hear the satisfaction in his voice. I don't think anyone has ever sounded that proud to claim me before. Warmth fills me and I feel guilt for having doubts in Luke.

But then... they start talking again. Luke's voice is drained

"...When she finds out you were using her to get close to her girl."

My heart beats double and then it feels like my blood runs cold and everything slows down. It's like being in the middle of a time loop, where your world is crashing around you and all you can do is watch.

"If it comes out, Red and I will deal with it."

Whoa. Okay, what the fuck is this about. What would Luke want with Gabby? And I know immediately she's the one Ford is talking about. Memories filter through my brain. Starting out the only time I saw Luke was when I was with Gabby. I remember asking him if there was some reason, and I also remember how he denied it all. There's so much I'm going over in my brain, it's like a miniature movie. I struggle to listen to more, despite the pounding of my heart, pumping blood through my body and echoing in my ears.

I have to the fight the urge to confront Luke. I know logically that it wouldn't be smart until I have him alone, but I really want to demand he explain now.

"It will come out," Ford offers. "These things always do."

I step back, moving so I'm hid by the wall. I close my eyes, my chest tight.

What secret is Luke hiding? Is he using me? Is he using me just like Dewayne did?

I walk back to Daisy's room, my heart thundering in my chest.

Am I being played the fool again?

Just the thought leaves me feeling sick to my stomach...

I don't know what I'm going to do.

Chapter 32

Grunt

"You're quiet."

Something has changed. I don't know what it is, but Jasmine is different. She's not talking to me, but her silence is speaking volumes. I don't have much fucking experience when it comes to relationships, but I'm pretty sure that when a woman goes silent, something is wrong.

Jasmine has barely said two words since we left the club.

I'm uncomfortable as hell, because until tonight I never saw my shortcomings as Daisy's father. A few things opened my eyes tonight and I'm kicking my own ass. The fact that Jasmine probably saw that I've been a shit father doesn't make things better—just a lot fucking worse.

"Nothing to say," she murmurs, staring out the window. I brought the truck tonight, but my skin is itching to feel the outdoor air. I should have been on my bike. I didn't because I wanted to talk with Jasmine, feel her body beside me and hold hands with her.

Sentimental shit, but that's what I wanted.

Instead, she's not talking, she's not beside me, but about as close as she can get to her door. We're not holding hands, and I'm pretty sure if I tried, she'd jump out of the damn truck.

"Daisy seemed to really like you."

"She's a sweet kid."

Christ. I let out an irritated breath, rubbing the side of my jaw and gripping the steering wheel way too hard.

"You're going to have to tell me what's wrong Jasmine, I apparently suck at a lot of things tonight and mind reading is just one of them."

"Nothing's wrong, Luke."

"Bullshit. Don't play games with me. Tell me outright what has you pissed and let's deal with it. I don't think you understand yet, but I'm not giving you up. So, whatever bur you have up your ass needs to be dealt with."

"Bur up my ass?"

"Exactly."

"There's nothing wrong. I'm tired, that's all."

"I don't believe you," I mutter, knowing that she's lying to me.

"I don't know what to tell you, then," she shrugs and damn it, she's yet to look me in the eye.

"Red, talk to me."

"We are talking," she mumbles and Christ, women are difficult.

I grunt under my breath, figuring this is going nowhere. I'll wait until I get her home and then maybe I can fuck it out of her.

"Do you think we're moving way too fast?" she asks at last, her voice sad and she's still looking out the truck window.

"Fuck, no."

"We really don't know much about one another," she says. She's speaking so quietly that I have to strain to hear her.

"Jasmine, we've been over this before. What's between us is real. We'll learn more about each other as we go along."

"I've only ever had one other relationship, Luke."

I frown. Honestly, I don't want to hear shit about who she was with before me. Maybe that's stupid, but I have the urge to kill anyone who might have touched her. Jasmine is mine, and I'm so fucking possessive over her that if she knew it'd probably scare her to death. Hell, it scares me. I've never experienced anything like it before.

"Red..." I want to tell her to just stop, that I don't want to hear about her other relationship, but I don't want to come off sounding like an asshole either.

"I thought it was love, honestly I was kind of desperate to find love, someone who could love me as much as my father loved my mother. I'd grown up watching them and I knew that was exactly what I wanted one day."

"Are your parents that close?" I ask, unable to talk about the rest of what she's telling me. I keep my attention on the road and decide to just listen—that seems to be what she needs.

"Dad thinks the sun rises and sets on my mother. All of the men in my family are like that," she says and when I glance over, I see this ghost of a smile on her face as light from an oncoming vehicle flashes through the cab. It might be a smile, but the sadness is so thick on her face that I have to fight the urge to pull over and hold her. "I grew up surrounded by men who adored their women like that, though. I thought that was just what adult relationships were. I didn't realize that you couldn't trust love."

"That kind of thing is fucking rare, Red," I murmur, wondering if it's real at all, but not wanting to hurt her more.

Red is mine. I'm obsessed with her and the feelings I have for her are stronger than anything I've ever experienced. *Is that love?* I've never truly believed in that word, then I had Daisy and I definitely love her, still the love for a child is different. It's pure. I've never seen that kind of emotion work between two adults. Then again, I've never experienced anything like what I feel for

Jasmine. How I feel about Jasmine is fucking intense and nothing I ever knew existed.

Either way, I don't know shit about love, that was proven tonight. I know I need to make some changes.

"Yeah, tell me something I don't know, Luke," she laughs, but there's no humor in it. "Still, I thought I loved Dewayne, convinced myself he loved me. I threw myself into that relationship, all while ignoring the warning signs."

"What warning signs?" I ask, trying to keep the jealousy out of my words.

"Too many to list. I can see them now, but I was oblivious back then. I ignored everything but creating this fictional world where all that mattered was the two of us." She stops talking and I thought the conversation was done, but eventually she adds another sentence, her voice so sad that it's painful to hear. "I changed who I was to fit what I thought he wanted."

"Like what?"

"Things he wanted sexually, choices I made personally, different things," she shrugs, but there's a bitter edge to her sadness now. "I can't lay the blame totally on him. I was young and I was experimenting, I thought it couldn't hurt."

"And it did hurt?"

"Things hurt when people lie, Luke."

"Jasmine—"

"Are you lying to me, Luke?" she asks as I pull into my drive.

"What?"

"If you're lying to me, Luke, tell me now. I survived Dewayne's lies because my feelings for him really weren't what I tried to make them be. I didn't really love him. If you hurt me..."

I turn to look at her, guilt churning in my stomach. I've not really lied to her, but if she finds out what I am doing, how we met...How I encouraged her to invite her girl down here... How will she react to that? It might not be an outright lie, but it sure as hell is hiding things from her.

I start to talk to her about it all, but something stops me. I'd like to say it was loyalty to my club, but the truth is, it has everything to do with the fact that I don't want to lose Jasmine.

"Come here, baby," I tell her softly. Her eyes look stormy. She's confused and I can see that even in the pale light from the moon. I feel like I'm holding my breath, wondering if she will slide closer to me. I'm about to give up hope when she finally does. I slide my hand against the side of her face holding her there and then I place a short, sweet kiss on her lips, not deepening it, just needing the feel of her lips pressed to mine, to feel that she's here.

Her head goes down and her eyes close after the kiss. I feel a small shudder run through her body.

"Luke," she breathes.

"I know how special you are, Red. I'm not your fucking ex. I don't want you to change, I don't want you to be anything but who you are. *Just you.* I want you here with me and that is one hundred percent the truth."

"And that's it?" she presses. "No secret agenda? No hidden motives. You're not keeping anything from me?"

"Jasmine, where are all these questions coming from?"

"I heard you tonight," she says, looking up at my face. "Daisy needed her Bear-Bear and I went into the kitchen to get it. I wanted to see you, so I came to the room. I started to go in, but I heard you and Ford talking."

"Jasmine," I groan.

"Why would you need me to get close to Gabby, Luke? What's really going on?"

Fuck...

"Ford is interested in Gabby, baby. Not me. I promise you. You're the only woman on my mind these days."

"Why?" she asks. "What could Ford possibly want with Gabby. She's too young for him," she mumbles.

It's wrong I know, but I don't correct her when she immediately jumps to the wrong conclusion. I never thought I was a weak man, but being afraid to lose a woman is a new fucking thing to me.

"Some would say you're too young for everything I want from you Jasmine," I respond and that, at least, is fully truthful.

"What do you want from me, Luke?"

"For starters, tomorrow, you and I are going to look for a new place to live."

"Uh...come again?" she asks, pulling back and looking completely startled.

"It took having you meet Daisy. Seeing your reactions and really talking to my daughter to realize I've fucked up."

"I'm listening," she says, and even in the semi-darkness, I can feel her gaze appraising me. I should worry, I guess, but the sadness is out of her voice and I let that soothe me. I should have come clean, laid all my cards down on the table with Jasmine, but I can't.

Not yet.

I need time to get her addicted to me, make her feel for me what...

What I'm starting to feel for her.

"Fuck, baby. I don't know a damn thing about raising a kid but finding out my daughter has been waiting a damn week to get a lightbulb changed in her room... Shit, she had cereal for dinner and was forced to go to bed early. I took on the responsibility of being her father, but that's as far as it's truly gone. I love her, but I've been a shit *dad*. Help me find a place I can bring my daughter home to."

"Oh...I can do that if you're sure," she murmurs.

"I'm sure. I'm also sure that I want you in that home."

"Luke, this is—"

"You said your father loves you. You are secure in that. I want that for Daisy. I want you to show me."

"I think that's something you just have to build, honey. You may not believe this, but you've got a good start. Daisy adores you."

"Then stay with me because you want to be a part of what I'm building, Jasmine. Stay because you want to be with me."

"You're serious..." I hear her exhale, the sound broken and jittery.

"Baby, you've been running from me so much lately. Isn't the fact that I keep coming after you proof enough? I admit, I'm getting frustrated with the way you keep trying to pull away from me, but from what you said about your ex, I guess I can kind of understand it. Still, what's it going to take for you to realize that I'm in this for the long haul. I'm not your douchebag ex."

She giggles and I smile because it's the first time tonight that her voice has felt light-hearted.

"What?" I prompt, when she doesn't say anything.

"It sounds kind of funny listening to your big, gravelly voice say douchebag, but it's so true," she laughs.

"Stay with me, Jasmine. Go house shopping with me tomorrow."

"Don't make me regret this, Luke."

"I'll do my best," I promise, and I hope like hell I can keep that vow.

I really do.

Chapter 33

Jasmine

"Jaz-min! Jaz-min!" I jerk up in bed, clutching the sheet to my chest, blinking. It takes a minute to focus. The clock on the wall says eight-thirty. Now, it should be said that I don't normally sleep in—truly I don't. Last night, however, Luke worked me over and I think it was four orgasms and three in the morning before I finally crashed.

Still, I wouldn't have thought I was that out of it. Obviously, I would have been wrong, because Luke—dressed, looking damn good with a to-go bag from the local doughnut shop under his arm and a very excited Daisy come into the bedroom.

"Jaz-min! I'm here! Daddy says I get to stay here with you!"

I blink. *Oh shit.* I mean, I hated leaving Daisy at the club last night—I really did. She was sleeping however, and Luke didn't mention getting her and I figured it wasn't my place to question him. Honestly, when I left, I wasn't sure if I was even going to stay with Luke. I still don't know if he's telling me the complete truth, but I want to believe him.

I also love him and it's real. It's not the weak emotion that I felt for Dewayne and tried to force. It happened before I knew it and it fills every part of me. Daisy jumps on the bed and I clutch the cover to me even more, wishing I'd put on a nightgown of some sort last night.

"Yay!" I tell her, clearing my throat. "That's awesome. I know it will make your daddy really happy to have you with him."

"And you, Jaz-min! You too. Daddy said you live with him."

"He did?" I ask, going bug-eyed and looking at Luke like he's lost his damn mind.

Luke gives me a wink, smiling at me with a look that instantly makes my insides melt. The damn man should be marked lethal.

"Yep! We can watch movies tonight, can't we, Jaz-min?" she asks, bouncing excitedly.

"Sure kiddo," I answer immediately, hoping that will make her settle down before she bounces on the bed so hard that I can't hold onto the quilt and she asks me why I'm naked in her daddy's bed.

"Yay!" she yells and hurls her body at me. I'm forced to catch her which sucks because I can't grasp the sheet. I hug her tightly, but I narrow my eyes at Luke now that Daisy can't see me. I warn him without words that he's in for it later. His grin deepens as Daisy pulls away. The cover slips but I grab it quickly, barely averting disaster.

"How about we go get breakfast dished up while Jasmine gets ready, Daisy?"

"Okay, Daddy," she says, dutifully, then she bounces into Luke's arms. He catches her like it was perfectly timed, even though there's no way he could have guessed she was going to jump like that. Seeing them together tugs at my heart and I have to clear my throat before I can talk again.

"What am I getting ready for?" I ask, feeling a little lost for several reasons.

"We're going house shopping, Red," he says and then

surprising me he bends down and gives me a quick kiss on the lips. My heart squeezes in my chest.

"You kissed Jaz-min," Daisy says, as if in awe.

"Yeah, I did," Luke says, winking at me yet again.

"You like her?" Daisy asks.

"Definitely," Luke responds, in a way that makes it impossible to doubt him and that squeeze on my heart intensifies, but it stops beating and somersaults in my chest with Daisy's next words.

"I should kiss her too, cause I really like her," she says, nodding her head slowly.

"You can kiss her when she comes and eats," he says.

"Okay," she accepts. "Don't let me forget, Jaz-min."

"I...I won't baby," I answer, my voice hoarse as emotion clogs my throat.

I barely stood a chance against Luke when it came to protecting my heart.

How do I fight both of them?

Chapter 34

Grunt

"What do you think, Red?" I ask, but I already know what she will say. She's going to give me the same answer that she's given when I asked about the other four houses we've looked at today.

"I think it will work well for you and Daisy, Luke."

And there it is.

"Daddy! There's a swing set out back! Did you see?" Daisy asks excitedly.

"I didn't. Do you like it?"

"Yes! It has a slide and everything. Can I go play?"

"Sure baby. I'll be here talking to Jasmine," I tell her. I asked the realtor to leave us alone to look at this one. She's pretty easy-going, because she's stayed back at her car at each property. That works to my advantage right now, because Jasmine and I are about to have it out—yet again.

"Red, you and I need to talk," I grumble, when she goes to the French doors to watch Daisy play.

"We do?" she asks, looking up at me like she's clueless. Hell, maybe she is.

"Damn it, woman. You've said the same thing about every house we've checked out today."

"That's because they've all been great homes, Luke," she mumbles.

"But don't you have any opinion on which you like better?"

"Not really. What does it matter?" she sighs.

"Because I want my woman to like the house I buy for us?"

Her eyes go big as saucers and I swear to fuck she steps away from me.

"Whoa, maybe you need to slow down here, Luke."

"The fuck I do. Do you think we're just playing house here, Jasmine?"

"I, uh...Luke maybe we..."

"I'm trying to plan for the future here, Red. I don't know where your head is at, but I fucking love what we have going on between us."

"Luke, I think—"

"Do you, Jasmine?"

"You know I do," she murmurs.

"I thought we had this out last night, baby. You've got to quit pushing me away."

"But, I'm not..."

"Then tell me which house you like," I respond softly, pulling her into my arms.

"I don't think it's normal to take a girl you've just started dating to look at houses, Luke."

"Baby, I don't date."

"You don't?" she questions, but her lips are fighting a smile.

"Shit, no," I laugh.

"Then, what do you do, Luke?"

"I see what I want and take it," I purr, dropping my head down so my forehead rests against hers. Her arms wrap around me and I grin down at her.

"Just like that, huh?" she breathes.

"Oh yeah, and then, to make sure she wants to stay, I do my best to feed her dick."

"You know, Luke, I think I've heard this story before."

"Then you should have listened baby."

"You really want my opinion on a home you're buying for you and your daughter?" she asks like she can't believe it.

"And you, Jasmine. I see you in my future. Don't you see me in yours?"

"I want you there," she qualifies, but I'll take it.

"Then tell me what house you like the best? Or do you think we should keep looking?"

"What if we don't work out long term, Luke?"

"What if we do, Red?"

She holds my gaze and I can tell that she's thinking. I don't even blink.

"Fine, then, if you want the truth, I liked the first one the best."

I think back to the ranch home and I have to admit I'm surprised. It was probably my favorite too, but it's not as fancy or as high-end as the others have been. It's not one I'd imagine a woman picking at all.

"Why was that one your favorite?" I question, curious to know her answer.

"It was all one level. I never liked the idea of those houses with the master downstairs and the other bedrooms upstairs, like the second one we looked at. Then, with this one, there are only two bedrooms. You want at least three or four bedrooms."

"Why do I want that many bedrooms?" I ask, believing I already know the answer, but wanting to hear her say it. Needing her to have the courage to admit it.

"In case you have more kids."

"Are you going to give me kids, Red?"

Keeping Her

"Luke..." she exhales, the sound ragged.

"Answer me, Red."

"How about we make it one week without fighting and then, I'll answer that question?" she bargains.

"That ranch house doesn't work for me, baby."

"It doesn't? Why?"

"The master was on the same side as the kid's rooms."

"So?"

"I plan on making you scream and beg often and I'd rather Daisy not hear it."

She licks her lips as she pulls away, putting just a little space between us. I let her go, although I grab her hand and link our fingers together.

"Then, I guess you better tell the realtor to find some more ranch homes," she responds and I grin fucking bigger than I think I ever have.

"Daddy! Jaz-min! I want ice cream!" Daisy yells as she comes running back into the house.

"I could use some ice cream too," Jasmine says much softer than Daisy.

"Well, I guess I better take my girls out for ice cream," I laugh and suddenly today might be one of the best I've ever had...

Chapter 35

Jasmine

"Luke, you have to quit," I moan, knowing that him stopping is the very last thing that I want.

"Fuck, no, Red," he murmurs from between my legs, the sound vibrating against my clit as he sucks it back into his mouth.

"Daisy will hear," I hiss, as he pulls my legs over his shoulders, eating at my pussy with a ferocity that will soon have me coming.

I'm trying to hold on, but I woke up with Luke's head buried between my legs and I'm not sure I can keep resisting. My hands clutch against his head, my fingers tangling in his hair, the heels of my feet pressing into his back.

"You will need to come quietly," he growls, and I toss my head back and forth, not so much as in denial, it's more about the pleasure bombarding me as he thrusts his fingers inside of me, all while working my clit with his mouth.

"Luke," I moan, feeling my orgasm starting to barrel through me.

"Come for me, Red," he demands, his fingers biting into my hips with bruising force, as he grinds me against his face.

Keeping Her

"Fuck," I hiss, losing control and unable to hold back any longer.

"That's it, baby. Come all over my face," he groans and that just makes me come that much harder.

The urge to scream is so huge that I grab a pillow and push it down on my face, biting into the fabric. I come so hard that my entire body quakes, my muffled screams escape as I bite into the pillow so hard that I can feel the fabric tear. It's so intense, unlike anything I've ever felt before, so much so that I begin to wonder if I'm going to pass out. I may have lost consciousness, because the next thing I remember is Luke, slowly tonguing my pussy, soothing the tortured area. Then, I can only assume time has passed, because Luke is pulling the pillow from my face. He's got a towel wrapped around his hips and he's smiling down at me, his eyes sparkling.

"Luke," I moan, stretching, because he's beautiful and being with him is unlike anything I could have guessed existed.

"Don't really want you to smother yourself, Red. If you're into that kind of thing, we may have to do some research first," he jokes. I try to roll my eyes at him, but it requires way too much effort and he's already worn me out.

"What time is it?"

"Nine-thirty."

"Daisy—"

"Still sound asleep, baby. Checked on her after you went comatose on me," he says, bending down to kiss me.

"I was not comatose."

"Sweetheart, you were snoring," he laughs.

"Whatever," I mutter. "Have you already been to the club?" I ask, sitting up in bed.

"Yeah, can't say it was much more fun than yesterday. There's shit going on there that I'm completely lost on."

"Aren't you the club muscle? Supposed to have your finger on the pulse of everything that's going on?" I ask, rubbing my tummy. I want bacon and eggs, but there's no making them here. I sigh out my disappointment.

"The only thing I have my finger on the pulse of lately is your clit," he mutters, leaning down to kiss me.

"If you're expecting to hear me complain about that, hot stuff, you need to think again."

"Hot stuff?" he questions, giving out a startled laugh, as he sits down on the bed.

"Oh please, like you didn't realize that you're all that and a bag of chips. If your swagger gets any bigger you won't be able to fit through the door with that ego of yours."

"I swear, baby I'm starting to think if you don't have anything to bust my balls on that you invent shit."

I shrug, not really able to deny the claim, which just makes him laugh again. It's a *real* good thing that I like the sound of his laughter.

"Any word from the realtor?" I ask him, mostly just changing the subject.

"Closing was delayed again. It's rescheduled for next week."

"That sucks," I mutter, and it does. I'm still worried about moving in with Luke full time. I mean, at this point, it's a pretty foregone conclusion that I'm in love with the big dummy. Still, it's a huge thing to move in with someone when there's an understanding that what you're doing is building something long-lasting—especially when there's a child involved. A child that I'm starting to love as much as her father. If this doesn't work out, it will truly destroy me and I'm worried that it will hurt Daisy too…

"I know, Red. Trust me, I feel the same. I want out of this place too."

"This from the man who thought it was fine before," I mumble, shaking my head.

"That was before I had you in my life and discovered how

Keeping Her

much I like it when you scream out my name when you come. Something that you can't do with my girl so close by," he responds softly, his words wrapping around me like silken lava.

"I didn't see you complaining this morning," I murmur, held hostage by the dark promise in his eyes. Jesus, after what Luke did to me this morning you would think my hormones would be in hibernation for the rest of the day.

"Oh, I wasn't Red," he replies, his voice a low rumble. "But, I don't think the pillow can stand much more of your biting.

I was so hypnotized by him that until just now, I didn't realize that he was holding the pillow I used earlier and clearly the fabric has been stretched and torn where I bit into it.

"I guess we could just not have sex until we—"

"Don't even finish that sentence, baby. We both know neither one of us can do without it, even for one night let alone a week." I can't really argue with him, so I just shrug. He rewards me with a quick kiss on my lips. I sigh because I remember my conversation last night with my mom. I know it's something I need to discuss with Luke.

"Well, shit. I know that look," he mutters.

"What?" I ask, surprised.

"Why are you running now, Red?"

"What?" I question again, wondering what in the heck he's talking about.

"We've gone through a quiet spell. It's been, what, a week since our last argument? Anytime you get that look I know you're about ready to run on me. So, tell me why and let me get that cleared up before I go wake up Daisy and take you guys out for breakfast."

"You're being a jerk right now, Luke."

"I'm always a jerk. Luckily you like it most of the time," he replies with a smirk. He's not wrong, which is annoying.

"This is *not* one of the times I like it," I huff.

"Duly noted. So, spill, baby."

"It's nothing bad and I'm not *running*. Mom called last night while you were reading Daisy's bedtime story."

"Shit. You didn't tell me. Did she upset you again? Maybe I need to talk to—"

"Oh, good Lord! Will you stop? My parents aren't bad people. We may be oil and water sometimes, but the fault lies on all three of us. She called to remind me about Kayden's baby shower tomorrow. She'd like me to be there and, really, I need to go. I'm not extremely close to Kayden, but I like her and we're family."

"Family?"

"Yeah, she's Uncle Dragon's daughter."

"Uncle...*Dragon?*" Luke snaps and I guess that name clicked in his head. I knew it would, and maybe I should have confessed all of this sooner...

But I didn't...

Chapter 36

Grunt

"You have got to be shitting me," I growl, standing up to walk around the room. Jesus how could I have been so blind. Slowly things are clicking into place. Jazz knew how to handle herself in my club. She knows about the biker lifestyle. Shit, her best friend is the daughter of the Devil's Blaze president. It was all right there in front of me and I was a blind fucking fool.

"Luke..."

"Don't you Luke me, Red. Not right now," I growl.

"What are you so pissy about?"

"Your fucking uncle is Dragon West, the baddest, most ruthless motherfucker in Kentucky, hell, maybe several damn states and you don't think you should mention that?"

"I didn't see a reason," she shrugs, and if the woman didn't have me tied up in knots and own my fucking cock, I'd choke her right now.

"You didn't see a reason? You didn't see a fucking reason?" I bark.

"Will you keep your voice down? You're going to wake up Daisy!" she snaps.

"I can't believe you didn't tell me this, Jasmine. The Savage Brothers and my club aren't exactly on great terms, you know. This is a fucking mess."

"What did you do to us?"

"Us? Jesus, fucking—"

"I know Uncle Dragon. He's a fair man—"

"A fair man..." I whistle, thinking my Red just might be delusional.

"Exactly."

"Your *Uncle* Dragon once shot off a man's dick and watched him bleed to death—while laughing."

"Hmm..."

"Hmm? That's all you have to say, Red?"

"Are you saying you haven't done worse, Luke?"

Motherfucker, she's got balls of steel. How did I miss this?

"You should have told me Red," I finally growl, sitting back on the bed and staring at the woman that I'm not sure I ever knew.

"If I can accept you, Luke, then you should be able to accept my family."

"Your family?" I murmur. "Just how deep are your ties to the Savage Brothers?"

"Pretty deep."

"Jasmine," I warn.

"My father is his second."

"You father is Dancer?"

"Yeah."

"Your father is Dancer, the Savage Brothers Vice President?"

"I'm guessing you know him?" she says, and I can see the trepidation on her face, but she doesn't back down. She stares at me and doesn't even blink.

"Yeah, baby, I know him, and we've got a fucking problem."

"I can't imagine what," she mumbles with a shrug—as if she doesn't have a care in the world.

"How about the fact that your old man's club and your father's club hate one another?"

"Do I have an old man?" she asks, purposely ignoring everything else I said.

"What in the hell does that mean, Red?" I bite out the question, wondering how in the hell this woman can get me from relaxed to pissed off in a matter of seconds.

"It means, it seems like you're getting ready to head for the hills. Are you scared of my family, Luke?"

"Fucking hell..." I growl. How the fuck she can be with me all this time and then ask that fucking question blows my mind. I get up and walk out. I walk out and don't bother looking back.

Chapter 37

Jasmine

Luke stayed out all day yesterday and last night until the early morning hours. When he got home he reeked of alcohol and smoke. He went to the club. I didn't have to ask, I knew. My stomach churned. I wanted to ask him if he had been with another woman, but I didn't.

I should have faith that he wouldn't do that to me, but my head is a mess. Hell, maybe he sees nothing wrong with that. Some men in this lifestyle don't. If he did, it would kill me and I don't think that's exaggerating one bit. I had no idea how I was going to feel about Luke, how deep it would go, or how much it would consume me. Now, I'm afraid there's no way around being hurt—and that's something that I swore would never happen again.

"What are you doing?" I squeak out, when Daisy and Luke walk out of the house.

"Taking you to the baby shower," Luke says, his voice brokering no argument.

"My family will be there," I tell him, saying it more as a dare.

"I know. Despite what my woman thinks of me, I don't give a shit about facing them."

I sigh, because I knew when I said that to him that it was a low blow. I don't figure there is much that Luke is afraid of, I was just mad at him. Although, if I'm honest, it might be good if he is a little afraid of my family.

"Daddy, you shouldn't say shit. Jasmine says it's a bad word," Daisy chastises.

"She does?" he questions, and despite looking pissed at me, when he turns to talk to his daughter his face softens, and his voice is almost sweet. My heart squeezes, because I could really use that sweet right now.

"Yep. Don't you, Jazz?"

"I do, sweet thing," I murmur, acknowledging as I respond to her that I really love that little girl.

And her father.

"I called Gabby. She's going to come and get me," I tell him, in case he feels obligated. I don't want that.

"You can just call her and tell her that your family is going to bring you."

"My family?" I ask, those two words making me feel nervous, even unsettled.

"Yeah, Red, that's what me and Daisy are. Right, Daisy? We're Jasmine's family."

"Right!" Daisy cries. "We love you, Jaz-Min!"

"You do?" I find myself asking, but it's not Daisy I'm looking at, it's Luke—whose face has gone back to being stern and immovable.

"Daddy! I forgot Bear-Bear!"

"Go get him, baby," he says softly, opening the door back up. "We'll wait on you."

"Okay!" she cries, taking off in a run.

"No running!" I yell, afraid she'll fall. I'm pretty sure she's ignoring me, but at least I tried.

"Gabby will come and get me. There's no need for you to go to Kentucky with me, Luke."

"She lives at least two hours from here, Red. What were you going to do? Sit outside that entire time?"

"Seemed better than having you standing in the same room with me and not talking," I reply with a shrug.

He lets out an irritated breath, staring at me. "I was pissed," he finally says.

"I could tell," I reply. Because really, what else is there to say?

"Call your girl and tell her that Daisy and I are bringing you," he orders, and I sigh.

"What if I don't want you to, Luke?" I breathe out.

"Damn it, Jasmine," he growls, but I shake my head no.

"Where were you last night?"

"I went to the club and had a few drinks," he says, his eyes narrowing.

"Anything else?" I push.

"Are you asking me if I fucked another woman, Red?" he spits out, his voice quiet, but the anger is coming off of him in waves.

My gaze goes to the door, to make sure that Daisy is not there.

"Did you?"

"Jesus, you think I'm a punk ass bastard who is scared of his shadow and will go from fucking you every chance I can get to sticking my dick into someone else? That's a great opinion you have of me, woman."

"That's not answering me, Luke."

"I didn't, although if I knew you were going to pull this bullshit maybe I would have."

I moisten my lips, trying to sort through all of the bullshit running in my brain.

"I don't want you to do that, Luke. If you did...I think it would kill me."

"Why's that, Red?" he asks, pressing me, not letting me get off easy.

"I love you, Luke," I murmur. I keep my voice so quiet that I can't be sure he can even hear me.

"Don't think I heard you, Red. You're going to have to speak up," he complains, arms crossed at his chest.

"I said I love you, you asshole."

"Then, come over here, Red."

I think about denying him, but the truth is, I ache to be in his arms again. I'm standing outside in the heat because I was miserable inside, thinking he was about ready to end everything. So, I go to him quickly, without another word. Before I even get there he opens his arms up and envelopes me in them as I fall into him. I crush the side of my face against his chest, taking in a big gulp of air.

"I was a bitch and I know you wouldn't be afraid of my father or the rest of the club," I mumble against his chest.

"Fuck that. I might be afraid. A little fear keeps a man smart and on his toes, Red. But, I wouldn't run away from them or you. Get that straight."

"Got it," I murmur.

"Maybe we're making progress," he mutters.

"What do you mean?"

"You just ran outside today. There was a time you would have gone back to Kentucky," he says and for the first time since this mess started, I see a ghost of a smile on his face.

"Well, technically, I *was* going back. I just had to wait on my ride," I feel the need to point out.

"Yeah, but not so long ago, you would have taken a taxi or hitched," he says, pulling back to look at me. He puts his hand under my chin, his thumb brushing against my lips and sweeping along my jawline.

"Probably," I admit.

"So, see? Progress."

"It really would have killed me if you'd been with another woman," I tell him, pointing it out, even if I shouldn't.

"I wouldn't do that to you Jasmine," he promises. "Besides, there's not a damn thing out there that can compare to the way you take my dick."

I blink, then laugh, the sound freeing after the way last night was spent.

"You're such a sweet talker," I laugh

"I try."

"I got Bear-Bear, Daddy. I had to potty first," Daisy announces, coming out of the house. She immediately runs to us and hugs us, her body pressing against my leg and thigh. I hug her close, my eyes closing as the sweetness of this moment surrounds me.

"What are you thinking, Red?" Luke asks, and I force myself to open my eyes and look at him.

"Just thinking what a wonderful family I have," I respond.

"That's my girl," he praises, and it does feel like a praise. "Let's load up and go meet Jasmine's family, Daisy baby," he says picking her up into his strong arms—all while keeping one arm around me.

"But, Daddy! You said we were Jazz-Min's family. Aren't we?" Daisy asks, looking at me, confused.

I smile because I like the broken way she says my name, stressing the Jazz part and rushing the last. My smile deepens, because she clearly doesn't want anyone else taking her chance to be part of my family.

"You are, baby," I hasten to assure her. "But, I have a mommy, a daddy, and a bunch of other family that will love meeting you and claiming you as part of their family too."

"Babe," Luke warns, and I look up at him, shaking his head.

"They will," I tell him, answering his unspoken question.

"They might her, her daddy I'm not so sure of."

"You planning on letting me walk away anytime soon, Luke?" I ask, already knowing the answer.

"You can try, Red, but in case you haven't realized it yet, I'll always come after you."

"Yeah! We'll come after you, right, Daddy?"

"Right, sweetheart," he says, his face softening as his smile deepens.

"Then, they'll either accept you, or they'll lose me."

Luke doesn't say anything, choosing instead to secure Daisy into her car seat. He had used the remote to start the truck when Daisy went in to get her stuffed bear, and I can feel a blast of cool air hit me as he makes sure his daughter is safe and snug.

"Just like that?" he asks, rising up to look at me. His face has gone serious, his eyes deepening in their dark color. I could lose myself in those eyes and maybe I already have to a certain extent.

"You and Daisy are my family. A girl would be crazy to give that up," I tell him softly.

His hand stretches out to hook along the side of my neck, his fingers forcing pressure on the back of my skull as he holds me perfectly still, unable to move.

"Fuck, Red, I love you," he rumbles and my heart squeezes in my chest.

"I thought you weren't the kind of man who believed in love."

"I wasn't," he confirms. "And then, I met you," he adds.

He kisses me after adding on those sweet words and his kiss is magical, because it heals every open wound I had inside from my past. For the first time in a very long time—maybe forever—I feel whole.

When we pull apart, I know he can see the unshed tears in my eyes, but I don't care. They're tears of happiness. He opens my truck door and I climb inside, barely breaking eye contact with him.

"Call your girl and tell her you don't need her, Red."

"Okay, Luke," I tell him softly. He still doesn't close the door. He just stands there looking at me. "Sweetheart?" I question after a moment.

"I'm thinking I understand why I didn't believe in love before you, Jasmine."

I rub my lips together and dry my suddenly sweaty palms on my pants leg.

"Why's that?"

"I never wanted anyone's love until you came along. Before you, it wouldn't have mattered. It would have just withered and died. Yours has taken root inside of me, baby," he says, slapping his hand against his chest where his heart is.

"Luke," I murmur, thinking if I live to be a hundred, that nothing will ever hit me as sweet as what he just said.

"You best believe I'm going to nurture that, and not let it go. I'm not letting *you* go. I'm keeping you forever, Red."

"You're going to make me cry," I warn him, already feeling the wet tracks as the tears leak from my eyes.

"Call your girl, baby," he says, softly.

"I will," I nod, trying to suck it up and not bawl like a baby.

"Good," he grins and before he can close the door, it's me who stops him this time.

"Remember when I said I thought I was in love before, Luke?" I ask, but I don't give him time to answer, because I can already see that he isn't a fan of that reminder. "I was a stupid fool," I hasten to explain. "Because before you, I wasn't capable of love. I had too many holes, too much missing inside of me."

"Red—"

"You made everything whole," I tell him. "You made me feel safe enough to just be me... I never felt that was good enough before," I tell him, my eyes dropping down as I hear Daisy singing to her Bear-Bear in the background.

"You can banish that fucking thought, Red. You're everything and more," he rumbles. Then he gives me a quick kiss. "Call your girl, baby," he urges again, and I pick my cell up and start dialing, as he closes the door.

And I do it all while wondering if it's illegal to be this happy.

Chapter 38

Grunt

"Hey."

I look over to see Jasmine's brother walking toward me. Fuck, I could use something to drink. Unfortunately, all I've seen at this place is some kind of pink punch.

"Sup," I mutter.

Hawk laughs. "You're looking a little out of place here, buddy."

"Until I saw you I didn't think there was any testosterone here besides mine," I mutter, rubbing the back of my neck.

My gaze goes over to the corner where Jasmine is laughing with Gabby and a bunch of other women that I don't know. My body relaxes when I see the way Daisy is curled up in Jasmine's lap and her hand is lovingly combing through Daisy's curls. My baby girl looks like she's in heaven. She whispers something to Jasmine and Jasmine stops talking to smile down at Daisy and kisses her forehead.

"You love her."

My gaze jerks back to Hawk. "Do you really think I'd be here if I didn't?"

Keeping Her

Hawk shrugs as if he doesn't understand and that's the minute I start to piece shit together. Jasmine may understand and know about the clubs and shit, but Hawk seems rather clueless. Hell, he's even dressed in gym shorts and a white and blue Kentucky Wildcat t-shirt. I don't know why I find this interesting, but I do. You would think the only son of the Savage Brothers MC VP, would be a biker because it was in his blood. I've got to wonder if this guy even knows how to ride a bike.

"Jazz is headstrong," Hawk says, and I give a small laugh, a crooked smile on my face.

"Yeah, that's a fucking understatement," I agree quietly.

"She's got a heart big as the fucking ocean though, man," he says, as if he needs to explain that shit to me.

"Not telling me anything I don't know, Hawk," I respond, using his name, because if he's got the balls to talk to me about his sister and defend her, I can show him respect. Besides, from hearing Jasmine talk, this is the one member of her family who has her back no matter what.

"Good. Jazz was hurt enough in the past. I don't want someone using her to try and get an in with dad's club or some stupid shit."

"That's rich," I laugh, although there's no humor in the sound.

"What's that mean?"

"Listen, I'm trying to be civil here because you're looking out for your sister and I can respect that, but you need to stop before you piss me off."

"Frankly, I don't give a damn if I piss you off," he says and the boy might dress like an overgrown kid, but he's got balls.

"Man, until yesterday I didn't even know about your old man or his club. I wasn't exactly happy to get the news and I'm not sure how he's going to react to me claiming his daughter. I also

175

don't give a fuck, because I'm not giving her up. So, while I respect you looking out for your sister, you need to step back."

"What's going on here?"

I turn to see Jasmine walking my way. My eyes instantly tracking Daisy who is playing with another little kid about her age. She looks so happy that contentment fills me. Until today, I don't think my baby ever had anyone her own age to play with.

"Nothing, Red," I tell her, opening my arm up for her to slide into, which she does.

"Are you behaving little brother?" Jasmine asks, and I laugh, quickly turning it into a cough to save the poor bastard a little of his ego.

"Screw you, Jazz. I was just talking with your new boy-toy."

"Hawk, the next time you call Luke my boy-toy, I'm going to give him permission to snap your neck."

"Are you two at it again? Can't I go one place where my children aren't trying to kill one another?" My body tightens as Jasmine's mother comes in close. My hand tightens on my woman and I know it has everything to do with the fact that I need to be ready to defend Jasmine. I don't know her mom, but I know she made her cry last time they got together. Theirs is a relationship that I don't quite get. Then again, I never had a mom, so maybe I'm missing something that is obvious to others.

"Jasmine is just busting my balls, Mom," Hawk says, kissing his mother's cheek. Jasmine leaves my arms to go and hug her mother and I let her—reluctantly.

"Jazz, I've missed you," her mom whispers, hugging her tightly. I watch as the woman's eyes close and it's clear she loves Red, so I'm not sure what the push and pull is between them. Maybe now that Red and I've cleared the air, I can get her to open up to me more. Trying is definitely on my to-do list.

When they pull apart, the woman looks over Jasmine's shoulder to see me. Her eyes go large with surprise. It's clear that she wasn't expecting me. I really need to talk to my woman about preparing people for what they don't know. It would have saved me finding out about her family last night the way I did.

"Hello," she says, not taking her eyes off me. In fact, her gaze moves over me, cool and calculating. I get the feeling what she sees might not measure up to what she wants for her baby girl. That's just tough shit. Red is mine. To prove that, Jasmine immediately moves back into my arms. One hand is flat against my stomach as she talks to her mother.

"Mom, I'd like you to meet, Luke, my...old man."

I snort, "Baby."

"It didn't sound right calling you my boyfriend, Luke. You don't exactly do dating. Remember?" she questions, looking up at me, her eyes sparkling.

"Yeah, Red, I remember," I laugh, kissing her forehead.

"You're the man who has practically kidnapped my daughter and held her hostage?"

"Luke, this is my mom, Carrie. She has a flair for being overly dramatic, as you can tell," Jasmine says with a sigh.

"Oh please, like you don't act just like me Jasmine Nicole," Carrie snaps, making me laugh.

Jasmine rolls her eyes.

"Jazz-Min! Jazz-Min!" Daisy says, running toward us and breaking up the tension that's started to build. Jasmine bends down as Daisy runs into her arms, hitting her with such force that Jasmine rocks on her feet.

"What's up, sweetheart."

"I got a new friend! Auntie Gabby says I can stay at her house and play with Ty! Can I, Daddy?" she asks, finally looking up at me.

"Auntie Gabby said that did she?" Jasmine mutters as Gabby comes up behind Carrie.

"Oh, come on. Let her. You and Grunt can come and get her tomorrow," Gabby says.

"Let me think on it, okay, baby girl?" I tell Daisy, not sure how comfortable I am with any of this. I don't know any of them and with the things I know concerning Gabby…

"Okay, Daddy," she says, clearly dejected that she didn't get an immediate yes.

"Hey Daisy, did Ty show you where the swing set was?"

"There's a swing set?" she asks excitedly.

"There is and it has a playhouse and everything on it," Gabby laughs, trying to bribe my daughter.

"Yay! In the new house that me, Daddy and Jazz-Min are buying. There's a pool, and a playhouse, and I have my own room!"

"Shit," I hear Jasmine mutter under her breath and a smile pulls at my lips.

All eyes are on us, but mostly it's the heat of Jasmine's mother's stare that I feel the most.

"You're house shopping together?" she asks.

"No," Jasmine says immediately. I grin.

"We've already bought one. They just moved our closing, or we'd already be living in it," I tell Carrie.

Jasmine gasps, elbowing me. Hell, there are two or three women around us now and they all seem to be making that noise. My woman is the only one I'm looking at though, with her flustered look and the fire in her eyes that says she might just want to kill me.

"You bought a house Jasmine Nicole?" Carrie snaps.

"Jasmine *Nicole*? You been keeping secrets from me, Red?" I murmur.

"At least one of us can keep secrets, Luke," she grumbles.

I wrap my arms around her and pull her so her back is pressed against me, bending down to whisper in her ear. "I got the woman I love moving into a house with me and my daughter. Why would I want to keep that a secret, baby?" I feel her body tremble against me. They're all watching us, but I don't give a fuck. They're not important, only Red.

Always Red.

Chapter 39

Jasmine

I let the words that Luke whispers soak into me and I swear that's exactly what they do, they soak inside of me, filling me with their warmth.

"Quit being sweet. I'm not equipped to handle it in front of my family, Luke," I mumble, my legs feeling like jelly.

"Sorry, baby, not going to happen. I like what happens when I'm sweet to you," he laughs.

"Jasmine Nicole," Mom snaps, and reluctantly I pull my attention away from Luke.

"Yes, Mom?" I ask, trying to sound innocent—and since that has never been who I am, I fail miserably.

"Don't you yes Mom me. You're moving in with a man and you didn't think to tell your family first?"

"Well, that's part of the reason he's here, Mom. Meet the fam and all that jazz. Jazz, get it?"

Luke laughs and I elbow him in the stomach.

"Oof," he breathes out.

"Stop with the laughter back there, I'm drowning just fine without your commentary," I complain.

"I didn't think you were drowning until the lame ass joke, Red."

"It *was* lame, Sis."

"Shut-up Hawk."

"Hey, I was just helping a fellow man out. Those of us with balls have to stick up for one another when we're outnumbered," Hawk says.

"Thanks, man," Luke laughs.

"De nada."

"Are you two about finished?" I huff.

Luke and Hawk look at one another and Luke nods slowly, giving me a wink.

"Yeah, baby. We're done."

"Remind me why I keep you around again?" I ask him, my voice saccharine sweet.

"For my eleven-inch dick?"

"Lord have mercy," Nicole and Kayden both whisper. I'm afraid to look at them because Mom is standing beside them.

"Whoa, man, too much fucking information. I do not need to know how big your dick is, especially when it's my sister you're slipping it to," Hawk growls, his face filled with disgust. I hold my head down, pinching the bridge of my nose.

Luke does what he's famous for when he's been an ass, he grunts.

"Cool your jets, Hawk. He's lying anyway," I respond, knowing that Luke will make me pay for this later.

"Red—" he grumbles.

I grin at him, not backing down. Besides he probably is lying. We've not measured but I'm guessing it's ten inches tops. He shakes his head, his hand moving down to my hip, squeezing it and silently promising retribution.

"Well, duh, Sis. I'm not stupid," Hawk replies. "They don't come in that size unless you're a porn star with a daily dose of meds in your arsenal and I always wondered if those penis stretchers work. Remember that movie we watched once when Mom and Dad went to Vegas and we had the house to ourselves?"

"Dude, stop," B.B. says, laughing, but still able to get the words out as he joins the crowd—and proving that everyone in the damn room is listening. "You're destroying your own rep here. There's only one reason a man would ever wonder about something like that and that's if he was lacking downstairs."

"Fuck you," Hawk jokes—mostly. "What are you doing here? I thought you were going on a run with your Dad and Skull?"

I feel Luke's body stiffen behind me, and I know he's uncomfortable here. I snuggle into him.

B.B looks at Luke, and since Luke wore his cut today, he sees right away who Luke is—unlike Hawk, who has *nothing* to do with the club, Torch's son, B.B., is steeped in the Devil's Blaze and I have no doubt he knows who Luke is and more importantly who Luke's club is.

"It was canceled." That's all he says, but his gaze is locked with Luke's.

"B.B., I'd like you to meet my old man. Luke, this is B.B."

"Your old man," B.B. says, with a long drawn out wolf whistle. "You know you were fucking a Savage princess?" he asks Luke, mostly ignoring me.

I finally get up the nerve to look at my mom. She's staring at me intently, but I swear for the life of me, I can't read her face.

Luke...*grunts*. I've learned that this is really just his way of not answering. I sigh.

"He didn't know until last night," I breathe out, almost to my limit with this damn shower and it hasn't even started.

"Damn, I would have liked to have been a fly on that wall," B.B. says.

"What did you do when you found out?" My mom asks this

Keeping Her

question, surprising me. She's not looking at me now, she's looking at Luke.

I'm not sure that's a good thing.

"He left because he was pissed at me," I mutter.

"And you didn't leave him or tell him to fuck off when he came back?" Mom asks, and I frown. It's so weird to hear Mom say fuck. It's more than the fact that she's my mother, of all of the old women in the Savage club, Mom is the most reserved...

"Why would I leave?"

"Jazz, you always leave," Hawk laughs. "If anyone gets pissed at you, you take off. It's your M.O."

I look up at Luke, he's watching me closely.

"I don't always run," I mutter. I expected him to smile, but he doesn't.

"You do, Jazzie. I love you, but you always run," Mom says.

"Not anymore," I tell her. "Luke is stuck with me."

"Christ..." B.B. mumbles.

The rest of them and their voices blur. I'm lost in Luke's eyes and the smile on his lips. Pride fills me, because I know I'm the one that put that smile on his face and when he hugs me, I'm pretty sure I'm wearing the same smile.

Chapter 40

Grunt

"You can leave Daisy with me. I'll be watching Ty for Katie, because something came up for Gabby. Daisy will be fine with me," Carrie says, and I fight down the urge to say no.

I don't know why I'm being so cautious. Fuck, before Jasmine pointed it out, I didn't even realize that I was neglecting my little girl. Now that I do, however, I never want her to doubt that she belongs with me and I want her there.

"But—"

"I'm going to be honest with you, Luke," she says quietly. I look over her to see where Jasmine is. It seems that Kayden and Nicole have her attention, which means she's not going to bail me out anytime soon.

"I'd appreciate that," I respond, turning my attention back to Jasmine's mother.

"I'm not sure how I feel about you dating my daughter—"

"We're not dating, Ms. Blake. Jasmine is mine. I'm keeping her. Now, because Jasmine cares about you and her father, I'm hoping you will accept it, but I'm going to be honest with you, I don't really give a damn. I know how special Jasmine is and I'm not willing to let her go."

"Good Lord," she sighs. She looks down at the floor and then slowly brings her gaze back up to me. "You sound like her father." I shrug, because I'm not sure what I'm supposed to say to that. "I was so hoping she would find happiness in a normal life. She dated a cop once... Jacob wasn't extremely happy about that, but I'm not sure he would be thrilled about her dating you—no offense."

I grunt. Then, because apparently it needs repeating I add three small words. "We're not dating."

For some reason that makes her smile.

"In any event, my point is, Jacob loves kids. I gather from Bart's response to you—"

"Bart?"

"B.B. Torch and Katie's boy."

I nod, having no idea who Torch and Katie are, but since I remember the guy who sized me up earlier, it's neither here nor there.

"I'm guessing from Bart's response to you that your club and theirs is not on great terms." Since they're not really, but if Ford gets his way, it will only get worse, I remain silent. "Right, I thought so," she says, judging my silence successfully. "Daisy is a delightful child and sweet."

"Thank you," I respond, clearing my throat.

"I'm thinking if Jacob spends the night getting to know little Daisy, it might let him think twice when he hears that Jasmine is moving in with a man he doesn't know, in a club that he doesn't like, and a man who..."

"Who?"

"Who will probably give his daughter the kind of life that he never wanted for her."

"I don't understand."

Carrie sighs. "My husband is a complicated man. He loves his club and the life we've built, but he wanted different for his kids. He wanted them to live a life where there wasn't... consequences."

She's wording it nicely, but I get it. Nothing our club does is really by the book. We live by our own rules and we make those rules our laws. It's different from the life outside of our club and sometimes there is blowback. I will bust my ass to protect Daisy and Jasmine, but the threat will always be there. I'd be lying if I said it wasn't.

"You're suggesting this to make him accept me...*easier?*" I ask, wanting her to explain it and make sure I'm on the same page as her.

"I am."

"No offense, if you were hoping Jasmine would end up with a cop, why would you even try to make things easier for me?"

"Because I saw something in my girl tonight that I've never seen."

"What's that?" I ask, and I have to admit this is the first time in this whole conversation that I really want to hear her answer.

"She's happy, Luke."

I nod. "I plan on keeping her that way."

"Then, let Daisy stay. I promise you the only harm that might come to her is an overload of sugar," she says with a smile.

I don't know what I expected when I came here today. Hell, part of me thought I might die. After all, I showed up at a rival club's property, personal home of the President—although I just found that out about an hour ago. Still, finding an ally in Red's mom is surprising... I'm not about to turn it down.

"Daisy can stay. Jasmine and I can get her tomorrow."

"I'm starting to think my daughter has finally made a good choice, Luke," she says, then she walks off.

I'm left standing there wondering if I just got Jasmine's mother's approval.

Damn.

Chapter 41

Grunt

"Harder, Luke, oh God, please," Jasmine begs, her voice almost as sweet and addicting as her body.

Her fingers press against my ass as I'm pushing inside of her. Her legs bend, coming up as she does everything she can to bring me in deeper.

"How big does that dick feel, Red," I demand, withdrawing only to slam into her again. I hammer in and out of her, fucking her hard, pinching and pulling on her nipple with one hand, and never stopping my onslaught.

"So fucking big...." She moans, dragging the words out like they're torture. "Luke," she gasps, her body tensing as her climax begins to build.

"I got you, Red," I growl, grabbing my pillow by her head and pulling it down to slide it under her ass, tilting her body to accept mine. "It's never enough," I moan. "It will never be enough, baby."

"Never," she agrees, gasping as her body quakes underneath me, signaling her orgasm. She brings me with her, just like she always does. When we come together, it's like our bodies are completely in tune with one another, it's easy, natural, and so fucking good that I can't describe it.

"It gets better every single time," Jasmine breathes out with a sigh. I usually stay in her longer—long after we've come. Today though, I kiss her lips quickly and walk into the bathroom to get a washcloth. I've ridden her hard and this is like the third time straight since we got back from Kentucky. I should feel like an ass, but I don't. I've quickly discovered that fucking my woman when there's a kid in the house is a hell of a lot different. It's one of the reasons that I'm working so damn hard to get the closing done on our house. Having bedrooms which are on the same floor but far enough apart that I can have Red the way I want her will be like fucking heaven.

I wet the washcloth with warm water and then come back to find Jasmine, curled on her side, looking at me, her pillow bunched up under her head and the sheet pulled up to her hip.

God, she's beautiful—every fantasy I've ever had.

"I could get used to that view," she croons with a smile.

"Quit trying to be sweet. You still have to make it up to me for telling everyone I was lying about the size of my dick," I rumble, trying to hide the smirk on my face. I walk to her and start rubbing the cloth between her legs, cleaning and hopefully soothing her sweet pussy at the same time.

"If this is how you punish me, I'm just saying I may do it again," she laughs while stretching.

I throw the cloth down on the floor and climb back up in bed. Jasmine immediately curls into me, throwing a leg over my hip.

"I love you," she says, kissing my chest.

"Love you, too, Red," I respond, gruffly.

"My mom liked you," she says, her voice thoughtful—quiet.

"I'm not so sure of that, baby. Seems to me like she had her heart set on you ending up with someone on a different side of the law."

I feel her body tense even before I get the words out and I swear to God that I can feel her withdraw from me.

"I'm hungry," she complains, while sitting up. She tucks the sheet tight under her arm, shielding her body, turning to throw her legs off the bed.

"Did it get cold in here all of the sudden?" I question, sitting up behind her. I don't allow her to leave the bed. Instead, I wrap my arms around her waist and pull—a clearly resisting—Jasmine to me.

"Let me go, Luke. I need to find some kind of snack food in this damn apartment. How you ever lived here is beyond me."

"I never did much, until you came along."

"Oh yeah, I forgot, you only started not staying at the club when you needed a place to stay with me. Heaven forbid you keep me around the club."

"Why are you trying to pick a fight with me?" I grumble, refusing to rise to the bait she's dangling.

"I'm not."

"Tell you what, baby—"

"What?"

"You want to start staying at the club, that's exactly what we'll do. We'll move into the club. Hell, I'll even cancel the closing on the house."

"I don't want that," she bellyaches—sounding a lot like Daisy does when she gets in trouble and she pouts.

"Then, tell me, what you do want?"

"To find food, so let me go," she huffs.

"I thought you told me you weren't going to run away anymore, Red?" I growl, refusing to let go even though she is pulling against me to get free. Then, all at once, the fight seems to go out of her, and she goes limp against my body.

"There's a difference between running away and not wanting to talk about something, Luke."

Keeping Her

"I get that, but you're going to have to tell me sometime, Jasmine."

She breathes out, the sound achingly sad.

"Red..."

"You may not know this about me, Luke, but sometimes I make very bad decisions."

I move her thick mass of auburn curls to one side, placing it over her right shoulder, and then press a kiss against the base of her spine. I move so that I'm cradling her body, keeping my arms around her waist, wanting her to feel surrounded by me—surrounded and secure.

"I know that, baby," I tell her tenderly, my fingers brushing comfortingly against her stomach.

She tilts her head to look over her shoulder at me. "How?"

"Because you chose to hook up with me. But, I'm smart, so I'm not about to let you talk yourself out of it now," I respond, and she may not realize how honest I'm being, but I do. Jasmine deserves much better than me and I'm still worried she'll find out the real reason we met. I need to talk to Ford about everything, but he's not listening to reason. I understand it. If someone hurt Daisy, I'd be completely pissed, but risking going to war by bringing an innocent girl into the mix...

I push those thoughts away, much like I've been doing for a while, choosing to concentrate on Jasmine.

"I happen to think falling in love with you is about the only wise decision I've ever made."

I snort out, unable to form a word. I slide my hand along the side of her neck and then I kiss her, trying to give her a sample of the emotion she strikes inside of me, without voicing it.

She drops her head down and rests against my chest. I let her have her silence. I don't want to rush her and if she doesn't want to tell me, ultimately, I won't make her. I will find out eventually, however.

"When I met Dewayne, I was stupid," she laughs, the sound holding no humor.

"Red—" I growl.

"I was. I was going through shit. Believe it or not, it's not easy growing up when your father and uncles are the most notorious MC heard of in the last two decades," she admits. "Dewayne seemed different. He wasn't afraid of my family and on the flip side, he didn't seem to care about it at all. I thought he wanted to be with me because of me, not because of whose daughter I was. It was a good feeling."

"But that wasn't the case?" I question, wanting to understand.

"No..." she says quietly, but there's a wealth of emotion in that one word. So much so, that you can hear the pain ooze from it.

"You don't have to tell me if you don't want to, Jasmine. Whoever this asshole is, whatever he did to you, it doesn't factor in on who we are," I tell her, vowing that I'll find out without Jasmine telling me somehow.

"Dewayne knew my father. I didn't know that. To me he played it off like he'd never really heard of him. I stupidly believed him—and yes, I know that was stupid."

It was, of course. If Dewayne was a cop anywhere near the Savage territory, then he knew who Dancer was, he knew who the whole club was. Chances are he'd had dealings with them, or read reports where others had.

"You weren't stupid, Red," I try to reassure her. Kissing the top of her head. "Naïve, maybe."

"Turns out he had a deeper idea of who my father was. Dad went to jail before I was born—before he and my mom ever got together really."

I rub the side of my neck. This is a touchy subject and I don't know how to approach it. I can't promise her that it won't ever happen with me. My club's rules and society's laws don't exactly mesh from time to time. A man has to do what he has to do to make sure no one ever fucks with him or his family and sometimes that involves fucked up shit...*deadly* shit.

"Red—"

"Don't worry, Luke. This wasn't about club stuff, although I'm not a stranger to that life, at all. Luckily Uncle Dragon and the others are very careful on what they allow, afraid of blowback on their families."

"Is that what happened to you, Red? Were you a victim of blowback?"

"Yeah, not that Dad ever knew. He didn't even know Dewayne, hadn't met him except for the couple of times I brought him to the house."

"I don't think I understand, baby."

Jasmine's body is pulled taunt, like if she moves she might snap and break into a million pieces. She's in my arms and yet, she feels like she might as well be a million miles away.

"When Dad was in prison... things happened. Shit messed him up really bad. He even tried to kill himself, drove his vehicle over the dam..."

Several things become clear to me. Things happening in prison could mean a hell of a lot and none of it is good. My hold on Jasmine tightens without thought. The next thing that comes to mind is the evening I found Jasmine at the dam in Kentucky and she spoke about someone else's demons, she was speaking about her father's.

"He tell you that?" I ask clearing my throat. It's a shit thing for a father to lay on a child. I'm a crap father, trying to do better, and even I'd take that to my grave, not involving my daughter.

"No, Dewayne did," she says and now it's clear that she's lost in her memories.

"Baby, maybe we—"

"Dad didn't know Dewayne, but he knew Dewayne's uncle,

and before he died he was the one raising Dewayne. He made sure to tell Dewayne all about just how he had one of the Savage MC head men under his control and everything he did to my father."

"Fuck..." I hiss, my imagination going everywhere, but the thoughts and questions running through my head aren't ones that I will ever ask her—none that I would want her to answer.

"When my father got his revenge, it left Dewayne without a home and bent on getting revenge. I was clueless, naïve and innocent at the time..."

"Blowback," I sigh, the sound weary to my own ears.

"Yeah. I gave myself over to the relationship. Trusted him to take care of me. He made me feel loved. When he asked for things that I wasn't comfortable with, I did them because I loved him, and I thought he loved me. I told you that before and I'm not blaming him. I was adult enough to be in charge of my own actions and whatever else Dewayne is—and he's a lot—he didn't force me."

"He didn't want to force you."

"No, it was more fun for him to get me to do it willingly," she confesses.

"How did you find out?"

"He took great pleasure in telling me after a night of partying with him and two of his buddies, laughing the whole time. Bragging how he made the Savage Princess beg to be a whore for the children of the men who made her dad their bitch."

I make a sound that is more animal than man. A wounded cry, filled with fury. I'm going to kill the motherfucker. There's not a doubt in my mind.

"I was ashamed, shocked, sickened... until that moment I didn't know any of my father's past. I don't think I ever knew the world could be that ugly."

"Your parents have no idea you know, do they?"

"No. They think I have no direction, maybe that I'm a lost cause. Maybe I should talk to them, but if my father knew... It'd bring it back. It would open those wounds. It would hurt everyone."

"So, you let them think the worst of you. Christ. How could your mother ever like this motherfucker?"

"Dewayne can be very nice and unassuming. I know I never once saw the evil that lurks inside of him and I'd like to think I can read people pretty damn clearly most of the time."

"Please tell me the asshole has left you alone since this happened?"

"He pulls shit every now and then. He had me arrested for parking tickets once. None I had received but dated back to almost when we first started dating. He had a friend of his write them and turn them in, so my parents or his superiors couldn't trace them back to him. Dad was so upset with me that he let me spend the night in jail, a night Dewayne volunteered for duty and took pleasure in taunting me. Luckily, it was county lock up and there were too many people and cameras for him to do much."

"Jesus Christ."

"I can't blame Dad. He had no idea the tickets were bogus. He just thought his daughter ignored over a year of tickets because she thought they would magically disappear. The speeding tickets, the shoplifting allegations, they were all part of me running wild."

"Jesus, Red. Why didn't you tell me that shit? This ass-clown has made your life hell," I bark, not able to control my reactions to everything she's telling me. Part of me knows that she's also glossing over this shit. She's completely skating over it, her voice monotone—telling me without words that it's worse than anything I'm imagining in my head.

"There's no point. There's nothing you can do, and Dewayne

has pretty much left me alone for the last few months. I figure maybe he's grown bored."

"Or maybe you've just been in Virginia and he hasn't seen you enough to cause you shit."

"Maybe," she agrees with a shrug. Then she turns her head to look at me, I can see unshed tears in her eyes, glowing, but I also see a strength. It glows on her face and she looks at me with a purpose. "I'm not a whore, Luke."

"Damn it, Red, don't you think I know that?"

"The things I did, what happened, I thought it was a safe relationship. I thought I was loved. I didn't particularly enjoy parts of it and maybe others I did—"

"Red, stop," I tell her, hating that she's beating herself up over any of this fucking shit.

"Still, it's nothing I would want long term. It's nothing I want with you. I love you, if another woman touched you, I'd want to kill her," she says, her voice defiant.

"Baby—"

"And I never want another man touching me but you. You need to believe that," she's daring me to argue, everything about her defensive.

She's breaking my heart.

I pick her up then, no longer content with her body just pulled against mine. I pick her up so that she's cradled in my lap. Our gazes lock and I don't waiver, I don't even blink.

"Your past is yours. I have one. We all fucking do, Red. It marks us, makes us who we are. You don't feel ashamed of it. You hold your head high. You are one of the strongest women I've ever met. You walk into a room and you fucking own it. I'm so damn proud that I'm the fucker you've claimed, Red. Don't you ever forget that. I'm thankful as hell you want to be a part of not only my life, but that of my daughter and one day, when Daisy grows up, I know she's going to be a strong woman too, because she will have learned from the best."

"Luke..."

"She will have learned from you and so will any other children we have."

"You want kids with me?" she asks.

"I want everything with you, baby."

"For a man who has a reputation as someone who doesn't talk, Luke, you sure know how to make a woman's knees grow weak."

"Just being honest, baby."

She nods, and a lone tear slides from the corner of her eyes. I find myself catching it by kissing the salty droplet.

When I pull away, her overly bright eyes are shining like diamonds and I feel her body trembling in my arms.

"I love you, Luke."

"Show me," I tell her, kissing her, because I need to physically make love to her, bare the emotions I feel without words. I want to prove to her, mind to mind, body to body, flesh to flesh, that she's loved. Somehow, I know that will mean more in this moment.

I don't know why I do, but I do just the same. This is how the two of us work together and I'm damn grateful.

Chapter 42

Grunt

"I don't have anything against you..."

Whenever someone starts off a sentence like that—especially one of the first sentences they've directed at you—you can pretty much translate that to mean they have everything against you. From the look on Jasmine's father's face, that's definitely true right now. We're out on the back deck of their home. He brought me out here under the pretense of showing me his bike—which was a sweet, classic Indian, but that was neither here nor there. We both knew what the topic of conversation would be. I'm not looking at him. I'm looking through the wide expanse of glass in front of me, which is really three sets of French doors surrounded by large glass panes that look over the Appalachian Mountains. The house is made of hewn logs and is definitely gorgeous, fitting in its surroundings perfectly. That's not what is holding my attention though. It's seeing Jasmine sitting on the floor, working a puzzle with Daisy, while Carrie is sitting on a stool at the counter, laughing and talking with them. Jasmine is combing her fingers through Daisy's hair. She kisses the top of her head and speaks softly to her in a way that I've only seen women have the

Keeping Her

ability to do. I tear my gaze away from my girls to look at Jasmine's father.

"I'm not giving her up," I respond, laying my cards on the table. I figure I might as well cut to the chase. I get why he's not happy his daughter is seeing me, I do. It doesn't matter. The simple truth is that I don't give a fuck.

"You have to know, son, I know all about your club. You and I live similar lifestyles and you have a daughter. Can you tell me that you would want your daughter to sign up with a man like you?"

A man like me. If a man in my world is made of grit and determination then I guess that would be me. That grit right now is rubbing my insides raw.

"My first answer would be no," I tell him honestly.

"Then you can see where I'm coming from."

"I can, but I also know how I feel about Jasmine and I know that I will bust my ass to keep that light that shines in her eyes."

"Listen, Grunt," he says, automatically using the name that shows on my cut—as he has since I walked inside. Which is how it should be, but for some reason it annoys the fuck out of me that he's trying to act like what he's saying should be easy for me to understand.

"I also know that I will always protect Jasmine with my fucking life. If my Daisy found a man willing to do that and that man wasn't a good man, but he was willing to be good enough to make her happy, then I'd stand back."

Dancer just looks at me, not speaking.

"And that's what I'm asking you to do here. Stand the fuck back."

"If I refuse?" Dancer asks, his gaze appraising me.

I let out an annoyed breath. This is going to be hard all the way through. It's okay, I expected that, but it doesn't mean I like it.

"It won't mean shit to me. I'm not giving her up. I've come here as a man, not my club, and I came here because I won't let Jasmine travel unless I have her back. If we're going to be enemies, then we'll make arrangements when she wants to visit you. But, Dancer, you need to hear me when I tell you that I'm not letting her go. Not for you, not for any fucking-body. She's mine and I'm keeping her."

"Just because you want to keep a woman doesn't make them yours," he rumbles, and I immediately shake my head no.

"She's mine because she wanted that almost as much as I did. I don't fucking know why, but it's a gift and regardless what you think of me, I'm not a stupid man. That means, I'm not letting her go."

"You decide she was yours before or after you found out she was Savage MC property, motherfucker?" My gaze jerks over to the man that walks up the steps. Dragon. I've seen him before, from a distance. I doubt he took much notice of me, most of his dealings were with Ford. He's an intimidating asshole; lucky for me, I've never been one to give in to intimidation. I've been told I give as good as I get and I'm rather proud of that. So, in response, I broaden my stance, and cross my arms at my chest and give my best fucking grunt, because his damn words aren't worthy of a response.

My gaze turns back to look for Jasmine. She's still on the floor, Daisy in her arms. She's laughing up at her friend Gabby who is standing there beside Nicole—who I met yesterday, and another woman with red hair that I don't know. It's none of them that I focus on, it's the guy standing close to Gabby. Every so often Gabby will laugh and the guy's eyes go directly to her. They're standing apart as if they're not together, but clearly he wishes he was.

Motherfucker.

"You ignoring me, asshole?" Dragon barks.

I turn my gaze to him. "Your question didn't deserve an answer. Besides I already answered it yesterday. I didn't know who Jasmine's family was until two days ago. Trust me, I wish to fuck she had told me sooner."

"Would it have made a difference?"

This question comes from Dancer, so I stare at him, giving him the fucking honest truth.

"Not a damn bit."

He and Dragon both surprise me by laughing.

"Who's the guy in there with Jasmine's girl, Gabby?" I ask, when it's clear they aren't planning on killing me—at least not right here and not right now.

"That's my son, Dom. You got a problem with him?" Dragon asks, and Jesus Christ can't something go simple in my damn life just once?

"He just looked familiar. Could have sworn I've seen him around somewhere," I tell him.

Dancer changes the subject and I let him. My brain is scrambling. I'm going to need to talk to Ford and I'm going to need to do that shit the minute I get back to Virginia.

Chapter 43

Jasmine

"Are you okay?"

Something is wrong and I mean horribly wrong. Luke has barely spoken since we left Mom and Dad's. I was afraid that Dad had threatened him, but they seemed way too relaxed to be planning the murder of my boyfriend. Luke has been really uptight, though. Even when he was being nice to my mom and trading barbs with Bart and Hawk, he was tense. I could see it, even if others might have missed it.

The fact that he's been silent since we hit the road only solidifies it.

"I'm fine, Red."

"You shouldn't lie to me, Luke. I can spot bullshit a mile away," I grumble.

"Okay, I'm not fine, but the reason I'm not fine has nothing to do with you, baby," he tells me and that should make me breathe easier, but for some reason it doesn't.

"Then, my family?" I ask, wondering if I misread how relaxed Uncle Dragon, Bull and Dad seemed to be at the get together earlier. They all played and laughed with Daisy and I doubt seriously they would have done that while plotting to kill her father.

He grunts under his breath. It's this annoyed sound that immediately makes me sick to my stomach.

"What did they do?" I ask.

"Nothing, baby."

"Bullshit. I've had enough of this. If they can't respect me or my choices then, I'm done."

"Jasmine—"

"I mean it. I'm flipping done!"

"Flipping?" he asks, and he sounds amused, but I can't pay attention to that. I'm pissed and I'm letting my anger have free range here and my parents are going to feel the brunt of it.

"Daisy's here. She might be sleeping but little ears have sonar," I snip, and for the first time since we arrived at my parent's house, Luke is smiling. Too bad he chooses to do it when I'm planning to murder them.

"Baby, you need to calm down."

"No. No, I do not, Luke. You're upset and it has something to do with my parents. That means Dad and my uncles decided to be assholes to you and that is not cool. They have a right to doubt me based on my past, but they don't get to treat you like—"

My eyes go wide and I stop talking when Luke pulls over to the side of the road.

He shuts off the engine and I immediately start shaking my head no.

"Luke you are not going to get me to calm down by doing you-know-what beside the road. Our daughter is in the back seat!"

He looks at me, something coming over his face that I can't name and if I wasn't so upset, I might worry about it, or at least take time to try and decipher it.

"Red—"

"I mean, look at me!"

"Red—"

"I'm not a little kid anymore. I've been taking care of myself for a while now. I know I've made some big mistakes, but damn it, I survived, and I got smart—"

Before I can finish the word smarter, Luke's fingers press against my lips so that it comes out muffled.

"Baby, I need you to calm down for a minute. Can you do that?"

He looks so serious that my heart drums against my chest and I know a second of fear, afraid something is more wrong than just the fact that my family did something. I nod slowly. He takes his hand away.

"I don't know what's wrong, Luke, but whatever it is, as long as we're in this together, the rest will just be bullshit that we will overcome," I tell him, needing him to believe that, while silently plotting a way to knock some sense into my family.

"Did you mean it?" he asks. I don't know what I expected him to say, but that wasn't it. I just keep staring at him, waiting for him to explain. "Did you mean it?" he questions again.

"Luke..."

"Well?" he prompts, sounding impatient.

"Well, what?" I ask, thoroughly confused.

His brow furrows, his deep brown eyes becoming cloudy with emotion and what I think just might be a mixture of impatience. I just have no idea why.

"You just said *our* daughter was asleep in the back," he says. My gaze goes to the back seat to see Daisy asleep in her car seat.

"She *is* asleep," I respond, not understanding at all what he's getting at.

"Baby, you called her *ours*."

It hits me, and this sick feeling floods me, like a thick heat washing over my body.

"I...uh..."

"Did you mean it?"

"Luke, I didn't mean to overstep. I mean, I know she's *your* daughter."

"That's not what I'm asking, Jasmine. Do you think of Daisy as yours?"

I swallow. I wasn't thinking when I blurted that out. I have no idea how he feels about my slip. His face is giving nothing away. The instinct is to backtrack, but that wouldn't be truthful. I decide the best thing to do would be to lay my cards down on the table.

"I love her, Luke. I mean, I guess I shouldn't, but I kind of think of her as part of..."

"Part of?" Luke prompts, when I stop talking. I was hoping he'd let it go, because I am feeling exposed...

"Family... part of this family we're building. That is what we're doing, right? I thought that's what you wanted, Luke. You can't expect me not to get attached to Daisy. She's sweet and funny. She..." I let out a heavy breath. "I love her."

"You've claimed her."

"Luke—"

"You claimed her, like I claimed you," he says.

"Is that...bad?" I ask, wanting to understand. There's this small hope blooming in my chest, because he doesn't sound upset. He sounds...happy.

"We're getting married," Luke growls.

"I...wait... *What?*"

"We're getting married, Jasmine. I don't want you bitching about it. We're getting married and you're adopting Daisy so that she knows she's as much yours as mine. I want my girl secure before we have more children."

"Uh..."

"You can't back out now, Red."

"I'm not trying to back out," I snap.

"Then, what's the problem?"

"Nothing, it's just that I think you're supposed to *ask* me to marry you, Luke—not demand it."

"I can ask, but you're going to marry me regardless," he responds and I roll my eyes, because he's right. I'm about to give him hell about it anyway, when a siren and lights flash behind us, grabbing my attention. A cop car pulls in behind us, breaking the moment. Luke curses under his breath. I figure the cop is just being nice to check and see if we're stranded. I don't mind, although it is bad timing. Hopefully he'll leave soon, and Luke and I can revisit this conversation. I'm even jumping ahead in my mind, wondering how Luke would feel about us getting married at our new house.

All good thoughts flee however, once the cop gets out of the car behind us and I see who it is.

Dewayne.

Chapter 44

Grunt

"What's going on here?" Dewayne Lagger says, strutting over to my truck as if he's the big man on campus. He's got blondish-brown hair and has some muscles. For the swagger he tries to carry, the piss-ant definitely needs more. He's got dark sunglasses on and doesn't bother to take them off, as he comes to a stop across from me.

Jesus, Jasmine was so much better than this dick. She deserves better than me too, but this guy is ridiculous. He's definitely watched too many Hollywood movies and tried to emulate the cops he's seen on the screen. It's almost laughable—except there's nothing funny that this fucker is here trying to cause shit.

I know that's what he's doing too. I spotted that car a couple of times since leaving Red's parent's home. I thought he might play it smart and not bother me tonight. I figured he was just scoping shit out before he planned an attack—and I knew he would attack. Weak-ass men who can't handle their own shit always do. Sadly, Lagger is not that smart, so here we are. It's okay. I would have preferred not to have Jasmine and Daisy around when it happened and I'll have to let Officer Numb-nuts believe he's in charge for a bit, but I can deal.

"Get back in the truck, Luke. Let's just leave," Jasmine says, from inside the cab.

"That you, Jazzy baby? I haven't seen you in so long. How are you?" Lagger laughs.

"Fuck you, Dewayne," she hisses. "You need to leave. We're not doing anything wrong here."

"You're loitering beside a busy highway. It looked very suspicious," Lagger explains.

I look out at the empty road and then slowly bring my gaze back to him. "Yeah, it's really busy tonight," I respond, sounding bored.

"What's going on here, anyway? You stop beside the road to fuck her? Jazzy loves it in the open. She always was an exhibitionist," Lagger taunts.

"You have a point to this stop or did you just want to piss me off?" I ask him, still keeping my voice monotone. I'm not rising to this guy's bait. He wants to upset me. He has, but he'll never know it—not until it's too late for him to save his ass.

"I'm going to need to see your license and registration," Lagger says, his face tight, his enjoyment fading as I'm the one succeeding in pissing him off.

"Gee, Officer Lagger, I must have left that at home," I respond mildly, leaning against the side of my truck like I haven't got a care in the world.

"Is that a fact?" he responds, his mask slipping until you can see the ugly lurking below.

"That it is."

"I see you know who I am," he laughs.

"Jasmine and I don't have any secrets," I tell him, still managing to sound bored.

"Oh, I bet I could tell you more than a few things that you don't know about little Jazzy," he taunts.

Jasmine jumps out of the truck and stands beside me. I let out an annoyed breath. I need her to hold her cool, but I know my woman and that's not going to happen.

"You need to get the hell out of here, Dewayne. We're not doing anything wrong. If you keep this up, then I'll have charges filed on you for harassment," she huffs, fire practically spitting from her eyes.

"Red, get in the truck."

"Red? I guess that works, at least you won't get in trouble for forgetting her name. She's kind of a snooze-fest in the sack. That is, unless you bring a party. Jasmine here likes to get it from all ends, if you get what I'm saying."

"You bastard," Jasmine hisses, and lunges toward him. I wrap my arm around her stomach and haul her back.

"I'm sure you're enjoying yourself here, Lagger. But, if we could get a move on with this, I'd appreciate it. I got somewhere I want to be and it's not here with you while you try to see if you have the bigger dick. You won't win, so whatever it is you want, let's get it done and you go back to whatever hole you crawled out of."

"I don't have to prove that my cock is bigger than yours. Jazzy knows the truth. She used to love gagging on it while my buddy gave it to her up the ass, didn't you Jazzy? How do you like getting my sloppy seconds, man?" he laughs, no humor on his face, only hate.

"You asshole!" Jasmine yells, then she lunges at him spitting in his face.

Lagger hauls off before I can stop him or pull Jasmine to safety and backhands her across the face, tagging her cheek with his ring and splitting her lip. I pull Jasmine back, but seeing the blood on her face instantly has me seeing red. I pull her back against the truck.

"Stay fucking put," I growl.

Then, I lead fist first, planting it in Lagger's face without a thought. He falls back onto the ground, his nose spouting blood out like a stuck pig.

He draws his gun pointing it up at me and I freeze, never taking my eyes off of him.

"You better be a good shot with that, because I'll choke the life out of you if I live even a few seconds after you shoot me, motherfucker," I growl at him, my voice deadly.

"Put your hands behind your back," Lagger orders, spitting up blood as he scrambles.

"Fuck you."

"Put your hands behind your fucking back!" he yells, scrambling to stand up. I charge him, knocking the gun out of his hand.

I punch him again, knocking the gun out of the way.

Maybe I would have done more, I was mad enough to kill the son of a bitch. Two things stopped me, however. The first being my daughter who was holding her head out the truck door.

"Daddy?" she asks, worried and confused. Jasmine goes to her to hold her hand.

"It's okay, Daisy, get down in the back seat, okay, baby? We'll be leaving in a bit."

"You're not going anywhere," Lagger barks.

"Get down in the seat, Daisy." I order, distracted enough that I miss Lagger going for his gun again, I manage to kick it away, but it was too close for comfort with my daughter and Jasmine so close by.

The second thing that happened is another car pulls up behind Lagger's squad car. I curse myself for being stupid enough to start shit with my family so close by.

"Something going on here, Officer Lagger?" the other cop

Keeping Her

says, getting out and walking toward us. He keeps his hand on his gun, appraising the situation, but when he looks at Lagger there's a flicker of something there that I see clearly.

Disgust.

"Jasmine, you okay?" he asks, looking over at her, real concern on his face.

"I'm okay, Mike. Dewayne hit me and my fiancé was trying to protect me. Then, Dewayne pulled a gun and was going to shoot Luke," she says, her eyes bright with anger.

"Is that what happened, Officer Lagger?" he says, walking over and picking up the detective's gun. I notice however, that he doesn't offer to give it back to the guy. Instead, he secures it in the belt he's wearing.

"Of course not," Lagger growls, standing up and dusting himself off.

"Maybe we need to move this to the station and figure out what exactly did happen," the other officer that Jasmine called Mike suggests.

"That's bullshit. If he hadn't hit me then how do you explain the cut on my face from that stupid ring he's wearing. And who wears a class ring when they are knocking thirty? The eighties are calling you Dewayne, and they want you to go back in them and die," Jasmine snarls, holding her face.

"Daddy," Daisy cries.

Shit.

I hold my hand up to the one cop here that seems half-way legit and motion to my daughter. He gives me a silent signal and I walk over to her.

"Daddy's okay, honey. It was just a little disagreement," I tell her, looking at Jasmine, the blood on her face still making me livid.

"Like Auntie Gina and S'wedge have sometimes," she says, sniffling.

"Yeah, kind of like that," I tell her, wondering just what my daughter lived through before Jasmine showed me what a shit father I was.

I look over at the two cops who are now huddled together. Lagger is growling, demanding he take me to the station. We both know what he wants to do to me. He doesn't have his gun back yet, though and that's something that I'm keeping a close eye on.

"Luke..." Jasmine whispers, coming to stand beside me, her hand protective on Daisy.

I reach over and kiss her forehead. "Whatever happens, you take Daisy and get home. Call my club and tell them to get to me."

"Luke—"

"Do it, baby. Take care of our daughter."

"Jasmine, I'm afraid I'm going to have to take your fiancé down to the station, while we try and figure out what's going on here."

"This is bullshit," Lagger growls, clearly not happy.

"It is bullshit. Luke shouldn't have to go anywhere. He didn't do anything wrong here," Jasmine yells.

"Did you hit Officer Lagger?" Mike asks me.

"After he hit my woman, you better believe I did," I tell him, not even bothering to deny it.

"I want my fucking weapon and I'm taking this miserable shit in myself," Lagger demands, still spitting out blood. I must have broken a tooth as well as busted his nose.

"Stand down, Officer Lagger," Mike demands, his voice harsh. "Do I need to remind you as to who outranks who here?"

"I want the record to show I'm the arresting officer here," he barks, clearly not happy.

"Trust me, it will be noted," Mike sighs.

"And that the suspect admitted to hitting me," he walks off, pouting like a petulant child.

Keeping Her

"Listen guys, I'm really sorry about this. I'd send you on my way if I could. The simple truth is that even though Lagger is under an IAB review, he still has some connections high up, so I need to watch my back here. If you'll come with me, I promise I will protect you," Mike murmurs. His attention switches to Jasmine then, and even I can see the regret on his face. Apparently Jasmine's parents might have been blind to Officer Lagger's faults, but not everyone is. "Jasmine, get home, get safe and call your dad. Have him and Dragon get down to the station."

"No," I growl and they both look at me.

"I can take care of myself. You get me a call when I get there, I'll call my club in to take my back. I want Jasmine to get our daughter home safe."

"Luke—"

"No arguments, Red. Daisy and you are the important ones here."

"But I don't want to go without you, Daddy!" Daisy cries.

"Daddy will be back soon. You got to be a big girl and go home with Jasmine, okay?"

"Okay," she sniffles, clearly worried. I pick her up in my arms and close my eyes as her arms wrap around me, hugging me close. I kiss the side of her face and hand her into Jasmine's waiting arms.

"Be safe," I warn Jasmine, giving her a quick kiss. She nods, clearly not happy.

"You have a club too?" Mike asks, his gaze dropping down to my cut. I don't answer because I figure he knows that answer now. "Well, shit. Lagger is biting off more than he can chew," he mutters, and the man doesn't know the half of it. I was merely kicking around the idea earlier, but when Lagger hit Jasmine, he signed his death warrant. I'm going to take great pleasure in killing the son of a bitch.

And I'm going to make it painful.

Chapter 45

Jasmine

"Dad, I need you," I murmur quietly into my cell. My gaze moves into the rearview mirror to look at Daisy who is playing on her tablet. Until today, I had no idea she could even unhook the latch on her car seat. It might be time to invest in a better version.

"Jasmine? Honey, are you okay?" Dad asks, immediately concerned.

"Jacob? What's wrong with my girl?" I hear Mom asking in the background.

"Dad, it's Dewayne. He stopped us, starting crap. He hit me and Luke kind of snapped."

"*He hit you?*" Dad's voice is deadly, chilling and cold. I knew his reaction before I even called him and I know Luke told me to get home, but I can't do that. I don't know who there will listen to Dewayne and I can't let Luke get hurt because of me. Still, this is just one of the reasons I never truly told my father anything about Dewayne and what happened.

"Mike showed up and kept him from killing Luke. Dewayne

had pulled a gun, but Dad, I'm worried. They're taking Luke into the station."

I'm whispering the words, not wanting Daisy to hear them.

"I'll call Dragon and we'll get down there, Jazz," he says, and I swallow down the small amount of regret I feel. I can only imagine how difficult it is for Dad to be in a police station. He doesn't realize I know his past and I'd never tell him, but it hurts me just the same.

"Thanks, Dad. Could you...Can Mom come too? I'd like for her to get Daisy and take care of her while we deal with everything. I want to give my statement and get photographs of where Dewayne hit me. It might help, Luke."

"It won't be necessary, but I'll make sure she's there to get Daisy, baby."

"Thanks, Dad."

"I've failed you haven't I, Princess?" Dad asks, using my childhood nickname that I haven't heard in years.

"No, Daddy. Life just got hard."

"That it did, baby. That it did. Where are you at?"

"Just coming back into town, out by the house on the hill that I always liked, the one that was on television."

"Okay, sweetheart. See you soon. Be safe," he says and I think I can almost hear the smile in his voice.

When I was little, I wanted to see the famous house that had an elevator in it. Dad drove up to it and paid the owners to let me take my own tour. I remember feeling like my daddy could do anything in that moment and in some ways, that feeling never left. That's the main reason I called him, despite what Luke asked. This is Kentucky and not Virginia. If anyone can help with this mess, it's my dad and his club.

Luke will just have to understand.

Chapter 46

Dancer

"Jesus H. Christ, what the fuck did I do to piss off karma that landed half of the Savage MC Crew and the Devil's Blaze in my office?" Police Chief Garner growls, storming into his office.

His very crowded office—because he's right. The tiny room has me, Hawk, Dragon, Dom, Thomas and Bull standing behind Jasmine, who is sitting in the chair in front of me. Beside us is Skull, Torch and B.B. Gabby is also here, sitting beside Jasmine and holding her hand, claiming she was here for moral support.

"Your dipshit officer hit my daughter and then arrested my future son-in-law," I snap. Jasmine reaches up and grabs my hand holding onto it tightly. I look down at it and this feeling of warmth hits me. Her hand has grown, but this is exactly what she would do when she was scared and made me come into her room to get rid of any of the trolls that were hiding under her bed. I used to tell her a bedtime story ages ago that I mostly made up to make my Care Bear smile. Jasmine loved it though and made me tell it to her every night. I was kind of proud until she began to think she had mean trolls hiding under her bed every night.

Keeping Her

The memories make me smile, but I lock them down for now, needing to concentrate on the here and now.

"I have quite a few dipshit officers, Dancer, buddy. You're going to have to get a little more specific," Garner replies.

"Dewayne Lagger," Jasmine says, her voice so angry that hell... she reminds me of myself.

"Shit," Garner hisses, looking at my little girl. "I'm sorry Jasmine. Did he do that to your face?" Garner asks. Garner is a good guy. He came on the job about the time Crusher left for Tennessee. He's worked well with the club through the years and has always been above board. I respect him, and I can't say that too often about the boys in blue that I've dealt with.

"Yeah. He thinks he's in the eighties and it's cool to wear his fucking class ring even though he's thirty," Jasmine growls.

"There's nothing wrong with rings, querida. A man just has to have the balls to wear them correctly," Skull says, giving her a wink.

"Daddy, please, I'd rather not hear about your balls," Gabby admonishes.

"I'm still trying to figure out why you are here, asshole," Dragon grumbles. "This concerns my club, not the Blaze. I swear, I bailed your ass out of one jam after another and asked you for help one fucking time and now I'm stuck with you for life."

"I came because my Gabriella and Jasmine are close. Jazz is like another daughter to me. Besides that, mi hermano, you know that without me you would be like a sheep lost in the cruel world, vulnerable to the wolves."

"Christ," Bull mutters under his breath. Torch throws his head back and laughs.

"I really should have cut your tongue out the first time you tried to get Nicole in your bed."

"Not this story again," Dom and Thomas say in unison.

"It's bad form to remind me of that when you know that I

thought mi cielo was gone forever," Skull grumbles. "And to make it clear, it wasn't my tongue you threatened to cut off. Although my Beth says I am legendary—"

"La, la, la, la, la, I can't hear you!" Gabby cries out, putting her fingers in her ear.

"Fuck a duck, will you all just button it. Garner. I want to know what you're going to do about this fuck-wit who hurt my daughter. And I want my son-in-law released immediately."

"Hold up. Have we charged your son-in-law? Shit, did you get married, Jasmine? Why wasn't I invited to the wedding? Damn it, Bull, you know how much I love your wife's banana pudding. How is Skye anyway?"

"She's married," he growls. "And why don't you just keep your fucking eyes off of her."

Garner laughs, flipping him off and Bull returns the gesture. I pinch the bridge of my nose, wanting the fuck out of here. Anywhere near jails and police stations have my skin crawling. The walls begin closing in and I just need to get the fuck out of here—drive fresh air into my lungs.

It's been a lifetime and a past that I quite literally buried and put behind me, but the memories still cause reactions that I can't control—even if they don't tear me apart like they used to.

"I didn't get married, Chief Garner. I'm engaged. I'll be getting married in a couple of weeks when our house is finally ours and we move in."

"You are?" I ask, this being news to me.

"I love him, Daddy. He's good to me. He wants me to adopt his daughter and have more kids with him. I'm happy," she says, looking up at me with stars in her eyes. "He's like my father, one of the best men I've ever known."

She's still holding my hand. For a minute, the past and the present collide, and I see my little girl as six-years-old again, telling me she loves me and that I'm her hero.

"Are you sure, Princess?" I ask clearing my throat from the sudden emotion that threatens to choke me.

"He's my troll," she whispers, my eyes closing as the sweetness hits me.

"Troll? Did she say troll? That doesn't sound like she loves him. Sounds to me like she needs to drop kick him in the balls," Torch says, and I got to admit there's part of me that wants to do that very thing. Instead, I clear my throat and bring my attention back to Garner.

"You need to handle this shit—"

"We're here to collect our man!" An angry looking man with thick wavy brown hair, covered in tattoos says, after pushing the door open so hard it slams against the wall. For a minute I wonder if it's going to break, but it doesn't. There's three men, and they none look happy. They're also wearing cuts that say Demon Chasers—cuts like my future son-in-law.

This fucking shit just got a hell of a lot more complicated.

Chapter 47

Grunt

"Here you go, Chief Garner," the cop says that leads me into the police chief's office.

A very crowded office.

I look first to see, who I assume is Chief Garner, wave the cop away. Then, as I continue looking around, there are so many people that I don't know how they are fitting in the room. I rub my wrists where the handcuffs had been and before I can do much more than that, Jasmine is in my arms.

"Luke," she murmurs, her arms going around me.

"Red? Where's Daisy?"

"My mom has her," she says, as I wrap my arms around her.

"Baby, I told you to get to safety," I complain, and I should be mad, but it feels damn good to have her in my arms.

"Uh, Luke, I'm about as safe as a woman can get. Do you see all of my family here?" she asks, standing back to look up at me. That's when I focus on the people around us. My gaze takes in Jasmine's father, watching us closely and then, her brother, and Dragon. I see the guy that was with Gabby too...Dragon's son, Dom.

"Decide to go to Kentucky and cause a shitload of trouble, my man?" I turn to look at Ford, instantly aware. He walks to me, his hand slapping against mine in greeting, pulling me in and then slapping me on the back.

"You know me," I mutter, my gaze going to Gabby automatically.

"How long have you been here?" I ask, clearing my throat.

"Just got here, but from listening to the talk, it seems the muscle of *my* club has been adopted by another club," he says, and it's clear he's not happy with that. I'm pretty damn shocked myself. After the situation at the party, I was left wondering, but having them all here was not what I expected—at all.

"Just because we accept him, doesn't mean we will welcome your club into the fold. You stay in your territory and we'll be in ours," Dragon warns.

I see that muscle ticking in Ford's jaw. I don't have to be a mind reader to know that this isn't going to end well.

"That's big words coming from a man who had to pay me to even show his face in my territory," Ford taunts, reminding Dragon of the one time our clubs had dealings together. Dragon wanted to bring some nomad to our territory to show him why club borders were important. I thought it was stupid. We would have just killed the nomad for breaking protocol, but we got money and guns for it, so our club was the definite winner in that transaction. "As far as I'm concerned, you can take your fucking club and stuff it up your ass," Ford growls, spitting in Dragon's direction.

"You motherfucker," Dragon yells, going after Ford to tear him apart.

Ford, for his part, doesn't even move, he's waiting for Dragon to take the first punch—which, I don't think is entirely wise. Dragon might be older, but he's stacked like a damn brick house, and him mad should make any-fucking-body think twice. Ford isn't exactly a slouch either, my money would probably be on him, but it would be a coin toss on if I'd win or lose.

Dom and the other guy, who I assume is Dragon's son too, because he looks a fuck of a lot like his father, hold Dragon back—which is no small feat.

"Jesus Christ, if I'm going to get in the middle of a fucking club war, it's not going to be in my gaw'damned office!" Garner yells, pushing members of the Blaze and Savage clubs aside to get between two men that look ready to tear each other apart. "Do we have a problem here?"

"You better fucking believe we have problems. I will not be disrespected in my fucking territory," Dragon growls.

"And I won't have your dumbass son breaking my daughter's spirit and leaving her in pieces!" Ford barks out in response and I follow his eyesight to see Dragon's boy standing close to Gabby—who looks way too much like Lyla. Ford always was a smart motherfucker. Suddenly, I know this is going to go bad.

Really bad.

"What the fuck are you talking about?" Dom snarls, letting go of his father and going after Ford himself—or rather tries to.

"Christ, I'm too old for this shit. I picked the wrong month to give up drinking coffee," Garner mutters, rubbing the top of his head and mussing up his hair.

"I'm talking about you, you motherfucker. Waltz in and steal my daughter's innocence, knock her up, then drop her like she's got the plague when you can go back to the woman you're using her for."

"Jesus H. Christ," I groan. I didn't want the club to go to war over this shit. It all felt too much like fucking high school bullshit and here we are—and it sounds just like teenage crap.

"Hold up. Luke? Do you want to explain this to me?" Jasmine says, and shit, she's as pissed as the rest of her father's club. In

Keeping Her

fact, right now, with fire shooting out of her eyes, she looks more deadly than Dragon.

"Red—"

"Don't you Red me. You told me it was Ford that was interested in Gabby and I told you she was too young for him."

Fuck.

"Hold up. Mr. Melt-Your-Panties was interested in me, but you didn't tell me?" Gabby cries walking into the fray.

"*Mierda*, Gabriella, do not talk about some man melting your bragas in front of your padre," Skull responds in broken Spanish.

"No offense blondie, but fucking you would be like fucking a cheaper version of my daughter. Never going to happen."

Gabby blinks... "Whatever, but honey, I'm not cheap," she mutters, hand on her hip.

"This I can attest to," Skull responds, apparently not bothering to take offense with Ford, which is one very small mercy in this mess.

I don't have time to worry about it, however, because I'm busy getting death glares from Jasmine and the rest of her family.

"Red, baby," I start, hoping her face might soften, some of the anger leach out of her—it doesn't. She continues staring. I sigh, rubbing the back of my neck. "Okay, fine. I *let* you think that, because it was easier at the time."

"By easier, you mean I wouldn't leave your ass when I found out you've been using me all this time."

"That's bullshit, Jasmine and you know it. I haven't been doing my job for the club—"

"That's definitely something I can agree to," Ford says, and I cast him a look over my shoulder. He's still pissed, so maybe it's not wise to talk to him about this shit just yet.

"It's a weak-ass punk who tries to lead and can't control his men," Dragon snaps.

"Yeah, how'd that work out for you? Last time you were relevant in my world, my *father* was talking about how you went into hiding not long after one of your own men tried to kill your woman and family," Ford accuses.

"I'm going to have such fun in cutting you up in little tiny pieces and feeding you to the birds, motherfucker."

"You can try, old man, you can try," Ford responds, laying it down.

"This, Red!" I growl. "This bullshit was what I was trying to contain. I figured if I could locate Dom and maybe talk to him man to man about Lyla, this shit could be handled easily. I should have known better though, because where you're involved nothing is ever fucking easy," I huff.

"Wait, so now all of this shit is my fault?" she asks, her eyes about to bug out of her head.

"You never do what you're told!"

"Oh shit," Hawk hisses.

"Well, fuck a duck. It looks like I'm not going to be getting a son-in-law after all," Dancer adds, and he sounds entirely too happy about that.

"I'm thinking that's a good thing, since we're riding into war against his club in the morning," Dragon replies.

"What's wrong old man? You need a power nap first? Have to go home and drink your Ensure before you head to Virginia?"

"I'm going to start with your tongue, cutting it out first would do the fucking world a favor," Dragon threatens.

"You seem to have an unhealthy fascination with tongues, mi amigo," Skull tells him and Jesus, he looks like he's enjoying all of this bullshit.

"What the fuck is your problem?" Dragon growls, apparently picking up on the laughter in Skull's words, along with the smile on his face. "If I go to war then you do too, motherfucker. We're allies."

"I'm ready to fight by your side, Dragon. It's just..." he

Keeping Her

shrugs as if he's trying to form the words carefully—which might be wise. "I'm just glad that your sons have decided to give another father a headache instead of me," he finally says with a laugh.

Dragon growls under his breath, I wouldn't be surprised if the man could truly breathe fire.

"Do what I'm told?" Jasmine asks, so quietly that I can barely hear her over all of the angry breathing in the room.

"I told you to go to our house and protect Daisy. *If* you had done that, then this scene right here wouldn't be happening."

"So, all of this is my fault?" she cries.

"If the shoe fits, Red," I growl.

"Damn, that boy has balls. No brains, but balls," some guy standing beside Hawk says. I have to look twice at him because he's wearing a t-shirt that has a warning sign on it and then shows stick figures of a woman giving a man head. Underneath it, it reads:

Warning, choking hazard.
Package contains large parts.

Then, underneath the words is an arrow pointing down. If I wasn't worried Jasmine may try to fucking run again, and Ford would try to kill the head of the Savage crew, I'd laugh.

"I was trying to help my old man. That's when I thought I *had* an old man. Don't worry, I won't make that mistake again," she snaps.

"You definitely have an old man. I'll remind you of that bullshit when we get out of here."

"Not likely," she huffs.

"We both know I can get you under control in three minutes," I boast.

"You get any of your appendages near me and I will go feral on your ass and bite them off," she says a little too sweetly, her eyes scary.

Maybe I ought to rethink my attraction to redheads. Jasmine's temper is something to behold.

"Can we bring the attention back to my daughter? If you want to avoid a club war, I want your son's head on a pike," Ford growls.

"I'm thinking we need to move this bullshit out of my station. If there is a war, I'm going to use what is said here against every last one of you motherfuckers," Garner growls.

Everyone ignores him.

"His head on a pike? And you call my ass old?" Dragon laughs. "How did you even get a club? Did you start while you were in kindergarten and still wearing your damn diapers? Watch too many old war movies to try and sound cool?"

"The only one wearing diapers around here is probably you and your crew. Do you singlehandedly keep Depends in business, old man?"

"You got jokes," Dragon says, with a deadly smile. "Jokes that are going to get you killed.

"Bring it. If you don't have your son at the Virginia state-line by the Exxon station in the morning, you won't need to worry about what I'm going to do," Ford promises. "Because I'll definitely show you."

"Man, you're crazier than hell. I don't even know your daughter," Dom interjects.

"You're lying."

"The fuck I am," Dom growls, and I'm starting to wonder if his temper might rival his father's.

"You haven't even seen her picture to see what my daughter looks like. How could you tell me if you know her or not?" Ford points out.

"The only pussy I've been getting is in Kentucky," Dom snarls. "It comes looking for me motherfucker. I don't have to go to another state to hunt it down."

Keeping Her

"I...I have to go," Gabby says, and it's clear her face is crushed, you can already see the tears in her eyes.

"Gabriella," Skull calls, but Gabby is already out the door.

"Shit," Dom hisses, but he doesn't follow Gabby out.

Jasmine looks up at me and I nod my agreement to her.

"This isn't over," she warns.

"Didn't think it was, baby," I admit and when she goes to walk by me, I grab her arm and pull her into me and kiss her. "Love you, Red," I tell her, softly. "The rest is just bullshit. You were mine from the first moment I saw you."

"I can vouch for that. You're all the asshole could concentrate on," Jonesy adds, maybe not so helpfully.

"You can grovel later," she mutters, turning away from me.

"Is grovel code for eating out your sweet cunt, baby?" I ask her when she gets to the door.

Her back goes straight.

"Motherfucker, now I'm going to tear your tongue out of your head," Dancer yells.

"Daddy?"

"Yeah, baby?" Dancer asks, while he and I stare at one another.

"Kick my troll in the balls," she instructs.

I frown, my brow creasing at my confusion as I try to figure out what the fuck she's talking about. It distracts me and because of that, I miss the fact that Dancer's leg kicks out and nails be right in the nuts with his steel-toed riding boots.

"Fuck," I hiss, grabbing my junk and trying to breathe to keep from passing out.

Jasmine walks out, leaving me in pain.

"That's Daddy's little girl right there," Dancer brags, looking at me like he's still not satisfied.

"Well, she's my woman and I hope you weren't wanting

grandkids other than Daisy, because I think you caused permanent harm," I hiss trying to straighten up.

"A fucker can hope," he shrugs, not one bit sorry.

"Let's get out of here. The air in Kentucky is choking me," Ford orders.

"It won't just be the air, come morning. Better enjoy your last night on earth motherfucker," Dragon warns.

"It was me."

One voice comes out of the silence as we all stand there looking at one another.

Then, Dragon's son comes up to stand in front of his father.

"You?" Ford asks.

"If Lyla is your dau...daughter then, yes. I didn't kn...know she was pregnant."

"Well, she is," Ford says, sizing up the man who apparently has balls enough to take responsibility. It's clear he has an issue talking, whether that's nerves or something else, I can't be sure. He sure as hell doesn't look nervous though. He looks...*resigned*.

"I want to...to talk to her."

"Then, you can come back to Virginia with me and my boys," Ford says, crossing his arms.

"The hell he will. Motherfucker, I don't like you. I sure as hell don't trust you and there's no way my son is going into your territory," Dragon all but roars.

"I give you my word he won't be harmed. I'll send him back to you and give you twenty-four hours before war truly starts between us," Ford says, as if he is discussing the weather and not a club war that will end up in a bloodbath.

"Your word is about as dependable as a monk in a room full of easy pussy, motherfucker," Dragon responds to Ford.

"I don't get it," B.B. replies. The t-shirt guy slaps him on the back of the head.

"No dick is going to turn down free pussy," the man instructs. "Even a monk."

"But—"

"Unless his old lady has his dick in her pocketbook," the guy finishes. Everyone stares at him. "What?" he asks defensively. "You motherfuckers act like the rest of you aren't controlled by your old ladies' pussies. At least I'm man enough to admit that my sweet Katie owns my cock."

"Shut up, Torch," Skull grumbles, but he doesn't argue with him.

"I'll go with my boy," Dragon says. "We'll stay at the hotel that's on the state line and you will bring your daughter to us."

"Yeah, amigo, that ain't happening," Ford says, his Texas cowboy roots coming out in him. Hell, if he had on a Stetson, I could see him on the set of a western.

"You can stay in the hotel," I suggest.

"Damn it, Grunt—"

I hold up my hand, to my President, giving him a silent plea to hear me out. That muscle tightens on his face—the one that always warns you when he's about to lose his shit, but he nods.

"You and two of your men can stay in the hotel and I'll come and personally take Thomas to Lyla and deliver him back to you safely."

"Motherfucker, I don't know you either. Why would I trust you?"

"Because I love Jasmine and when this is all over, I want my woman by my side in Virginia, happy. I don't think she'll be happy if she feels like her parents can't ever come and visit her."

"You agree to this?" Dragon asks Ford. Ford looks at Thomas and then back at Dragon and nods.

"Then it's settled," Dragon growls.

"Good, now you motherfuckers get out of my office. Jesus, I need some coffee," Garner growls.

"You need to lock down your officer," Dancer warns him.

"Man, he wouldn't even be on my payroll if I had my way. He's got friends with a higher pay grade than I do. I'll use this to tangle him up in an IAB investigation and give him a slap on the wrist for the incident. That will keep him busy for a few months. I'm sorry, Dancer, but I figure that's the best I'm going to be able to deliver."

"What about me?" I ask Garner.

"You're free to go. You struck out because you were worried about Jasmine. She already gave her statement and detailed how Lagger pulled his weapon on you without call. If you want to file police harassment papers and get a lawyer, I can't really help you."

I snort. I'm not doing that shit.

"Now all of you assholes get out and let's make it another year before I see you again."

Everyone mutters under their breath, not happy, but figuring that at least for now, matters are settled. Just as I'm about to follow them all out of the room, wanting one last word with Jasmine's father, Garner speaks up again. "Hey Bull? Don't forget to tell that pretty wife of yours that I said hi."

"It's like you want me to kill you," Bull growls, storming out and leaving Dancer and Garner to laugh.

Jesus, I need to get back to Virginia.

Chapter 48

Grunt

"You still pissed, Red?" I ask as we drive up to our new home.

It's been four days since the throw down at the police station in Kentucky. Lyla hasn't been feeling good and Ford wanted to wait a couple of weeks before Thomas came to Virginia. I got the feeling that it was Dragon that wasn't happy about that, or maybe Thomas, but in the end, they agreed. Part of me wonders if it's not Ford just making Dragon and his crew cool their heels. I wouldn't put it past him, but I can't say as I blame him either.

She looks back at Daisy—which is the real reason we haven't hashed any of this shit out. "I'm fine," she mumbles.

The incident in Kentucky bothered Daisy more than Jasmine and I could have imagined. She's had trouble sleeping and has been crashing in our bed every night. I'm hoping that will change tonight when she has her very own room. Jasmine has been telling her some kind of bedtime story about a princess and a troll and it seems to be helping. I wonder if she's supposed to be the princess in the story and if I'm the troll, since that's what she called me when her father nailed my nuts to the end of his boot.

She assured me that the story was about her parents, which is confusing as hell. It's also leaving me to wonder if I am equipped to raise girls. They're freaking complicated.

I know that Jasmine's answer is just code for the fact that she doesn't want to discuss any of this right now.

I sigh. We finally got the closing done and the keys to our new home and yet, this bullshit is hanging over it all.

We get out of the truck, with Daisy's happy cry, and unload the shit we brought with us. Jasmine ordered up a fuck-load of furniture and had it delivered yesterday, so there really wasn't much more than personal belongings for us to bring. Jasmine had a suitcase full and a few things she had collected, but next week—if we're not at war—we are going back to Kentucky to finish packing up the shit that she has at her parent's home.

Which should be loads of fun.

We go to the door and I unlock it. Daisy runs through immediately

"I'm going to my room!" she cries.

Jasmine starts to follow her in but I grab her, letting my crap fall and picking her up in my arms.

"What are you doing?" she asks. She's not hostile to me, but it's clear she's not fully forgiven me yet. She's not running away either, though and that shouldn't be overlooked.

"Carrying you over the threshold, baby."

"We're not married," she points out and she sounds more than a little sad over that fact. I bend down and kiss her gently.

"It's going to happen," I respond, and it will. It's just that we both decided to wait until after the mess between my club and the Savage Brothers is done. We'd rather not have people here at each other's throats when we're celebrating.

"I'm still mad at you," she mutters, proving my girl is great at holding a grudge.

"But you love me," I remind her.

"If I didn't, I wouldn't be here," she admits, her face still betraying her sadness.

"I love you, Red. I did when I didn't even believe in the emotion. I want us to raise Daisy and our other children in this home. I want you by my side for the rest of my life as my old lady, as my wife. It's all going to be okay."

"Ford hates my father's club and Uncle Dragon despises him," she points out and that's when I know that the club war is bothering her more than the shit with Gabby, Dom, Thomas and Lyla.

"It will be okay," I promise her, and I don't know how, but I know that it will. I will bust my ass to give that to her.

"But your club..."

"If it's not worked out, we'll fucking move to Kentucky."

"You'd give up your club?" she asks, completely shocked.

"I don't think it will come to that, but if Ford chooses to hold onto a vendetta over this, when I think Thomas plans on manning up and being there for his child, then I will have to."

"But—"

"Baby, I don't want to follow a man who would lead his club to war over something like this if the guy is trying to do the right thing."

"He can't be with Lyla if he's in love with Gabby, Luke. It wouldn't be fair to anyone," she says as we walk through the door.

I put her down, letting her slide to the floor, while keeping her in my arms.

"You can support your child and not be attached to the mother, Red. People do it every day."

"Speaking of...." She stops talking, her cheeks flushing with color.

"Speaking of what, baby?" I ask, tenderly, knowing it's something important to her.

"Well, you said you wanted me to adopt Daisy," she says nervously.

"I do," I respond. "I *absolutely* do."

"What if her mother doesn't want that? I mean, I know she gave you custody and all... but—"

"Carla got paid forty-grand to even have Daisy. She was going to do away with my child. I paid her money and kept her up. The minute Daisy was born she disappeared. I'm the only parent Daisy has ever known. That's the way I wanted it, that's the way Carla wanted it and most of all that's what was best for our daughter."

"Where is Carla now?"

"Doing what she does best, thinking of herself, partying and fucking. It's none of my concern now, Red. You just need to know that if you want to be Daisy's mother, you can be."

"And that's what you want?"

"I want it more than anything," she answers and I can hear the honesty in her voice.

"Whatcha' want?" Daisy asks, as she comes in with a timing only a small child can master. "Daddy? Can I have a picnic in my new room?"

"No food in your room, munchkin," I laugh, letting go of Daisy to squat down to be more on eye level with my daughter.

"Aw man..." she mutters, instantly pouting.

"How would you feel if Jasmine became your mom, Daisy?"

"My mom? Like my friend Ty? He has a mom. I've never had one of those."

"Do you want one?" Jasmine asks, bending down to join us.

"Would I call you mommy?" she asks, studying Jasmine.

"Only if you wanted to. If not, then that's fine too. I like how you call me Jazz-min. I want you to call me whatever you want, Daisy. I love you."

"I think you'd be a good mommy. You already read me

Keeping Her

bedtime stories like Ty's mommy does and you fix me mac and cheese!"

"So, you think it would be okay if I became your mommy for real?"

"Yes! Daddy! I get to have a Mommy!"

"I know, baby."

"And my mommy is prettier than Ty's Mommy!"

"Uh..."

"She's right about that, Red."

"You haven't even seen Ty's mother, Luke," Jasmine laughs, her face filled with happiness—happiness that has been missing the last few days.

"I don't need to. I know that I have the most beautiful woman in the world. That's all I need to know."

"You really pick the worst times to be sweet, Luke," she mumbles.

"You can punish me for it later," I reply with a wink, making her roll her eyes.

"Can we celebrate Jazz-Min being my mommy with a picnic?" Daisy asks innocently.

"Let me guess, you want it in your room?" Jasmine laughs.

"I do. Can we, Mommy?" she asks. Damn it, Jasmine might have backed me up and said no food in her room until that moment. But as Jasmine and Daisy hug, Jasmine smiling at me with tears in her eyes, I know I'm having a picnic in Daisy's new room.

I'll probably be forced to drink soda from Daisy's new pink plastic tea dishes.

And I don't even care.

Chapter 49

Jasmine

ONE WEEK LATER

"Wow," I gasp, as Luke pulls away from my body and moves over me.

"My baby came hard," he purrs, his lips kissing along my neck, as his hand caresses my stomach.

"My man has a magic mouth," I laugh, sliding the palm of my hand against the side of his face, not minding a bit that it's wet with remnants of my orgasm.

"Just my mouth?" he asks, with a wicked smile.

"Everything about you is magical," I admit, kissing him, tasting myself on his lips and swallowing his groan as he kisses me deeper.

He's hard, having refused to come until he made me come twice. I feel his heavy cock pressing against me. His body surrounds me. He's full of heat and strength. He has this way of making me feel small, feminine and beautiful all at the same time.

"I love you, Jasmine."

"I love you. I have to say when you left the house today, I didn't expect this," I giggle.

"It's been a good day," he says, his hand wrapping around his cock. He lifts up just enough so he can angle the head of his cock, raking it through the wetness gathered on the outside of my pussy. Then he presses in, so that he breaches me, sliding just the tip inside. "And getting ready to be an even better night."

"You're torturing me," I whimper.

"I'm celebrating, baby. It's not every day an entire club war is averted, and my woman's father shakes my hand and invites me to dinner," he says, pushing in just a little more.

My eyes close from the pleasure, and I feel a new surge of wetness pool between my legs. I bring my legs up, working to bring him even deeper. Luke allows it, slightly, still holding his body back enough that he won't give in completely. He's determined to make me wait.

"Two things, baby."

"What's that?" he mumbles, his lips moving against my breast, as he flicks his tongue against my nipple.

"One, let's never talk about my dad while we're having sex again, because, *eww*."

"Got it. I need to up my foreplay game," he laughs, right before sucking my nipple into his mouth, teasing it with his teeth and proving he's a master at foreplay—and anything else he chooses to do to my body.

My entire body quakes as he tortures me with deliciously wicked movements.

"What's the second?" he asks, when he finally releases my nipple with a wet popping noise.

"Second?" I ask, momentarily sidetracked, but then it hits me. "Oh...my dad came by here once the clubs finished their meeting and he and Mom are coming by for dinner Friday, instead of us going there."

"Works for me. Are we done talking about your parents now?"

I nod my head, yes. I'm just glad he didn't ask me why there was a change in plans. I didn't want to be the one to tell him the reason is because Dewayne is back on full-time duty and upset him. Dad doesn't want either of us in Kentucky right now and I'm okay with that. My life is here in Virginia with my man and our daughter.

"Good, now I'm going to get back to fucking my soon to be wife. Okay?" he mock-growls.

"If you must," I breathe, letting out a heavy sigh as he slams inside of me with such force that it causes my whole body to shudder in pleasure.

"That's my good girl," he praises, as he begins to slide in and out of my body. I meet his thrusts with a moan.

"I love you, Luke," I cry as I can already feel another orgasm begin to build. "I really love you."

Luke swallows my confession, his tongue thrusting into my mouth almost as forcefully as he pushes into my body. He's too busy kissing me to tell me he loves me back, but I'm okay with that, because I know he does.

I feel it in his every touch.

Chapter 50

Grunt

THREE MONTHS LATER

I hear the door opening and smile. It's almost over. I'd be lying if I didn't say I wasn't finding pleasure in it.

I am.

I look over at Jonesy and then across from him is Ford. The two men I'm the closest to in the club. But standing in the corner by the front door is Sledge. It surprised me that he wanted to be here, but the fact he did means a fuck of a lot. I thought when I let the club know what I was going to do, he'd be the first person to give me shit and try to get the club to block it. It wouldn't have worked. I would have done it on my own if the club wasn't going to have my back. Sledge didn't do what I expected, however.

Hell, I got the feeling that he completely agreed with what I had planned. It was a surprise, but it made me feel closer to my club than I've felt in years.

My gaze trickles around the room to look at the two other men who are handcuffed—with cuffs that conveniently have Officer Lagger's fingerprints. They're not making any noise—of course they can't.

They're fucking high as a kite. Having sampled some of the finest coke the DC's could get their hands on—which means it is Grade-A, premium shit. They're also gagged.

Why?

Because, thankfully Dewayne Lagger is a forgetful ass wipe who leaves his extra handcuffs lying around his house.

It took me three months to locate all of the parties that were involved in Lagger's twisted game of revenge he tried to extract using Jasmine. It wasn't easy, because I wasn't about to ask Red to help me or give me names. I don't want her to have to remember any of this shit ever again. Which meant, I'd been watching Dewayne Lagger very closely the last few months. It soon became clear who the men were that Dewayne spent time with, and once I watched them all in bars and out in town, I knew who to go after.

That brings us to this point, with my brothers and I looking like crime scene investigators not wanting to contaminate a scene and waiting on the final piece to end this game.

The minute the fucker's squad car pulls up outside, we all hear it. That means we are all ready as the door finally opens up.

The asshole has his head down, humming some fucking song. He has no idea the hell he has just walked into. My men and I all stay in place, as the fucker closes the door. When he finally looks up the first person he sees is me. Then, again, that's how I wanted this to go down. I see his eyes dilate, as shock spreads on his face and it goes pale with fear. And the asshole is definitely afraid. He's literally shaking with it. I wouldn't be a bit surprised if he didn't just piss himself.

His hand trembles as he reaches down for his gun. I shake my head no and cock my own weapon.

"I wouldn't do that, Officer," I mock. His hand freezes.

"Listen, I know you're upset, but you got mixed up in this game between me and that whore. You just didn't know who you were getting involved with. There's no reason to let her get you mixed up in something that will send you to jail. She's not worth it, man. She's just a whore. You can find one of those anywhere," he says, his words spoken rapidly in his fear. He backs up a few steps and that's when Sledge comes out of the corner. Finally, Lagger looks around, too late realizing he's surrounded. His eyes go to his two buddies on the floor—naked, cuffed and high. That's when the extent of this starts to hit him. "What the fuck," he hisses, his face going even paler.

"This is going to go down one of two ways," I tell him, and he shakes his head in denial, which just makes me laugh. Ford tossed down a baggie of drugs—at least the first dose. Jonesy tosses down a bottle of cheap whiskey. The other bottles we brought have already been poured down his buddies. Empty bottles are lying around the room. To anyone entering, it's going to look like a real party took place here tonight. They wouldn't be wrong—at least not completely.

"Listen, nothing horrible has happened here, we can end this and—"

"This started when you fucked with the wrong woman, asshole. I'm just a little late serving up the justice."

"Come on, man. She's just a fucking pussy who likes begging for dick. Hell, she didn't even know you when I had her. This is crazy."

I close my eyes, my hand tightening on my gun.

"Dude, you need to shut the fuck up. My man Grunt, here, is going to make this painless for you, but you keep it up and it will go the other way in a fucking hurry."

"Think about this," Lagger says, ignoring Jonesy's very wise advice. "If you go to prison, you're going to be leaving your daughter without a father. It won't matter about Jasmine because you won't be here for her either," the fucker adds. "You do *not* want to do this."

"Mention her name again and you're dead. You will disappear and there won't be anything left of your body for anyone to find, let alone charge someone with murder."

"There's no way you can pull that off," he denies, but he knows the truth—it's written on his face.

"Come on, dude, you've pissed off not one but three fucking clubs by hurting Jasmine. Did you really think you wouldn't die from that shit? The only question is how you're going to die," Jonesy adds.

"I say we throw him in a wood chipper and then feed him to the pigs that Sawbone always insists our club keeps," Ford says, speaking up for the first time.

"Damn it, Ford, the last time we did that the guy screamed for twenty minutes. If you do that this time, you need to shoot the fucker first. Or at least go headfirst into the chipper. And I'm not cleaning that shit up this time."

"Shut up whining, Sledge. You enjoyed that shit as much as I did," Ford laughs.

That's when it hits Lagger that they're not kidding.

"I have a family to get home to. That means I want to make this quick. So, you're going to make your decision, or I'll let my boys make it for you, Lagger. You can choose to take the pills in that baggy and wash 'em down with that bottle of cheap ass whiskey, or you can choose to go the difficult route. I'm warning you however, that the first option is your best shot at dying easily."

"Don't—"

"Either way, you *are* dying. So, decide," I respond, interrupting him.

He doesn't talk. He just stands there looking at me, like I'm going to change my mind.

"Clock's ticking asshole," Ford says, coming to stand beside me. I don't blink. I just keep staring at Lagger, waiting. I know

Keeping Her

what he's going to choose. I know how these assholes always go. He's too weak to stand up and be a man, even when it counts.

There's silence for a few more minutes. I'm tired and I want to get back to my girls. I've been spending too much time away from them while tracking these assholes down. I had my gun down, waiting, but since it's clear this asshole is going to stall as long as he can, I bring it back up.

"Let's load him up. Sawbone can feed his pets," I growl.

"Damn it," Sledge grumbles. "You're cleaning up the chipper. That damn brain matter sticks everywhere."

Lagger reaches out, his hand trembling, grabbing the bag.

"What's in this?" he asks, as if he has a choice.

"That right there is X, dude—the good stuff. You'll enjoy yourself first, which I think is too damn good for you, but I was out-voted," Jonesy laughs.

"Ecstasy?" Lagger asks, shaking so hard that it takes him a couple of times just to get the whiskey opened.

"Yeah, you and your buddies here are going to have a butt party before you die."

"Christ, do I have to watch this shit? I don't have nothing against it if that's your speed, but it doesn't mean I want to watch a live porno version of it," Sledge growls.

"You complain more than any man I know," Ford laughs, although there's no humor in it. "Suck it up, watch and go home and take your frustrations out on Gina."

"I'd rather chop my own dick off than touch her at this point," Sledge says and that gets everyone's attention, although we don't question him about it. He'll tell us when or if he wants us to know.

Lagger swallows down all the pills, just like I knew the asshole would. While we're waiting, Jonesy holds up another bag. This one he will snort. Sadly, that might make him feel too good. It also might not kill him. If it doesn't, the third bag Jonesy has will and that shit is bad. He'll die and die painfully. It will look like he just got a bad dose of illegal narcotics. That's the one I'm hoping he'll end up having to get before his sorry life ends.

I can see when the drugs start to take effect. I sit there and watch, never wavering. I sit there through it all and when I inject Lagger with the bad drugs to end his miserable life, I don't get much pleasure out of it. I inject the needle into his vein, using Lagger's own hand to press the needle in so that it is self-inflicted —or at least looks that way to a coroner.

"See you in hell, Lagger," I growl, as his body starts convulsing.

"Let's load up, boys," Ford commands, and we get the fuck out of there, leaving three dead bodies that not a fucking soul will miss.

Chapter 51

Grunt

I DROPPED BY THE CLUB TO SHOWER. I DIDN'T WANT EVEN the smell from spending time with those assholes on me when I walked through the doors of home. I could lie and say I felt some kind of remorse, but I didn't. I was glad they were no longer breathing air. I was glad it was done. I know how idiots like Lagger operate. He would have made Jasmine's life hell every single time he got a chance. Besides, he sealed his fate when he hit her that day beside the road.

Plus, when someone is rotten on the inside, they aren't satisfied with being a pest. Eventually, he wouldn't have stopped until he hurt Jasmine even more, maybe killed her, and that made him too dangerous to live.

My world, my rules.

And it definitely helped that my club had my back.

I walk into my house, taking a deep breath of nothing but clean air. My home with Jasmine is a sanctuary. At thirty-five I've never had a real home, unless you count being part of the DC's. This house, building a life with Jasmine and Daisy, is a home. A true home and the first real one I've ever had.

I'm not stupid. I know that it's not the brick or wood that make it that. It's the fact that I share them with Jasmine. Hell, she even made me a father. Before her, I didn't have the first clue how to be there for my daughter. Now, I couldn't imagine being anywhere else, couldn't imagine Daisy being anywhere else except with me.

After making sure all the doors and windows are secure, and arming the alarm system, I stop by Daisy's room first. She's sleeping, hugging up to a ridiculous troll doll that her and Jasmine made together. She's named him Ty and I don't even want to know what that means for me in the future. I make sure the covers are pulled up and I kiss her forehead. Daisy doesn't even move. Her hair smells like sweet cherries and I grin, because I know that Jasmine is responsible. She is a born nurturer and she's spoiled my daughter—in all good ways.

Before Jasmine, I couldn't even tell you how often my little girl had a bath. Here she gets one every night for the most part, she gets one using the special bubble bath and shampoo that she loves. She loves them because Jasmine took the time to take her shopping and let her pick things out. It might sound stupid, but I would have never thought to do that. I didn't even know it mattered.

But it did matter to Daisy.

When they came back from shopping, it was all my daughter could talk about. She was so happy and all over something as simple as a shopping trip to pick out bubble bath.

I move on to mine and Jasmine's room and when I get there, I can't move. My heart is too fucking full, so full that I can hardly breathe.

Her red hair is fanned out over the pillow, the sheet has worked down to her hip and my t-shirt is tangled under her boobs, revealing her stomach.

If someone had told me a year ago that this would be my life, that I would come home to a woman who was everything good in the world, a woman who accepted my daughter as her own, a woman who taught me what loyalty and love are all about...

I would have called them a liar.

But it's all true. I have everything, and it all happened because of a beautiful woman, with hair the color of fire, looked at me one day and took my breath away.

"Luke?" she murmurs, as I get close to the bed. I tried to be silent, but maybe I wasn't good enough. Or, maybe, Jasmine is like I am. I swear I can feel her the minute she enters a room.

"Yeah, baby, it's me."

"Everything okay?" she asks, opening her eyes and blinking.

"Better than okay," I tell her, undressing quickly and sliding into bed with her.

Jasmine immediately flips over, giving me her back. I pull her back into me, my body spooning against hers, as she snuggles back into her pillow.

"You're late, I was worried."

"No need, baby. I'll always come home to you," I promise, kissing her temple.

"Mmm..." she says, already back asleep.

I lie there in the darkness, holding Jasmine in my arms and I breathe easy. Tonight wasn't fun, but I protected my woman—my family, and I'd do it all again.

Because they're everything.

Epilogue

Jasmine

Two Days Later

"Did we get anything good in the mail?" I ask Luke as he comes back in from outside. It's a quiet Saturday—quiet because Daisy went home with my parents. Bart has Ty this weekend, which means Aunt Katie has Ty and they've been asking for Daisy. I know they're only five and six, but I wouldn't be surprised if they aren't tied at the hip for life. The thought makes me happy and it makes me smile.

"We did," he responds, putting a thick envelope in front of me. I look up at him and he's smiling, so I figure it can't be bad. Then, I read the address and it's the Clerk of Courts. My heart beats harder and I open it.

My hand shakes, the television noise blurs in the background as I look at the papers. It's forms to fill out to start the official adoption procedure for Daisy.

"Oh my God!" I cry, looking up at Luke.

"I figured it's about time we make it official. I want your name on her birth certificate before we have another child and the way we go at it..." he trails off, but he has a wicked smile on his face and we both know what he's talking about.

We make love like rabbits, as in, every time we get a chance. Since we threw away my birth control this morning, it's just a matter of time.

"We have to celebrate!" I cry.

"We will," he responds with a laugh. "We'll go pick up our girl and she'll go with us. Maybe we'll drive down to Natural Bridge. Daisy would enjoy that."

"She would, but I don't think it's a good idea to be in Kentucky for long periods of time right now. Dad's right, we need to be smart. I mean, he feels that way and he doesn't even know the whole story. Maybe we could—"

Luke bends down and kisses me, not letting me finish. "We'll go get our girl and spend the day at Natural Bridge. They have a sky lift, right? Daisy will love that."

I start to argue, but as the universe often does in its infinite wisdom, it picks that moment to stop me in my tracks.

My gaze moves over to the television when I see a report that comes from my part of Kentucky. I fumble around for the remote clicking the volume up.

"...two of the three dead served as patrol officers with the Kentucky State Police Post there in London. Assorted drug paraphernalia and alcohol were found on the scene, including materials signed out of the evidence locker by Officer Dewayne Lagger, one of the deceased. At this time, no foul play is suspected."

I mute the television, in shock. My gaze slowly lifts up to Luke's resigned face.

"Do you know anything about that, Luke?"

"Red, don't start."

"This is where you were so late the other night wasn't it? It didn't have anything to do with a run you had to make for Ford."

"Red, you need to let this go," he says, walking away to put his coffee cup in the sink.

"But—"

"But nothing. I took care of a problem that needed taken care of. You're not a stranger to this life, baby. You know what goes down. There was a threat to my family, and I handled it."

"I'm sure that's what my dad thought all those years ago. What happens if this comes back and hurts Daisy, Luke? Or any of the children that we have in the future?"

"So, you're admitting we're having children in the future," he mutters, and I have to stop and do a double take, making sure he's not gone completely insane, or that I'd somehow misheard him.

"Of course we're having kids in the future. Weren't you the caveman who went all insane earlier and told me to throw my birth control away?"

"Just making sure you weren't planning an escape now that any illusion you might have harbored about who I am and the codes I live by have been ripped away," he mumbles.

"Now, you're just being asinine. I'm not going anywhere. I love you and I know full well what kind of world you live in. I've never asked you to change. I just happen to think that this was one thing that maybe—*just maybe*—we should have discussed!"

"I took out a threat, Red. You know as well as I do that Lagger had so much hatred boiling inside of him that it was twisting him inside out. You became the focus of that hatred and eventually no one would have been safe. It would have boiled over."

I swallow, because I do know what he's saying is true. It's all just such a shock.

"But, Luke..."

"But nothing," he sighs, coming over to pull me up so that I'm standing in front of him. He keeps his hands on each of my shoul-

Keeping Her

ders, his finger under my chin so I'm forced to look into his eyes. "He was a problem and me and my club took care of it. We protect what's ours, it's what we do. We made it look like these fuckers took themselves out and that ends the circle. There will be no blowback. Our daughter and any other children we have down the line will breathe clear and easy. They will be able to spend time with their grandparents and not have to look over their shoulders. Your dad will never have to know about the poison that was slowly building so close to his family, or that it touched his daughter. It's gone."

I nod my head in agreement, knowing he's right. I moisten my lips with my tongue and push any other thoughts away. I'm part of this world, and I know what goes on for the most part. I also know what kind of man Luke is and I'm glad that he is the kind of man who takes care of his family. Maybe that makes me a bitch, or coldhearted, I don't know. What I do know is that everything he said makes perfect sense and I'm glad. I'm glad that my man had my back, and even protected my father.

"I really do love you, Luke."

His eyes close and I guess until this very moment, I didn't realize he was worried that I might truly walk away or be unable to accept what he had done.

"Thank fuck," he growls, making me smile.

"You're supposed to say you love me too," I murmur.

"That goes without saying, Red."

"Promise me you'll never quit saying it, Luke. I need it."

"I promise baby, I promise," he vows, and then he kisses me. It might be the single, sweetest kiss that we've ever shared. It's slow, gentle, and full of love. When we break apart, Luke gives me the words that I'll never tire of hearing.

"I love you, Red. Always and forever."

What more could a girl ask?

Epilogue Two
Grunt

"I didn't know the whole club was going to be at the family dinner," Dancer says as he follows me to the grill.

"I didn't either. They weren't invited. I think it happened when one of the prospects reported that a Savage MC bike was spotted," I tell him, opening the grill and flipping the burgers over.

"Not much trust between our clubs," he admits.

"That's the truth," I agree, closing the grill.

"Would my two favorite men like a cold beer?" Jasmine asks, coming out of the house, holding two cold ones in her hand.

She looks fucking amazing today. She's wearing a bright green tank top and cut off jeans. Her hair is down, the mass of copper curls bouncing with each step she takes, and perfectly highlighting the beauty of her face. She's smiling bright and didn't even give a damn that the club showed up. Instead, she sent her brother down to the local store to grab more food.

She's perfect.

"Thank you, Red," I rumble, taking my beer from her hand

and then, unable to stop myself, pull her in and kiss her hard. "Love you."

"Love you too," she whispers, surprise on her face, before melting into a softness that's so full of joy it settles into my heart. Ever since she told me how much she needed to hear me say that I loved her, I try to never miss an opportunity. She hands the other beer to her dad and kisses his cheek. "Glad you're here, Daddy."

"Me, too Princess," he says, giving her a squeeze. "Looks like your troll might have turned into a prince after all," he adds, and I frown.

"He's a little rough around the edges," she says, turning her head to look at me. "But, he's getting there," she adds, laughing as she walks away. Her laughter echoes in the air and damn if it doesn't sound good.

"What is it with this troll shit? Why do you two keep calling me a troll?"

"She hasn't told you yet?" he asks, his attention on Jasmine as she walks to her mother who is playing dolls with Daisy.

"No, but she tells Daisy this story every night about a Princess Caroline and a troll," I respond, exhaling an annoyed breath, wanting to know the full story.

"She does?" he asks, and for some reason, I get the feeling that makes him extremely happy.

"Yeah, Daisy eats that shit up. You going to tell me what it's about?" I question, watching him closely. "Does it have to do with me?"

"No, not technically. It's a family story. Ask her to tell you tonight. She will," he says, his eyes going thoughtful. "I think I owe you a debt of gratitude Luke. That's not easy for a man like me to admit to."

"What do you mean?" I ask, taking a swig of my beer, while I watch Daisy, Carrie and Jasmine laugh and play.

"You brought my little girl back to me. I haven't seen that smile, that sparkle in her eyes in so long that I almost forgot it existed."

I clear my throat. "She's special." I'm completely understating everything that she is, but right now that's the best I can do.

"That she is. That's why I have an important question to ask you."

"What's that?"

"The report about Lagger's death. I didn't think too much about it, until I recognized the last names of the two other men. I thought I might just be overreacting. So, I did some digging and found that Lagger's mother had a maiden name I did recognize."

"Dancer, man—"

"I'm asking you man to man if my past hurt my daughter. If I was the reason that the light went out of her eyes, Grunt."

I take a deep breath, instinctively knowing I'm treading thin ice here, just from what Jasmine has shared with me.

"Not the way you're thinking. I don't know your story, but I know enough that I figure you carry a large enough burden. Don't take this on. Lagger was a poison that needed ending and that's exactly what happened. The others, I have no idea about, but I wanted to make sure I covered my bases."

"So, it was you," he says.

I shrug. "Me and my club."

"I should talk to Jasmine..."

"No, you need to let it go. I'm going to tell you that Lagger did not hurt Jasmine physically until he hit her that day beside the road. That's what got him killed. He was a twisted fuck, yeah, but Red, she can handle herself. She was fine. What she would not be fine with, would be having her father take on a guilt that he has no reason to feel. And personally, I think that's giving that fucker too much credit. The circle is closed now, you heard the news. Those fuckers died by their own vices and hands. There's no blowback. It's done. The past is dead and rotting. Dancer, I can't know what happened or what's going on in your head, but I think we both need to let it rot and concentrate on everything we have."

Dancer doesn't reply right away. He continues to drink his beer, watching Jasmine spin Daisy around.

"We have a lot," he says, and I nod, even though he's not looking at me.

"That we do."

"She's going to be trouble," he says, and I jerk my gaze to watch Gina walk up to Daisy and grab her by the arm, trying to forcefully pull her away from Jasmine.

"Fuck," I hiss, getting ready to go over there. That's when Dancer puts his hand on my shoulder and holds me back.

"Jasmine might be a girl, but she's more mine than her brother. She's got this," he says. I think he might be insane. I'm set to ignore him and walk over there, when I start laughing.

Jasmine grabs Gina by the arm, she twists it in a way that looks completely unnatural and really painful. Then, she brings her knee up and plants it in Gina's stomach.

"Get this straight bitch, this is *my* daughter. If you ever come around her and put your hands on her again, I will end you and I will bury you so deep you can kiss the devil's ass," Jasmine bitches.

The boys all go quiet and Gina looks around at everyone. She's had the run of the club for a while now, being the only old lady and there's been no one in the running to worry about replacing her, since apparently Ford has sworn off women in general. It looks like Jasmine may have just made her case as leader of the females in the club.

"Damn," I hiss, my cock actually getting hard seeing her in action.

Keeping Her

"Told you," Dancer laughs.

"Are you all going to let her talk to me like this? Sledge! Do something!" Gina demands. I tense, waiting to see what Sledge does, he's a wildcard at best. I feel Dancer come to attention beside me. Then, Sledge defuses the situation easily.

"Welcome to the family, Jazz," he calls out and every single one of my men hold their beers out, taking a drink, and toasting her.

"That's my girl," Dancer says, taking another drink, toasting her himself. Jasmine picks up my daughter and kisses her on the top of her head and our eyes meet.

"No," I deny him. "That's my woman."

I leave him behind, a forgotten memory, as I go and kiss the hell out of Jasmine, thanking my lucky fucking stars that I have her.

The End
(Turn the page for a sneak peek of the next book in the series)

Book Three

Prologue

Breaking Her
Lyla

"What are you doing here?"

I can't believe what I'm seeing. My hand automatically goes to my hair, which is a matted mess, mostly because I've rolled around on the couch all day, not having the energy to get up. There wasn't a point anyway. That also means I don't have makeup on. My hand goes down to my face. I don't know what I'm trying to do. Maybe if I put my hand over part of my face he won't see the pimples that seem to pop up daily—a complication of either being pregnant or binging on chocolate peanut butter cups. My fingers feel a sticky, wet smear of the chocolate on my cheek near the corner of my mouth, as if to mock me.

Okay, so the acne outbreak may totally be related to the chocolate binging and not pregnancy hormones.

"You're pregnant," Thomas says, and the sick, white-hot flushed feeling spreads through me. My stomach rolls.

Shit. Shit. Shit.

"What?" I croak, trying to figure out how to get out of this.

"You're preg...pregnant," Thomas says, giving away that he's not completely comfortable here either.

He always stutters when he's uncomfortable or upset. He's sensitive about it, but I never thought much about it. It embarrasses Thomas, but I didn't understand that either. You only have to spend a little time with Thomas to realize that he's special, the kind of man a woman would feel proud to belong to. At least that's what I always thought.

Until I discovered that he was only using me to nurse a broken heart...

I must remember that and never let my guard down around him.

"I have no idea what you're talking about," I bluff, furiously wiping some of the chocolate from my face.

"Bullshit."

"I'm serious Thomas, I don't know where you got this idea, but I'm not pregnant." I hope like hell he buys what I'm saying. Luckily the room is semi-dark, and as I stand up, I'm confident that my body is hidden under the overly large sundress that I'm wearing. I'm not that far along, but you can definitely see the small swell of my stomach when I wear more form-fitting clothes.

"Then, m-maybe you could tell your father that, since he's convinced you're pre--pregnant and I'm the father," he responds, point blank. He's clearly pissed and a lot of that is directed at me. I ignore it, because I have bigger fish to fry—so to speak.

"I'm going to kill him," I snap, talking about my father, although killing Thomas still sounds like a good plan.

"You've got bi...bi...bigger problems," Thomas says, and I

open my mouth to deny him, but Thomas immediately shakes his head no. "Don't lie to me."

"The way you lied to me, Thomas?"

"I never lied to... to you."

"Do you remember when we first met? You never used to have trouble speaking to me at all. When your stuttering started, that's when I knew you were pulling away from me. You would have trouble sometimes with others, but never with me. I convinced myself that meant I was special," I tell him. I hate that I sound weak and broken in front of him. I hate that I feel that way.

"You're acting like I m-m-made promises," he stammers, and I guess that's what makes me feel the worst. I clearly thought we were making promises *together* and he truly never did.

"Why are you here, Thomas?" I finally ask. "Don't you have a girlfriend to get home to?"

"I'm here because that's what you wanted," he accuses me. I blink, thoroughly confused, because I have no idea what he's talking about.

"What does that even mean?"

"You can't play dumb now, Sunflower."

My eyes close, pain so intense that it almost floors me. It feels like my heart is being frozen in my chest.

"Never," I spit out under my breath, because it's hard to talk. He can hear me though. I stare directly into his eyes and refuse to look away. "Never, call me that again."

"I guess I deserv-vv—ve that," he says, his face resigned.

"And so much more," I agree. "You need to leave."

"If only it were that easy, Su...Lyla. It's not though. You made it impossible for me to walk away."

I have no idea what he's talking about. I can feel panic begin to build though from just the thought of Thomas coming back into my life. I don't want him here.

261

Not anymore.

"I don't understand," I deny, shaking my head back and forth and backing away from Thomas as if he was Satan himself—which I think he might be.

"Your father tracked me down. We're on the v-verge of a club war and you and I are the only ones who c-can stop it."

"How? I never told my father who you were. I never wanted him to know. I never wanted anyone to know."

"Lit—little too late to be ashamed of m-me now, Sunflower."

I don't think. I lash out, slapping him across the face with the palm of my hand.

"I said, never call me that!" I scream. "And for the record, Thomas, I was never the one ashamed of you. You covered that particular issue all on your own," I add, walking away from him, sick to my stomach.

I don't know why he's here, but I don't need him. My hand goes to my stomach and I place it where the tiny life is hiding inside of me. My child doesn't need him either. He or she will have me, and I'll never leave it alone like Thomas left me...

Want to be notified when Breaking Her goes live?
Turn the page to learn how to sign up to be one of Jordan's Insiders!

Jordan's Insiders

Did you know there are several ways to see all things Jordan Marie, before anyone else?

First and foremost is my reading group. Member will see sneak peeks, early cover reveals, future plans and coming books from beloved series or brand new ones!

If you are on Facebook, it's easy and completely free!

Jordan's Facebook Group

Next, you can add me as a friend on Goodreads!

Goodreads

Then, if you live in the U.S. you can **text JORDAN to 797979** and receive a text the day my newest book goes live or if I have a sale.

(Standard Text Messaging Rates may apply)

And finally, you can subscribe to my newsletter!

Click to Subscribe

Social Media Links

Keep up with Jordan and be the first to know about any new releases by following her on any of the links below.

Newsletter Subscription
 TikTok
 Goodreads
 Facebook Reading Group
 Facebook Page
 Webpage
 Bookbub
 Instagram

Text Alerts (US Subscribers Only—Standard Text Messaging Rates May Apply):

Text *JORDAN* to **797979** to be the first to know when Jordan has a sale or released a new book.

Also by Jordan Marie

Savage Brothers MC—2nd Generation

Taking Her Down
Keeping Her
Betraying Her

Stone Lake Series

Letting You Go
When You Were Mine
Where We Began
Before We Fall

Broken Love Duet
(Spinoff of Stone Lake)

Mistakes I've Made
On My Way To You
A Song That Never Ends
The Broken Road

Lucas Brothers

The Perfect Stroke
Raging Heart On

Happy Trail
Cocked & Loaded
Knocking Boots
Home Run
Hot Summer Nights
Cowboy Up
A Hard Time

The Lucas Cousins

Going Down Hard
In Too Deep
Taking it Slow

Mr. Series
(Spinoff of the Lucas Brothers)

Mr. Heartbreaker
Christmas Carol (A Mr. Series Novella)

Savage Brothers MC

Breaking Dragon
Saving Dancer
Loving Nicole
Claiming Crusher
Trusting Bull
Needing Carrie

Savage Brothers Complete Series with Bonus Material

Devil's Blaze MC

Captured

Craved

Burned

Released

Shafted

Ride Me Sweetheart

Devil's Blaze Books 1-4 Boxed Set Edition

The Devil's Blaze Duet

Beast

Beauty

Beast Comes Home

Savage Brothers MC—Tennessee Chapter

Devil

Diesel

Rory

Fury

Filthy Florida Alphas

Unlawful Seizure

Unjustified Demands

Unwritten Rules (Steel Vipers MC)

Unlikely Hero

Unwilling Protector (Steel Vipers MC)

Filthy Florida Alphas Box Set (Books 1-4)

Filthy Florida Alphas Box Set

Titans of Hell

Ruthless Arrangment

The Fall (Coming Soon)

The Eternals

Eleven

Nine

Seven

Alpha Men

Branded By The Mountain Man

His Mail Order Bride

Doctor For Hire

Spreading Christmas Joy

Matched To The Movie Star

Made in the USA
Middletown, DE
02 April 2023